Ian Hopkins and John Duignan have written for Radio, TV and Stage.

Ian's writing includes:

Stage Plays: *Citizen Singh* (with Gurmeet Mattu); *Every Bloody Sunday* (with Gurmeet Mattu); *Albatross Soup* (with John Duignan).

Radio: *Naked Radio*; *Six of the Best.*

Television: *Not the Nine o' Clock News;*
Three of a Kind;
Naked Video;
Spitting Image.

Writing in progress: *The Buick Stops Here* a comic novel, sequel to *Skelp the Aged* (with John Duignan).
Your Other National Sport a comic novel (with John Duignan).

Screenplay on Thomas Muir, the Scottish political martyr and 'father of parliamentary democracy' (with John Duignan).

John's writing includes:

Stage: *Albatross Soup* (with Ian Hopkins)

Radio: (with Ian Hopkins) *Naked Radio*; *Six of the Best.*

Television: (with Ian Hopkins) *Not the Nine o' Clock News; Three of a Kind; Naked Video.*

Books: *Quantitative Methods for Business Research* (Cengage 2014); *Saving the Last Dance* (a novel, Kindle).

Katharine Black Doesn't Dance (a novel, Cider Apple Press).

Forthcoming: *Things To Do When The Music Stops* (novel, Cider Apple Press, Spring, 2016).

Skelp the Aged

An extremely serious novel of our time

John Duignan and Ian Hopkins

Skelp the Aged

Pegasus

PEGASUS PAPERBACK

A CIP catalogue record for this title is available from the British Library

ISBN-978-1910903-00-1

Pegasus is an imprint of
Pegasus Elliot MacKenzie Publishers Ltd.
www.pegasuspublishers.com

First Published in 2016

Pegasus
Sheraton House Castle Park
Cambridge CB3 0AX England

Printed & Bound in Great Britain

Dedication

To our wives, Margaret and Sheila, and John Lloyd for his encouragement, advice and support over many years

Disclaimer: *Skelp the Aged* is a work of fiction and all characters and events described are fictitious. Any similarities with real persons dead or alive are coincidental.

Disclaimer – Product placement: in referring to real products in this work of fiction the authors are in no way endorsing them either in their normal use or advocating any abuse or extraordinary usage of the products as described in the actions of the characters in the novel.

Parental Guidance: This work contains words with asterisks. There is one scene of not-quite total nudity, one act of violence and a couple of flashing images. Some of the physical manoeuvres described should not be attempted at home unless in the company of at least one responsible adult with first aid training.

Acknowledgements

Gordon Kirk, Jean Kirk, Graham Hyslop, Denis Martin and Michael Duignan read a draft and commented both critically and extensively. Their contribution is gratefully acknowledged by Ian and John. With thanks also to Margaret Duignan for reading the final proof. They are in no way responsible for any remaining weaknesses in the content.

About the book: *Skelp the Aged* is a serious comedic novel. Mungo and Ethel Laird should have been entering their golden years in material comfort but Mungo's mismanagement of the family brewery and the predations of financial advisors on their pension pot, have left them in genteel poverty in the decaying family villa. They dream of a place in the sun where they can samba their days away fortified by warm breezes and even warmer fortified wines. Mungo borrows from loan sharks to secure a little villa in the sun while placing their house on the market. The book covers a period of a few weeks in which a diverse set of 'candidates' (some of whom have 'colourful' histories) view the house. All of them make offers as it has been deliberately undervalued by an unscrupulous surveyor conspiring with their estate agent. Mungo wants to take the first legal offer, but Ethel has other ideas and she decides to have a dinner party to choose – *discriminate* – between the 'candidates'. The dinner party misfires badly and Ethel and Mungo find themselves in deeper waters with the loan sharks scenting blood. But Mungo has a plan!

At the heart of the tale is the condition whereby today, the elderly, compared with all other groups, such as those based on ethnicity, religion, gender etc., can be bad-mouthed with impunity. Today the elderly are blamed for the National Debt, the crises in the NHS and for living too long. Political correctness has not yet invited the elderly into their 'Big Tent'.

Chapter 1

The First Temptation of Ethel and Mungo
they had a dram – a fan-ta-see.

The sun was setting over the Bay of Angels (*Baie des Anges*, as the French provocatively insist on calling it) and Mungo Laird was dozing lightly on the terrace of his *fin-de siècle* villa, his face upturned to embrace the butterfly kiss of the cooling breeze, as the land almost imperceptibly turned from the richest burnt sienna to a deep purple.

The only sounds that penetrated Mungo's slumbering consciousness was that of the aforesaid breeze riffling the palm fronds and the evening traffic on the *Promenade des Anglais* a few kilometres away in Nice. On the table before him lay a jumble of magazines: *The Telegraph, The Daily Mail* (€3: worth it for the racing card) and a brochure from *The Night Soil Association*. There were too, a few cocktail glasses that had been for too long discharged. Then he heard the music seep from the open terrace windows – it was Stan Getz, *Menina-Moça.*

Still dozing in his lounger (*Bronze 'Havana'*, Debenham's, €150 plus delivery at time of writing, *atow*), Mungo began to move his body to the sinuous rhythms of the music and he knew that in a few seconds, if he opened his eyes, Queen Ethel would snake her way out on to the terrace, and he would join his love of loves in a display that could have graced the barrios of Rio, the bars of Porto Banus or the Barras of Barrowland (just off the Gallowgate, Glasgow, and worth a visit for the multi-cultural suppers – pie, fish, Mars bars and deep-fried sushi).

With a great sense of anticipation at the thought of the passions that would be unleashed and ultimately sated in the time-honoured fashion this balmy evening, and with his eyes still closed – there was always a slight problem of rheum if he closed them overlong – Mungo called out for his houseboy to replenish the glasses.

"Mourinho, por favor. Dios Buckie coladas. Obrigado."

"Mungo."

Mungo felt the gentle touch of his queen on his shoulder, and smiled and postponed the moment when he would open his eyes and drink-in the vision in taffeta and organza that would stand lovingly over him, a generous vista of well-supported bosom on parade waiting expectantly to be...

"Mungo!" He felt a blow on his shoulder that made him think he had staggered into one of the palm trees that lined the garden all the way down to the summerhouse and gazebo. But how the bl*zes if he was in his chair on the terrace, how come a palm tree had struck him on the... and there it was again!

Then Mungo woke up.

'Ph*cque', he thought but did not say. His dream had been all wrong – it was supposed to be set in Portugal. As for the *Baie des Anges*, he had only ever seen it in a cheap print of Dufy's daub, and he found the French appalling. Not only that, apart from the natives, it was packed with English and gangsters and Labour politicians from Lanark (North and South). Something was out of kilter, Mungo reasoned as he prised his eyelids open.

Another thump on the shoulder and he was in the 'drawing room' of *Villa Laird* with his lady wife Ethel looming over him. This room variously described as: *living room* when they felt democratic or a sense of faked humility; *music room* when the piano was used to plank something like a bottle; or *drawing room* when they could not remember another name for it. And now the source of the affectionate blows was revealed, for Ethel his wife was towering over him and not only was she not shoving her embonpoint into his fizzug, (der. *physiog* – abbr. *physiognomy*) she looked as if she was going to hit him with her rolled-up copy of Yellow Pages that accompanied her just about everywhere, and which she now brandished in her hand.

And Mungo was glad he had only thought the expletive *ph*cque* on awakening for of course swearies were not advisable in the Presence. Unless of course Ethel Laird herself gave permission in the way that granddames of the past might have said: *gentlemen you may loosen your ties, light your cigars and pass the port, but not one post-prandial flatulation will be tolerated below the salt.* Then and only then, when the signal was given, was it allowed to use a sprinkling of colourful epithets. But never before eight at night and never after ten.

And now he had been disturbed in his dreams by the arrival of Ethel and a couple of accompanying clouts on his shoulder, and no wind chimes to signal a change of mood. But why? What was so special about this day that his beloved consort felt moved to thump him, rather than just plump cushions vigorously where he lay on the old couch, causing not just the stoor to get up his nose? Then it all came back to Mungo and he felt a shiver of anticipation as he thought of what lay ahead that fateful day. Though it could have been the draught from the old sash windows.

Chapter 2

The Stuff that Dreams are Made on – and how to pay for them.

"Mungo, today could be one of the most important of our lives. Do you recall the object of all this? Yes? Mungo?" She was in her headmaster mood and sometimes this distracted Mungo – he would imagine her in black, flowing gown, mortarboard and tawse nicely concealed over her ample shoulder just under the gown. Is there any more arousing vision one could imagine, imagined Mungo, thinking that he might need to change into his baggy trousers, when Ethel hauled him back to earth with a start and no warning wind chimes to say the dream was over before it had even been fully formed.

Ethel waited for a response.

"Wait: I know that one – no, don't tell me," Mungo called out, thinking that if he got this right, the baggy trousers might still have their use before this day was out.

"Got it: sell the old place. Be shot of family home. Be liberated. Get the money for the place in the soleil..."

"No! No! No! Mungo." Ethel crashed her Yellow Pages on the kitchen table – for they had repaired there, even though the table now needed repair.

"You are being deliberately obtuse. I know your game, my man. You are being swinishly provocative. *Sell the place*, indeed. Nothing so stark... so crass. Think about it, Mungo: this has been our family home for... for ages. Been in the family before that even – three generations. We are reluctant to part, but given the passage of time..."

And at that Ethel did an inspiring imitation of a salesman of the most lugubrious and plausible type.

"Garden too grand. Ed the gardener consigned to the bosom of his family as his arthritis takes over his life; we have many of the rooms – My Father's Mansion... not too biblical. Halls that should be echoing to sound of children's laughter... And so on. So, Mungo: what we have today is a series of *interviews*. The people who come here are not prospective buyers – they are *candidates.* Candidates to become the elected custodian of this ancient monument to Victorian excess. They will need to display qualities above the ordinary. Bluntly put: we are not going to sell to any Thomas, Richard or Harriet. Damn it, Mungo, we owe it to our memories, we owe it to ourselves."

"We owe it to Hammerhead Loan Sharks, Ethel," Mungo murmured then added vigorously, "Bo*locks to all of that. It's not been a home proper since the children skedaddled – rarely to be seen again. No use pretending otherwise. Heaven's sake, Ethel, it's not Balmoral or the Castle of M*r. It's only a house now. Large house. Too large for us. Deteriorating at a rate faster than we can... well faster than us. Little matter of our new place in the sun? Our friends at Hammerhead may become just a little bit, well, pressing. Solution? Sell to first one to offer what we know we want. What we need."

With that outburst, Mungo thought he might really have gone too far. Now was the time to become emollient or the baggy trousers were definitely suspended *sine die*. He turned on his most wheedling voice – if he got it right he would have an asthma attack and Ethel would become quite concerned and it would be an excuse for both of them to overdose on *Salbutamol.* (Among the listed side effects there is no mention of the one discovered by Mungo, of which more later, but no blame attaches to GSK, milud.)

"Ethel my dear, it is for both our sakes, after all. Remember?" He paused and listened for the wind chimes effect, but when they were not forthcoming he hummed a samba, did a few fluid steps, and briefly had Ethel in his arms in a vertical Boston-crab; and for a moment she was almost with him, then her superior self-control took hold and she shrugged him off, but not before a faint blush had suffused those sculpted cheeks (facial variety – think Mount Rushmore with weather-ravaged capillaries).

"No Mungo! I know you think you can melt me all too easily with your facile seductive charms. But not this time. We have too much on our plate. In fact we don't have enough on our plate and so we must sell. One of us must maintain a business approach. And we both know you have no business sense. Remember? No offence intended, but... successful family brewery, piss-up, organise? *only you couldn't, but you did* rearrange *it rapidly* into a rundown organisation. Am I being unfair? Enough said."

Mungo sighed for he had been here before. Many times. Oh b*llocks, he decided, why bother. He recovered his composure and drew his shoulders back.

"Ethel my dear, you can count on me. Line up the *candidates*, let the interviews commence and s*d the consequences." And with that he marched smartly out of the kitchen and held his breath until he was in the hallway where he exhaled thus: "*Candidates*? All b*llocks."

"And Mungo!" Ethel called from the kitchen where she was having a quick tonic wine for the day ahead (*Buckfast* fortified ecumenical wine: see Appendix 6 for tasting notes) to stiffen her sinews – actually she had no need of the latter since she was criss-crossed in varicose veins. But the Buckie always helped in times of crisis.

"Yes dearest?" Mungo stuck his head through the serving hatch.

"I don't want to hear one of your 'b*llocks' again. Ever."

"Yes, dear. But it's just that sometimes depending how I walk – you know the old regimental stride – they tend to click a bit. Maybe I'll stick some cotton wool down my truss… when I find it."

Chapter 3

Everyone needs good neighbours. Oh really?

Villa Laird, the residence of Mungo and Ethel Laird, was not situated on the French Riviera, but stood above the little Sc*ttish town of Borrfoot. And like the Lairds, husband and wife, it had seen better days.

It was built in 1885, the year in which other auspicious events included *The Mikado* opening at the Savoy Theatre in London, Arbroath beating Bon Accord 36-0, and Chief Sitting Bull joining Bill Cody's *Wild West Show*. There is no official record of Sitting Bull having stayed at the Lairds' residence. However, Appendix 1 shows how the great man might have looked in 1885 had he done so.

The house was erected on an outcrop of rock that stood above and looked down on Borrfoot. It was built of a lovely honey-coloured local stone that became nicely weathered over the years (eroded and soot-begrimed); the timbers were of Oregon pine and oak and the roof was of blue Welsh slate. (More of the Welsh slate later.) In 1885 the Lairds, wealthy brewers and stalwarts of the Unionist Party (Scottish Conservatives by another name), had owned much of the land in the valley of *The Bevvy* that flowed into *The Clyde* via *The*

White Cart, but since the 24-hour Tesco had opened at Silverburn, the *White Cart* became known as *The Trolley Cart*.

The area surrounding Borrfoot was once a place of agriculture and gracious living – known internationally for the *Nullson Cattle Show* that took place every year on the first Saturday in May. (See Appendix 2 for flavour of the event.)

Behind *Villa Laird* lay fields of whin (*Ulex, Fabaceae*) and gorse (*ditto)* in which ruminants straight off shortbread tins and Highland Toffee wrappers trained for the Cattle Show. (See Appendix 3: Selfie: *In training for Nullson Cattle Show.*)

But over the years since Mungo and Ethel had inherited the family home things had changed, and not always for the best. The town upon which they looked down – in every sense – had changed: in the past the lower orders seemed to know and accept their lot as they worked in the fields and the dye works or the Laird Brewery for a pittance; and they seemed happy enough, though no one had ever tested the opposite proposition. But now in Mungo's lifetime it had been transformed from what had looked like a rural idyll from above, into a grasping industrial powerhouse in which class relations broke down: the working class got uppity, and an even uppitier middle class emerged.

Borrfoot became the global centre for lavvy-pan making and companion pieces in glazed china, and over time the lower orders did not even know they were lower. And families like the Lairds were marginalized and even regarded as a species whose time had passed. But much worse, as the working class in the town grew in number and became healthier and better educated (intended or unintended consequence of universal free education and the NHS?) they were even exhibiting signs of sympathy and compassion for the declining old Borrfoot families that had ruled their parents' and their grandparents' lives for so long through their control of business and the cooncil (tr. *council*).

The house had passed-down to Mungo and Ethel through Mungo's side of the family. And yes, they were cousins who in the dim and distant past had been kissing cousins. In fact a bit more than that – and so they had to marry.

Mungo was *un homme d'un certain âge* (and a bit more), of medium stature and when he was quite a bit younger and had enough of the stuff, he had sandy hair that matched his skin colour and went well with his twinkling blue eyes. It had been his hope as a young man to develop a paunch that would be the outward sign of inner contentment, but he was still working on both.

As the scion of the brewing family, Mungo had spent a couple of summers in his youth with a competitor, and by the time they were finished with him, he knew less about brewing than when he had started. But that mattered little as there was a tradition of nepotism that was kept in the family that smoothed his passage, so that when he assumed complete control of the company, Mungo could say with some pride that he had worked his way up from the top. And just at that point, the old fellow who had been really running the thing and was not of the family, jacked it in. This should have been the time to panic. But Mungo failed to spot this and so, in his later years he reflected that he had now achieved some sort of double-first: he had not only worked his way up from the top, he had managed to work his way down from the top when the company crashed.

Mungo was now, in his view, a youthful seventy-six (some rhymester says somewhere that all men look out with the eyes of an eighteen-year-old – he might have had Mungo in mind). And yet in his youth he had been burdened with the epithet: *'Old before his time'.* He always had been. It was even written large in his school report card. Indeed it was the only qualification his inferiority complex would allow for him being chosen as Head Boy at St Kentigern's Academy, an increasingly exclusive (numbers falling each year) private school – Motto: *Born for better things*. It had had a motto in Latin but the only one who could remember what it meant was the jannie, and he wasn't telling until he got his back pay and a working lino-polisher. Mungo *looked* the part – the only boy permitted to wear leather patches on the elbows of his school blazer and to dry-smoke a pipe – though this privilege was somewhat tarnished by the fact that his mother had the housekeeper sew-up his pockets for medical reasons.

Mungo's brother, Buffy – two years older and precocious in life – had always thereafter referred to Mungo as the *Principal* Boy. Buffy's view of public tom-schoolery in general and St Kentigern's in particular, was that it was a pantomime without a dame, for families who often didn't have a dime (he had adopted certain American ways). When he was sixteen Buffy had spent the summer working at the family brewery – more accurately one week of three-and-a-half days – after which he composed a very erudite letter to the trustees of the firm whose task it was to safeguard the interests of Buffy and Mungo. A slightly different slant on this letter (which no longer exists), was that it was a skilful forgery purporting to be from a solicitor acting on his behalf and demanding his 'cut' of the firm forthwith or sooner, otherwise there would ensue a lengthy test case in the courts out of which no one would emerge with credit (or with much loot) (apart from the legal profession).

With his well-earned pre-inheritance in his metaphorical back pocket, Buffy embarked on a relationship with the school cook. The relationship was carnal in that Buffy and the cook – an ex-army major of dubious provenance – were dealing jointly (no single or double pun intended) in the sourcing of St Kentigern's and other private schools' meat and veg; an arrangement that involved Irish horse traders who had an interest in the pet-food industry and piggeries. In their defence, milud, there is no scientific evidence that BSE existed in the British public school system in the early 1950s, the first recorded case being in the 1980s. No matter, Buffy was eventually expelled from St Kent's and the ex-major became a magistrate in the north of England, Buffy having kindly produced convincing documentary evidence of his qualifications and unblemished character as a valedictory gift. After which Buffy prospered in different climates, but never forgetting his little brother the Principal Boy, to whom he sent irregularly but generously, postal orders of significant value – some of which he had not manufactured.

Chapter 4

Mungo meets Ethel and learns about slates.

Caught between admiring Buffy and being just a little envious of his derring-do and success in life, and not a little hurt by Buffy's soubriquet for him, Mungo consoled himself with the panacea of the weak-willed and those destined for worse things, with the scientifically dubious proposition that '*he who laughs last laughs longest'.* And so with Buffy gone, Mungo took over the family brewery from their early-demised tee-total and vegetarian pater – you would think there would be some sort of lesson there, but alas he was poisoned by a wild mushroom (*amanita phalloides* – said to be very tasty, but how this is known is not certain).

During this self-same period he had set eyes on Ethel for the first time. Although she was a cousin, despite the advice of the family doctor who knew a little about genetics and inherited characteristics, the two of them had not been kept well-enough apart, as the family's interpretation of nepotism was broader than that given in the *Oxford Dictionary* (or any other dictionary for that matter other than the *Concise Cahulawassee River Dictionary of Words and Acceptable Practices with Relatives* – see *Deliverance,* 1972, dir. J Boorman. 7.8/10. Available on NetFlix).

ANYWAY, Mungo first set eyes on Ethel when she was bent over the prostrate form of the town's first traffic warden. The *victim* – if such a word can be used during an epoch in which Foucauldian Discourse Analysis had reached these fatal shores and Glasgow Uni: we were all culpable for the violence and rapine that was committed upon us – had, some would say, rightly incurred Ethel's wrath as he had attempted to ticket the family Vanden Plas (the 1960 *Princess Limousine*), just as she was egressing Julian and Clive's *Salon de Cheveux et de la Beautie* (known locally as *Salon Shug*; *appointments not always necessary*).

Mungo was smitten by her presence, and by the fact he could see all the way down her décolletage to her belly button and even beyond. That was the first time for both of them. It was also one of the last times he would catch such a glimpse of paradise, though they were engaged and married within a twelvemonth.

Although from the rebellious branch of the family, Ethel was the seventh daughter of a Seventh-Day Adventist (who after 1960 spent much of his time travelling the country watching *The Magnificent Seven* wherever it was shown). She had been a glorious failure at the most expensive girls' school in the city (details on request), and so, on the advice of the careers advisor Ethel trained as a careers advisor before segueing into social work (which is a sort of safety net for scooping up those who have been victims of the Careers Service). But she found that mixing with the *hoi polloi* tended to coarsen her view of humanity and so she retired from the field and duly, as noted above, married Mungo whom her family had mistaken for his well-do-well brother, Buffy.

Between them they had two children: a girl called Two-Dogs Ph*****n* (no – that was Sitting Bull's thirteenth lass); Mungo and Ethel's girl child was called Jane, which most people plainly forgot, and a boy called Mongo, which Mungo tried to forget, but still thought of him as Mango especially when there was chutney for tea in the afternoon.

In the eyes of the rest of the world, their children were the sort of unsung heroes that songs are never sung about: Jane was in the Jungle somewhere in South America or South-East Asia or some other of the few places left that still had a jungle deserving of the name, where she worked as a midwife. Mongo was doing something else equally worthy – building latrines and schools in some godforsaken country where the government only had enough money for nuclear weapons, conventional ordnance and well-cut uniforms for the army that kept it in power.

Mungo thought they – the fruit of his loin – were mad. There had been a history of insanity in both branches of the family, but hitherto it had never manifested itself in acts of unpardonable folly, tending instead to erupt in a lot of arson about the family businesses or those of close competitors in the brewing industry.

He had had high hopes at one time, that either or both of their children would buy the old house. And to this end, one Christmas, when both were coincidentally taking a break from their worthy international labours – and equally coincidentally recovering from the same tropical affliction – Mungo had put this proposition to them. A look had passed between brother and sister, and rising from their sick beds in the infirmary wing, they as one pronounced that they felt so much better now and they had planes to catch. *Adios* they said, but in different disparate local languages and were off.

Ungrateful wretches, Mungo had thought, but had let it pass in the hope that the next fever they had would seriously interfere with their reason, and at that moment of vulnerability, he would get a signature on the relevant contract. Meantime he would obtain copies of their signatures.

But that was all in the past and Mungo and Ethel had to set aside these little local difficulties and deal with the *actualité* as it encroached from above (in the form of rain) and from below in the form of the baying mobs that were getting ever closer as they, Mungo and Ethel, resorted to ever more desperate measures to keep the hordes at a distance.

Since the war, the town had grown rapidly and had spread its influence almost as far as Villa Laird. Why, even on what had been their personal carriage driveway to the front of the villa, middle class bungalows and worse – quite tasteful villas – had sprung-up on land that once belonged to the Lairds. Mungo and Ethel hated these – especially in view of the fact that they had sold-off the land upon which these bungaloid excrescences had erupted like pustules on the face of a plague victim with impetigo who had mislaid the *Clearasil.*

While those looking up wistfully to the villa from the town below, or even from the street below, thought that someday, they might too live up there, Mungo and Ethel knew better. There was no way in H*ll that Ethel would sell to the plebeians of the town. Unless Mungo was absolutely forced to.

Had Villa Laird been featured in any of *Town and Country*, *House and Garden*, *Scottish Field*, or the local estate agents' free sheet (excellent for wrapping fish suppers), it might have been characterised as *fin-de-seedy*. The truth was that apart from lording it over a rather ordinary town, there was nothing remarkable about the villa other than it was bigger than those it looked down on. Truth to tell, it was an ordinary but remarkably ugly Victorian construction – with any beauty in it being in the eye of the beholden or perceived by those who saw beauty in the face of a Jack Palance, a Lee Marvin, a Jack Elam or a Lloyd Webber – the kind of beauty that only a mother could see and love.

On top of the faded glory of Villa Laird, there was the problem of the blue Welsh slate – aforementioned. The roof leaked even in the dry season. Mungo would call a roofer and the older grizzled version of that species would appear in due course and, after duly inspecting it, would come down and pay tribute to the longevity of the ph*cquing Welsh slate. Nothing like it in the world today. Will last for another ph*cquing hundred years. Much better than the modern synthetic materials or tiles. You don't get them like that today and so on and so on. Then why the ph*cquing h*ll does it leak even in the dry season – which lasts about one week and which, like Easter on the calendar, cannot be predicted with any degree of certainty? Mungo thought often.

Nail fatigue, more than one wise old roofer had said, while praising the longevity of blue Welsh slate. *Nail fatigue*? echoed Mungo. What? The nails are tired? They've been working for more than a century and are feeling just a wee bit kn*ckered? Well boo-hoo, thought Mungo, and meantime invested his cash in plastic buckets and whistled philosophically as another grizzled roofer of the old school explained that the new nails did not have the same character as the old ones and... ENOUGH! Let's have a peek inside the villa.

What would have been called ‘the lounge’ by the new lower middle class; (see for example *Abigail's Party*, 1977, dir. M Leigh); or ‘the living room’ by those of the working class who had not fallen into the trap of ‘buying’ their own houses yet (that delight awaited them), the Lairds correctly called the drawing room. It not only looked down over the town but also doubled as the music room and the smoking room – so called because the chimney was blocked by nests and every time a fire was lit the place was smoked out and stank of roasted crow (think of the scent of the Algarve). Mungo used this also as his refuge for a quick puff at a cigar – the window was easiest to open and had a large ledge upon which he could lean and allow the smoke to drift over the town adding to the fog from the river that pleasantly obscured the view.

(For an (incomplete) inventory of the contents of the drawing room/smoking room/music room see Appendix 4.)

As for the drawing room itself, it was the nerve-centre of the Laird household – it was where Ethel and Mungo got on each other's nerves at some point each day. Most of the other rooms were sealed-off, the exceptions being a couple of lavatories, (Original Shanks – not your Armitage-Shanks faux-wally), the scullery that adjoined the kitchen, and of course, the master, or in this case, the mistress bedroom, and some odds-and-s*ds.

But life in the raw for the Lairds was lived mainly in the drawing room, which had a high ornate ceiling, ceiling-to-floor bay windows (original sashes, that rattled even on calm days), and was warm for a few hours if the sun shone. There probably was a smaller, cosier room somewhere in the house that would not have taken a fortune to heat, but Ethel was determined to maintain some standards of the life that they had briefly enjoyed before the brewery had gone, and before they had discovered how successful their financial consultant had been with their pension funds. And they used the room because Mungo liked to look wistfully from the open window as he smoked a stogie, and wonder what life would be like on the outside.

Chapter 5

In loco parenthesis.

ANYWAY, his dream had been disturbed and Mungo briefly stuck his head once more into the serving hatch and listened closely to his spouse – or tried to make her think that he was listening closely to her. After all, this was a special day.

Today, this special day, Mungo was wearing a double-breasted blazer that had seen better days, striped shirt (navy-on-grey, yeah, our thoughts too) with de rigueur frayed collar, Faculty of Dental Hygienists tie, and beige cavalry twills over aubergine suede shoes, and a frown designed to simulate concentration. He had also been dressed like that the day before which was only an ordinary day. It was how he liked to be dressed as he was comfortable that way. It made a change from his dressing gown, Carstairs-style pyjamas (no cords or pointy things or buttons) and slippers, in all of which he was inclined to incline until early afternoon at the earliest. But not today!

He smiled for his lover – whom he trusted was well out of earshot as he hummed the opening bars of *Dies Irae* – the original, not the Mozart rip-off.

That day of wrath, that dreadful day,
shall heaven and earth in ashes lay,

And like... (someone) on the eve of battle, he girded himself with his *Daily Telegraph* (under left oxter), a cup in one hand and his Ethel-assigned clipboard in the other. Oh, and clenched between his teeth was an old *Bíró* pen that had a range of uses including stirring his tea and cleaning his ears. This item, a family heirloom, still performed in its original function – which like the Rubik Cube is a tribute to the contribution that exceptional nation has made to civilization despite having a language that makes no anthropogeographic sense.

(On which point, a good question for a Pub Quiz is: *Name three famous Hungarians, excluding Puskas*.)

Just as Mungo made to sit in his favourite chair – furthest from the telephone which rested on one of the side tables (*ReUseIt*, 14 Muriel Street, Somewhere Near You) – and as he skilfully dragged another small side table with one be-sueded foot (with what Connolly terms the Glasgow 'broken-a*se walk') until it was next to his chair so that he could read and drink his tea at the same time; when just at the moment that he was about to lower himself into what passed as the state of *Nirvana*, there was a sudden clattering of water pipes from behind the wall or under the floor or in the ceiling.

A lesser man would have collapsed in defeat, but Mungo, still with paper, and cup in hand, *Bíró* clenched even more firmly in teeth, disconnecting his foot from the table, broke out of his broken-ar*ed walk and almost skipped to the nearest wall to give it a sound kick. The pipes ceased their racket.

How easily peace can be established in some domains, he reflected, thinking of all those Arab wars, that could have been settled had the weans been given a good kicking at the first hint of petulant truculence. He finished positioning his side table, and laid down the clipboard on it along with his cup. Finally settled down and in the act of opening his paper, the telephone rang with a shrill *dring-a-ling-a-dring* that AG Bell would have found comforting, albeit deafening, if he had been proximate.

He waited and tried not to listen to the monster of the Bakelite-disguised-as-ivory instrument. But the important thing from the perspective of the drama, is that to answer it Mungo would need to get off his a*se.

So he waited.

After about half a minute or so, during which the instrument persisted and insisted, Mungo gritted his teeth and bit all the way through the *Bíró* that he had forgotten was in his mouth and had belonged to his father. Now he would need a teaspoon *and* a cotton bud. Free at last to speak, he inclined his head towards the door and called-out at first in a wheedling way.

"Ethel? Will you get that dear?"

No response while the phone stridently persisted: *dring-adring-adring-adring*. (No *bing-bong Avon calling* here.)

"Ethel!?" he called. "Telephone! Rather busy, my dear."

He waited. The d*mned phone insisted on attention. With a sigh of the defeated he muttered "B*llocks. Do everything myself."

And rising he set aside his newspaper and knocked his cup over. Fortunately the *Zeigler* (Copy – see Appendix 4 or 5) Persian rug was pretty used to this and within a few minutes Albert Karmely himself would have struggled to assess the damage.

Just as he reached the phone, Ethel breenged in, brushed him aside, grabbed the thing and demanded to know who the h*ll was it.

"Laird residence!" she accused the phone. "Who the devil is this? Who? What? Yes, yes, no, absolutely not. What do you think this is? *Composting bin*, indeed! People surrounding us you want to give bins to. Put some of them in them."

With that Ethel slammed the phone down and glowered then stared at Mungo settling once again into his chair.

Not being able to find obvious fault with him immediately (her vanity precluded the donning of her specs (Poundstretcher – price unknown) other than in total privacy), and seeing him in a near state of peace she started to vigorously plump every soft furnishing that was remotely plumpable. And some that weren't. She even landed a blow on the tiger who was reclined, rug-ged and well beyond caring.

Eventually Mungo had to move about to avoid getting plumped himself, not for the first time. But in fact not for a long time, he sadly thought. He fought back thoughts of what he would give for a decent pl*mp. A real pl*mp. A proper pl*mp. And his thoughts segued neatly from the cushions to Nellie the pl*mp-ish waitress at the club for one, in the event that Ethel was not for pl*mping.

"Anyone important, dear?" Mungo asked, trying to sound like a man who cared. He saw she was riled and he liked this state of affairs. He knew he could make her even more riled if he was pleasant and pretended to be interested.

"Important!? I should think not. Bl*ody Council. Give us 'free composting bins'. 'Free', my posteri*r. Cut in council tax or whatever they call it this month, more like it. Parks, leisure. Library? Library? When did I have a need for a book?

Preposterous. When was the last time we had a use for a school? Anyway, sent them both to those private schools and look how that turned out. Saving the d*mned world instead of looking after those who suckled them. And what did I get for that?"

"Sore t*ts," Mungo muttered.

"Sore te*ts," Ethel said ignoring Mungo's vulgar intervention and inaccurate spelling. "Saved the council money we did. Pay-as-you-go, I say. If you don't go, jolly well don't pay." Then as if she was seeing him for the first time (which she was since she came in – slow not soft 'focus' being the problem) she stopped in horror, "Mungo! How are you dressed? What's the meaning of this…?"

"Val said that…"

"Val most certainly did not say to look like a Portuguese pimp masquerading as the President of France. What did Val say? Dress down, Mungo. To their level. Look at the time. Oh, will have to do." At this she left with a tragedian's sigh and a little sideways Parthian pl*mp of the cushion at Mungo's back.

(Note re pub quiz question above: Albert Karmely is Iranian (*Persian* if you believe in the Shah) by birth, and not, repeat, not a Magyar.)

Chapter 6

Class and criminality and the church that pretended to be a clock.

The Time. She mentioned the time. Mungo looked at his wrist – but he then remembered his watch was lodged with *Cash Convertors*. His eyes quickly went to the mantelpiece. The clock?! Or rather the no-clock? [*Edwardian French eight-day striking mantel; porcelain dial and Arabic numerals all held in a deep, almost black, green marble. Circa 1900 with an eight day movement striking on the quarters and the hour with a clear, melodious tone.* Manufacturer unknown.]

This clock was a fr*gging monster. So large was it that some Sundays after their lunchtime libation, Mungo could have sworn that he saw a congregation come out of the thing. But how the T*m Dalyell had it been removed? Burglars could never have done it. Lazy b*ggars b*rglars are.

[As an aside: Mungo's observation sheds light on one of the reasons that the main victims of the s*ds are the working class, within whose community, b*rglars tend to dwell. Only those middle-class folks on the edges of such locales suffer at the hands of these sc*mbags – a word Mungo had come across on the television Ethel allowed in the kitchen. She was an aficionado of *NCIS* and *Watercolour Challenge* or any other show that offered the grossest types of vivid imagery. Now middle-class crime is democratic, Mungo argued, because the criminals – the a*countants, l*wyers and b*nkers and ps*chologists – were able to rip-off people of all classes without moving their ars*s from their desks. If you had a couple of pounds in a saving account, or you wanted to buy some foreign exchange for that once-in-a-lifetime trip to Cala-something-or-other, or like Mungo and Ethel once had had, a pension pot that was supposed to provide for a decent life in their twilight-zone years, then you were at the mercy of these white-collared-pillars-of-society sc*mbags.

Mungo had developed his *theory of class and criminality* one Sunday after reading (nearly all of) the *S*nday P*st*. And with his *Bíró*, Mungo had fired-off letters setting out his position, to various publications. In return he got the usual solicitor's letter from the so-called *British Medical Journal* (BMJ) which he contemptuously placed on the pile – he had some knowledge of legal matters garnered from the (centre pages of the) *S*nday P*st*, and doubted that an injunction or even an interdict could apply to letter-writing. There was a more positive response from the *Anglers Times* and a vigorous debate ensued in its letter pages for a couple of issues (during the close season).]

"Ethel! The time? Where's the clock? Have you moved it again, Ethel, the clock?!" he called, getting just a bit irate. In recent weeks there had been a lot of this going on. Objects disappearing and then re-appearing in different parts of the house. Why, only on Sunday Mungo had found his trusty truss behind the coatrack. Which was a bit fortuitous since the coatrack itself had been found behind a hedge. And that was the first time he had noticed its disappearance. (What Mungo was doing behind a hedge is not germane to the drama – suffice it to say that his prostate could hold its own against any other prostate of the same vintage; except it couldn't, unless he held it.)

And now the damned clock was gone – it had been a gift of Uncle Brodie on what he had termed their *Formica wedding* – making it to six months of marriage without any physical damage. Mungo was especially attached to it because it was fashioned in green-black marble in the shape of the Greek Thomson Church that stands to this day on the corner of Saint Vincent Street and Pitt Street, Gl*sgow. His attachment to that particular church – still worth visiting – was unconnected to his love or indifference to architecture or to Alexander Thomson (9th April 1817 – 22nd March 1875), but because he had had his first kiss in the alley behind the church with a girl from Craigholme School. It was the only tangible benefit he had reaped from being at St Kentigern's: had he attended a 'bog-standard state school' (Anthony Charles Lynton Blair; b.1953) he would not have got within sniffing distance of Jennifer Ecks.

But apart from any sentimental value Mungo attached to that clock, what made it really dear to him was that it was just big enough to *plank* (old Scots – *to hide*) a half-bottle of whatever happened to be his favourite tipple that week. And this without interfering with the sonorous chimes that reminded them both of a night of passion in Crieff. On thinking that thought, Mungo made a mental note to see if he could find an excuse to revisit Crieff. But he supposed that Ethel might just perversely choose to accompany him, and so he cancelled that thought and instead wondered if the generously fleshed Nellie at the club – the one who spoke to him as if he was human – had ever been to Crieff, which was just as well, as he had enough thoughts inside his head to last him for at least one morning.

Ethel barged into the room again and flicked at a fly with her *Yellow Pages*. "Clock, Mungo. Gone. Good price too. And there's no use in going to the garden because not only is the sun not shining, even if it was, it'd be no use. Sundial's gone as well. Antique's whatsitsname."

"But the clock, my dear. That had sentimental value to me. Remember Uncle Brodie..." Mungo began.

"B*lderdash, Mungo. Detracting from ambience. According to Val."

And with her eye still firmly on that fly – in fact it was one of the biggest bluebottles either of them had seen – she chased it from the room, and was heard to give it one mighty swat against the wall which ended like the sound of a pumpkin being blasted by a single-action twelve bore (side ejector). This started the pipes again and Mungo, with what passed for anger with him, did the kicking needful and collapsed into his chair and didn't even bother to read his paper.

"Oh b*llocks to Val," he muttered, then bounced out of his chair and stuck his head out the door and called after his wife, "Your precious Val said we should also shoot Polly. I was all for that but..."

Ethel re-entered knocking him over the cuspidor and right into the now forbidden, redundant, humidor.

"Exaggerate, exaggerate, exaggerate. Val said no such thing. Put Polly in a home she said. A care home. The best type. Get rid of the smell." And with that she took Mungo's unsullied *Telegraph* and plopped herself down on his chair.

That was the final straw for Mungo, his paper. The one little pleasure he had left in life, he told himself. Well that and... And... And...?

"Care home, shooting," he said pretty much to himself, though in the loud sonorous voice he sometimes affected at his club, when he was trying to attract the attention of the weasel of a bar steward who sucked-up to those who were not on their uppers while ignoring Mungo. "Same thing in end. Shooting more merciful. Quicker. Cheaper. Did you see that place? Hearse rank, outside. Says it all."

"Mungo! A very good home it is too. Recommended. Last year it won the Gold Medal for the... Awarded by the... To the... that most... Well I don't recall all the details. But it did."

"Name gave it away," Mungo said to himself. Then loudly to Ethel's back, which Mungo noticed was rather attractive this morning, "*Snuffit!* What a name for a care home."

"*Cooriedoon*, Mungo, not difficult to remember. So many to choose from today. All quality. When my time comes, I would want something equally apposite."

"Chri*t's sake, Ethel, it's a dog home. Better with the composting bin. Less trouble. Cheaper. Good for the tomatoes. There's a corner up by the crab-apples that gets the sun in the morning."

"Language, Mungo. Anyway, I find it comforting that the same company caters for people and dogs. There's a certain symmetry in it. I'm sure some Danish philosopher will have said that you can trust a person who treats his dog better than his wife. And it has a motto." She made a mess of folding his *Telegraph* and giving up, crumpled it and threw into the jaws of the tiger.

"Yes, it has a motto," Mungo said bitter-sweetly. "That's all right then. What was it again: '*You wouldn't treat your dog like this*'. Dog branch for me then. Best flight out East I ever had? *Air India* – treated us like cattle," he said to the room.

Meantime Ethel had ignored Mungo and was standing with a look of horror facing the mantelpiece, one hand shaking in anger and pointing at his cup which rested there and which he had no memory of placing thereon. Must have happened in the maelstrom of emotions prompted by the no-clock affair.

"Mungo! What have I told you about cups, Mungo? Never on the mantel, and never, never cups. What did Val say? Mungo?"

"B*llocks, to Val," he muttered below his breath, then as if in rote fashion before the schoolmaster – which in some ways Ethel was, he recited, "Cups. Ah yes. Liked that one, Ethel: cups – lower classes. Mugs, on other hand, show that people of class – such as ourselves – are comfortable with their station. Mugs are us, if not, we. I blame that poncy New Labour Prime Minster we had foisted on us, trying to appeal to his plebeian worshippers. Bet he had an advisor to show him what side the handle went. And by the way," Mungo went on, lapsing into the vernacular, "Val also said that about my much-holed cardigan. Didn't have the heart to tell her: my only one. All my money spent heating this monster." He trailed off, knowing he had overstepped the mark with that last reference.

"Mungo! Control yourself. Never, but never, mention the H-word." And Ethel shuddered so violently at the thought that she set off the ph*cquing p*pes again. While Mungo went off and kicked the wall, Ethel continued in a less emotionally charged vein.

"Val said: If by some chance, one of them raises the issue of the h*ating, well then? Well then?" She towered over him but he felt no fear – the Yellow Pages were missing from her great mitt. So he became ever more rebellious.

"Knit woolly hat, dear? Buy lap dog? Install treadmill? Should we tell them about the buckets in the attic? What did Val say about that?"

"How dare you?" and she began to shudder but, remembering the pipes, settled for heaving her bosom (which almost set Mungo off). "Mungo! Think fiscal prudence. I warn you." And with that she marched from the room only for her great head to reappear in the serving hatch. "And don't mention the b*ckets. Ever." Then she was gone before he could rush across to the hatch and plant a big slobbery kiss on her fizzug (der. *physiog*; abbr. *physiognomy*).

Mungo strolled about the room and mused on the turn his life had taken. He spoke aloud thinking he was alone, apart from the tiger in the tiger-skin rug. "Fiscal prudence? This is our home. The only home we've ever had – apart from the bedsit in Govanhill, which I was quite..."

At which Ethel's visage reappeared in the serving hatch. "*Shawlands*, if you please. Govanhill?! I shudder at the very idea." And she shuddered at the very idea, which took some doing given the Procrustean position she was in at the hatch. "*Upper* Shawlands. Bijou apartment, not a bedsit."

"Well, my love, I quite liked it," he said, hearing inside his head those wind chime things that they use in films to denote entering a dream sequence. Then he continued as if he was in a dream sequence:

"*Bijou* or not. Where else have we been able to lie in bed, cook a fry-up and answer the door at the same time?" Then he drifted off into a soft-porn corner of his dream: "While touching up a certain part of a certain person's nether regions with the other hand. *Visiting the Black Forest*, as Freud might have said had he not lacked a talent for imagery."

He (Mungo that is, not Freud), reached into the serving hatch and managed to get one of Ethel's arms through beside her notable body. He stroked it warmly.

"Ah, those days of wine and Benylin – it was rather damp, admittedly. We had some times there. Eh? No children. Not a concern in the whole world. That time we spent the whole weekend without going over the door?"

Ethel managed to shake herself free of his hand, but now she was in a rather vulnerable position as she was jammed in the hatch. That of course did not prevent her from entering into the spirit of the conversation with her soul-mate.

"As I recall, Mungo, that was because the door had jammed with the subsidence – not by choice. Had to be rescued by the demolition men. I shudder to think of it even now." And she somehow managed to shudder to think of it, despite her squashed condition, even now after all those years.

"Ah, they don't make them like that any more." Mungo said, listening for the chime things that would signal the end of the dream sequence.

"Indeed they do, Mungo. Called *Barrett Starter Homes*, or some such nonsense. Now, enough of all our yesteryears and help me get my arm out of this hatch. And Mungo!" she added quickly, anticipating his state of arousal. "If you go round into the kitchen behind me while I am helpless like this, I'll..."

And on that emasculating note, Mungo heard the rippling chimes that tolled the end of this particular dream sequence, and a few minutes later they were once again in a state of relative mobility.

Chapter 7

Not Chas and Dave.

Ethel was stocktaking in the drawing room, not wholly convinced by Val's supposed specialist knowledge on how one should present a house to the market, for Ethel had the inner conviction that the house and its history made it a bargain, even a steal for those arriviste, aspiring, *soi-disant haute bourgeoisie*. (She did not actually use that phrase, but it just about summarises in pseudo-sociological terms what she was thinking. Of course, it is also summarised in her view that prospective buyers were all *candidates* – try that one in a buyers' market.) Mungo was elsewhere – possibly seeking respite in the original sense.

"Coffee on, percolating nicely," she almost purred, then went to the serving hatch and sniffed hugely. "*Check.* Baking in oven, door open, the scent to waft seductively… *Check.*"

She looked about the room for any treacherous item that was out of place or belonged to Mungo or most likely both. "No clutter– *objet d'art*, trinkets, etcetera, etcetera removed – with the exception of one well-chosen family photograph – all etcetera stuffed in a bag to meet Val's '*no clutter rule*'. *Check.* Medium-priced sherry with appropriately sized glasses ready to hand for the reprise post-viewing."

She fondled lovingly the bottle of Harveys Bristol Cream (*Special Edition* – only 14 million bottles of it sold to date). Satisfied, she replaced it on the silver-plated tray – making a mental note to take the tray to *Cash Convertors* when it was all over – and counted the glasses.

"Four glasses. *Check*." Then with a quick shifty down the hallway and through the hatch (sequentially) she skilfully uncorked the bottle with her teeth, poured a generous jag without wasting a drop; recorked the bottle (still with her teeth) and replaced it on the tray. Saluting herself, (*Slainte*) she tossed-over the sherry and wiping her lips with the back of her hand, said with great satisfaction to the mirror above the mantelpiece:

"*Checkmate*, you wicked woman, you."

Just then the doorbell sounded. *Dring-dring-dring-a-dring-dring – dring-dring.*

"Mungo!" she fluted. "The door. That'll be the first candidates. And what's the magic word?"

In the pantry where he had been hiding reading the rescued but still crumpled *Telegraph*, he muttered, inevitably, "B*llocks?" Then added quickly in case Ethel had bugged the small room, "Only teasing, dearest. The word is '*Candidates*'."

Chapter 8

Still not Chas and Dave.

Dave Ashley-Cole-Cole and his wife Chelsea had had one horrendous journey north, and, not for the first time, they blamed each other for this life-changing urge to start afresh in a new country; there was also the urgent need to disappear into an anonymous bolt-hole, safe from predators like Her Majesty's VAT lickspittles and fellow businessmen of the creditors variety with the aggressive persuasion.

They had been sort of counting on the Scottish people being sensible enough to vote for independence. In which case Miliband's border posts – an anti-tartan Maginot Line perhaps dreamed-up by the kind of Labour politician who had spent nine years at university without ever graduating, had never held a real job in his life, but who still felt himself suited to be the next leader (branch 'office manager') of 'Scottish' Labour – were a very attractive proposition for Dave and Chelsea. As was Dave's belief that it would be years before there was an extradition treaty between the two countries.

But now the democratic process had been gone through and everyone was satisfied that it had been conducted transparently and without anyone waving Kalashnikovs in the air and shouting 'Allahu Akbar'. And the 'YESs' were pure sick.

The people had spoken. The bastards! Worse: the Jock bastards!

So Dave ('Dave') and Chelsea ('Chels') had taken the high road to what promised to be a pleuvian (or *pluvian* if you prefer) retreat, and by the time they had reached the promised land, night had fallen – as had Chelsea when a heel snapped as she left the car for a comfort break behind a convenient and largish toadstool (actually it was a yew that some daft b*ggar with more time than sense had shaped into a sort of toadstool). Luckily the faux fungus backed-on to a B&B and so they spent a passable night until at five a.m. a radio suddenly blared with *Farming News*. After initially covering his head with the duvet, Dave began to take an interest in the current market price of beetroot. One for the future, he filed away, in that entrepreneurial brain.

Dave described himself as an *entrepreneur*. He dabbled in this and that and a bit more of this than that. His most recent project had been a bit of both and all three.

Chelsea described herself as a photographic model. And there was some truth in this because Dave (and his mates) had some scorching snaps of her. She was what Dave called his *trophy wife* – and like the three previous, she would be destined to rest on the shelf a year or two down the line; but for now she was simply the best – better than all the rest… and having thought those two lines, Dave thought it would make a good opening for a song that he would write… but not now for he had other fish to batter into submission.

Chelsea (Chels) was not without her own aspirational entrepreneurial dynamic: she had run a chain of tanning salons, nail bars, t*ttoo parlours and charity shops that only lawyers and naysayers assumed were fronts for drug dealing (Class C only, it should be noted) and taxi companies.

As of yet there were not any little Ashley-Cole-Cole Colettes – though it was not for the want of. Because although Dave was a little man – he was like all men of that ilk (with one exception), big in aspiration and short where it mattered, and Chels was not an unattractive bit of tottie, after making due allowance for the strata of acrylic tan, the clapped-in cheeks (of the facial variety) and the fact that she thought it lacked class if she smiled or showed any sort of enthusiasm.

Chelsea had once been on the front page of Vogue – she had been paralytic after an all-night d*mino marathon in Upper Hackney for Charity. Charity being Chel's best mate since reform school and was now on life support for, well, for life, at least, due to an ill-judged experiment with Crystal Meth (a reggae singer from Lower East Hackney). And before Chelsea could fall over, Dave held her in his arms and gently dropped her onto the pavement outside the *The Don't Give A Duck* public house in Streatham; and it so happened just as her tight little cheeks (non-facial variety) kissed the pavement slab, an old copy of *Vogue* happened to blow along the street and came to rest just where her cheeks (facial variety) now kissed the ground. It was a sign, Dave thought at the time – symbolic in the... the Greater Scheme of... Fings.

But now, on the cusp of that life-changing (even, life-preserving) moment, they had arrived at Villa Laird to view the gaff. And so with no more ado, Dave pressed the bell. And pressed the bell, and pressed the bell and would do so until some f*cker answered it. And we know that it would be M*ngo Laird himself, as Ethel did not do door-answering.

Dring-dring, etc.

While Mungo was answering the door, Ethel fussed with her clipboard then struck a pose at the fireplace. With more horror she saw that Mungo had yet again left his teeth on the very spot where the clock had until recently rested. With a sweep of her arm that would have done an orangutan justice, she swiped the falsers off the mantel, and hid them behind the family photograph – she would personally insert them into Mungo later, she vowed silently. Just at that very moment Mungo entered with, according to Ethel's clipboard, the Ashely-Cole-Coles, their first candidates for the house.

Mungo led the way with a smirk on his face – he was looking forward to Ethel's reaction to these *chavs* – he had recently learned that word from the *S*nday P*st*. (Abroad Readers Page.)

The first thing that struck Ethel after she had managed to get her jaw up from her naval was that the candidates were... *colourful*, with a predominance of brass and... *Bling-bling-bling*. And *bright vermilion*. And that was just Dave.

Chelsea was dressed in what in another age – about two thousand years ago – was Classical Rome: toga and thonged sandals and not a great deal else (as Mungo had sort of ascertained by positioning her against the sunlight that had serendipitously streamed-in at that moment as they had passed through the hallway).

Ethel took one look and put the sherry bottle beneath the table, speaking simultaneously, "Thank you, Mungo," she pronounced icily. "There's a bottle of Buckie chilling on the stoop. Would you? For our guests."

"But there was a bottle of perfectly good sherry..." Mungo began with feigned innocence.

"Mungo!!" And she stamped her foot on the floor with such force that the pipes started to clatter again.

With one skilful Mungo-kicking thump, they ceased and Ethel thought she had covered-up the noise by coughing loudly, but succeeded only in bringing up some phlegm that was well past its expectorant date.

And at that Mungo left with a gracious bow to Chelsea and Ethel and a wink to Dave, who was just the sort of man that Mungo might have wanted to be in another life. And not just for the sake of getting access to the tanned Chelsea.

Meantime, Dave and Chelsea were casing the gaff – no, sorry, were inspecting the room with more than a hint of disbelief and as if Ethel did not exist – which for them could have been the case. They took out their 'mobies' and began to speak to each other across the room – we did say it was a big house.

Ethel looked from her clipboard to the couple and back again. Could she possibly be mistaken? For they had such a name redolent of *class* – with all those hyphens and first names that sounded like surnames and all those other subtle signs by which people of quality indicated their... well their *quality*.

She decided to grasp the nettle, but was unsure whether if she let go of the mantelpiece with her other hand she might keel over, such was the surfeit of emotion (tinged with a tincture of Buckie) that raged through the fabric of her being.

"And you must be... no, surely a mistake on my list – down here as the Ashley-Cole-Coles? Ashley-Cole-Coles? Are you from that council re-cycling mob? *ReuseIt*. Well, if so..."

Then she stopped because they were completely ignoring her and... inspecting the room, the windows, knocking the walls, and Dave even lifted one corner of a rug that had seen bad days and worse floorboards beneath. Dave now remembered what remained of his manners.

"In two, you gottit, duchess. I'm Ashley and she's..." He grabbed Chelsea and gave her bum a resounding smack that suggested a certain level of intimacy. "Go on, guess..."

But Chelsea, after squealing at the smack, stuck her tongue in Ashley's ear, then, because she could not stand the tension occasioned by the question, blurted out, "Cole. He's Dave Ashley and I'm Chelsea Cole. But we thought that sounded too common so we doubled up..."

"As we have been known to do from time to time," Dave interjected and caused Chelsea to simper like a bottle of over-mature, but just-fermented, extra virgin olive oil.

"And so we are the Ashley-Cole-Coles," Chelsea finished with a flourish and somewhat reluctantly avoided the hand that Dave had reached out for her other cheek.

"And so there you have it – more than a touch of class: the Ashley-Cole-Coles," Dave somewhat superfluously added.

"You wouldn't believe the number of people that ask Dave for his autograph. You know: Ashley-Cole. Gettit?" Chelsea said, then turned to Dave quizzically, seeing Ethel was frozen in horror as if she was a too-close witness to some road kill. Then, in what passed for a whisper at Haringey Race Track on a Saturday night before the shooting started, she said:

"Dave. Is she all right, the old duchess?"

"Yeah. Probably just a bit slow. In-breeding. Decrepitude. Comes to all gals. Gals especially prone. Especially prone gals. Ha, ha. If you get my double attendant? No, you don't do you, Chels? Not fair. Not funny to the Discharge side. Fair enough. No one can call me a messaganist. Not Dave. Never.

But God's a man, innhe? Spare ribs'n all that, init?" Dave was making a (right) fist of being a stereotypical Essex boy. He turned to a totally bemused Ethel.

"And trufe be told, our name has certain other pluses in dealings with the authorities. Sowing more than a little confusion at the Social and those geezers what keeps losing our tax details, which pains us both grievously, eh Chels? But then 'spect you know that – I mean who's ever heard of Mungo and Ethel? Nice one. Respect."

At this juncture Ethel took the opportunity to retrieve the Harveys, and poured herself a large one which she downed in a oner.

"Oh, the carpet. Look, Dave. Brilliant," Chels purred loudly. Then to Ethel: "Was here when you came, I pre-presume, darling?"

Then she spotted the piano and raced across to it and after puzzling how to open it up, she shrilled, "Oh look, Dave, a keyboard. In a cabinet. Did you ever? What class. Where's the plug? Never mind – was a... eh... restorical question. It'll need to go. Carpet as well." At which point she produced a tape measure and began to measure the room, then the window. Dave had a laser version of this and spent some time trying to blind Chelsea before switching his attention to Ethel, who was impervious to any sort of laser treatment, at which the laser packed in.

"Yeah, Chels, all gotta go," Dave said, then tried to move the piano for a reason he was about to reveal to all who had been watching him with amazement and unconcern for his chances of herniating something.

"Bar'll do nicely in that spot – amazing what a little bit of glass, chrome and concealed lighting can do." He cast an expert's eye upwards. "That ceiling. Oozes class. And some green stuff up in that corner. Some height. Don't get them like that today outside of Billericay, the sick bay at Strangeways or the trolley bay at Sainsbury's, never. Look, Chels. No way Pepe. That ceiling has got to drop. Drop it, oh, two feet-stroke-metre; sheet it wiv veneer – cedars of Lebanon – give it some class; wiv some spots – transform this into a nice little ambience."

He tapped the wall wiv his 'ead. "Solid enough; will take a bit of cork sheeting, no probs." And with one bound he was at the window. "Nice view, Chels – can see everyone coming. Double aspect. And trees. *Wow factor five* maybe, Chels?"

Meantime Mungo had entered carrying the bottle of chilled *Buckfast* and, being ignored by one and all, but especially by Ethel, he summed up the situation and poured a large measure of the tonic which he tossed-over without it even registering on his epiglottis. After all, he had a long day ahead of him.

Dave was still rhapsodising over the view. "I could stand here all day and rhapsodise over that view," he rhapsodised in an outburst that brought out the poetic streak in him. Then to Chelsea, in a demonstration that he wasn't only poetic, that there was also a sensitive side to him, he said out of the corner of his mouth, "Spot the drug squad a mile off, Chels."

From the window Chelsea articulated what Dave had already thought.

"The bush thingy, Dave, that'll need to go. Youknowwho could hide in that. Apart from that: *wow factor-four-and-a-bit*, maybe." Then she turned to Mungo who had difficulty holding up his lower jaw without hand-aid, so fascinated was he by this exotic pair – and he *was* referring to Chelsea's.

“Bet you know its name, darling,” Chels said addressing Mungo. “That bushy thingy. Fancy like and all that?”

“Indeed my dear. In Latin, I do believe we have... yes, *Rhododendron therzapolis*. Get rid of that and you have a clear line of fire.” And he mimed firing a rifle.

“Nice one, Mung,” said Dave genuinely. “Clocked you for ex-military, from second one. Scots Own Photo Copiers.” Wiv that Dave saluted and walked away before Mung could respond. Then he banged another wall by trying to pin Chels up against it as a sign of affection.

“Got Broadband, Mung?” Dave said apropos FA (f*ck al*).

“Little touch of it last year,” Mungo replied as if he had a clue as to what the other referred. “Nothing too serious. Strong coal tar solution. Fruit should come back next year.”

Chelsea (‘Chels’ to her friends) now turned her charms on Ethel.

“What’s’n other side, luv?” And she knocked the wall with one of her heels. And before Ethel could reply she turned to Dave. “Yeah, Dave, I see this knocked through, and an atrium like, brimming with fish. Capons. Gold ones.”

“Could that be *Koi*, my dear?” Ethel interjected coyly. “And setting aside any differences as to what you and I understand as an *atrium* – capons my dear, I think you might find are castrated cocks fattened for eating, and not noted for their capacity as swimmers.”

Dave held his cr*tch and limped about in real or simulated agony, while both sets of his cheeks were tightly clasped.

“No matter,” Chelsea continued to Ethel. “As long as they’re gold and can swim a bit, they’ll look great under spots. Dave, I see it: lights, lot of lights. Maybe a grotto. Yeah, got to have a grotto.” She swivelled to Mungo who was disappointed as he had been fully appreciating the swell of the toga around the Chelsea buns.

“Went to Lourdes last year but one – or was it Fatima, Dave? We took a wrong turning at Benidorm. No matter. Well, we ended up there, like for reasons that we won’t go into. Miracle we didn’t catch somefink. Inspired me with design ideas. Spiritual like.”

Mungo raised his glass in a benediction. “Ah, spiritual. To the monks! Crutches hanging in cruciform; proscenium of discarded zimmers.” He refilled his glass.

“Yeah. But tastefully done, Mung,” Chelsea said as she marched to the door. “Can we see the... you know... bedrooms? Where the action is. Or should that be *was?*” she said in a loud aside to her bedfellow who leered instinctively at her provocation.

Ethel, reluctantly but quickly, followed Chelsea but not before indicating to Mungo that he should accompany Dave on a separate tour. No way would she tolerate these two being supervised by less than a one-to-one basis.

Chapter 9

Salbutamol for all – all I need is the air that I breathe and to love you.

Dave gave Mungo a whirlwind tour, opening doors that had remained closed for yonks – sticking his bonce in, sniffing as if he was on the way to having a perforated septum, but an innocent explanation might involve dust and mustiness. Dave would close the door gently as if he had been moved by what he had espied, though it could have been that his hangover was making his nerves a bit jangled. Then, when they reached what Mungo thought of as 'the mistress bedroom', Dave followed his usual procedure – poked his head inside, sniffed and closed the door. Then he stood stock-still as Mungo made to go off. He opened the door again, regarded Mungo with a look of naked disbelief, and with a thumb indicated the room and said:

"Mung, you and missis Mung – you don't still share the old Uncle Ned? And before replying, you should know I've got a bit of a delicate stomach."

"Uncle Ned?" Mungo said, wondering if Dave was getting mixed up with Uncle Brodie, but how could he? They had never met and there had been no mention of him.

"Uncle Ned, Mung. Scratch Your Head? Bet Wif Fred? Why can't you speak the Queen's English like wot I do? Don't they learn you English-speak at your Jock schools? Bed, Bed. You and Dame Nelly Ethel Mermaid!"

"Ah, bed. Of course we do. We're still married," Mungo replied as if he was speaking to a real idiot.

"Give under, Mung. What age you? Combined – 160?" Then before Mung could reply Dave had a light bulb moment – which was just as well because as the sun set it got really gloomy in that part of the house. "Gottit. You *sleep* together. You know: in the old antique sense. You see what I mean how easy it is to get confused. That's because of my natural delicacy of manner. Had I been the intrusive kind, I would have said, 'you're not still givin' the old cod a right s*eing to'. You know. I can be sensitive in these matters." Then he put his face close to Mungo's and looked him in the eye. "You're not, tell me you're not."

Mungo, like any man of that age whose manhood is being questioned, not to say interrogated in this case, instead of getting on his high horse and whipping the cur to the other side of the county, hesitated, then followed Dave into the room where he stood looking with wonder at what he now saw in his fevered imagination, as an altar of geriatric lust covered in a patched patchwork quilt.

The silence hung heavy among the heavy damask wall hangings, the heavy Axminster (£22.50 square metre, *General George* – no relation to Colonel George who got his, standing up to Sitting Bull) and the even heavier oak-framed altar of lust. It was Mung who broke the tension – at one time or another he had broken most other things in that room.

“We do have our moments,” he said and immediately felt shame at the betrayal of the secrets of the boudoir. What he did not say was that too frequently these ‘moments’ did not coincide.

Dave turned slowly to Mungo with a look of the utmost respect (or it could have been utter scepticism; either that or a rare, not to say virgin, foray into shyness).

“Viagra! Gottit. You rascal, Mung. Had me going there. Where do you keep it?” and with another bout of shyness for which he was not generally, or ever, noted, he began to rummage in the bedside drawers but stopped almost immediately with the one on Mung’s side open.

“Bl*ody Norah, Mung. What these then?” And wiv that he scooped a handful of inhalers that are used by asthmatics and scrimshankers.

Mungo blushed. For Dave had discovered the secret that he had never shared with anyone not even his consort Ethel. And so he confessed everything – it’s good to talk.

When his asthma had been severe, a decade at least ago, he had got into the habit of generously exceeding the recommended dose. And although he knew nothing of the mathematics of correlation, (or even whether the term had one ‘r’ or two) after a time he did notice that these periods of self-indulgence in the demi-monde of Salbutamol-users coincided with an urgent need for his baggy trousers to ease frontal discomfort. (Think non-erectile dysfunction but not quite satyriasis.)

Naturally, as a gentleman of a certain age, Mungo welcomed this unexpected rejuvenation, and so after a time it became habit forming. He did consult the notes that came with the medicine – and no, his discovery was not recorded by Smith-Glaxo-Kline, but no fault on them, milud.

And then b*ggar it if the asthma did not disappear. But having read somewhere (probably the S*nday P*st again) that there is no cure for asthma, only alleviation, he stuck with the medicine. He briefly thought about writing a piece for the usual publications, but then the thought of all those anglers slugging from hip flasks and snoking (alt. *snoaking*) Salbutamol was too much, baggy waders or not, and so he kept the secret for all those years and kept the repeat prescriptions going in (wonderful service).

The only drawback (no innuendo intended) was persuading Ethel to share his inhaler, so he took to spraying the room before she was likely to enter, and even erected (again no innuendo intended) a mosquito net over the marriage bed the better to contain the aerosol; but that was eaten by the moths who grew fat and quite aggressive and went forth and multiplied. He wondered if that was an unintended consequence of the Salbutamol, but again no mention of moths in the list of side effects. No doubt some smart a*se academic would shine some light on this someday (or night).

At the end of all this – about ten seconds in real time – Dave offered to take some of the inhalers off Mungo's hand for a fair price. And Mungo did a quick (for him) calculation and held back enough inhalers that would see him out this side of eternity and beyond.

As they were about to leave the room, Dave hesitated and was almost reverential in the way he looked at the bed, and from that to Mungo and said:

"You really would do anything for your missus Mung, Mung. No limits. Yeah?"

"Anything," Mungo said and swelled his chest with pride (and some lingering motes of Salbutamol from the morning attempt). "No limits, Dave. I can also speak for my dear wife when I say we would swing for each other."

Dave's eyes lit up – which was really useful because it was now pitch black in the corridor.

Chapter 10

No horse's head in the Uncle Ned – but who could refuse an offensive stereotype?

Everyone held a glass of Buckie. Dave was encouraging Mungo to be a bit more generous with his elbow.

"That's it, Mung. I'm the designated driver, eh pisser, only having a laugh I think not. So, the name. Mungo. Rhymes wiv… nothing. Get you beaten up at school? 'spect so. Yeah cheers. To matters nitty, as we say. How much really do you want? I mean, tell me what you want, what you really, really, really want."

And as if on cue – which it was – Chelsea stomped badly and sung abjectly: "*I'll tell you what I want what I really really want…*"

"Piss off, Chels, we're at the business end now. Chelsea does a really really great Madonna, really, Mung."

"Really? Lourdes influence, I expect. You were saying…?"

"Saying? Was I? What?"

"Business? Remember before the immaculate Chelsea intervened?"

"Ah. Business. Gotcha, Mung. Chels, what about you and Eth paying a visit to the little slappers' room? Freshen up. Mung and me are about to enter into negotiations. Boys' talk."

"Nice one, Dave. Eth, shall we take the bottle?" Chelsea trilled.

Ethel sprung and grabbed her clipboard. Looking over it she addressed the current candidates. "Slave to time and all that. Other candidates due as I speak. So, if you will, Mr Ashley-Cole-Cole, a few last details to complete your application." And with that she gave a firm tap of the clipboard with her pen.

"Suit yourself." Chelsea frowned and flopped onto the couch next to Mung.

Mungo was now far from frowning, despite the stoor-induced coughing of Chelsea in his ear, as she gave Mungo a very friendly squeeze on his thigh.

Dave laughed shortly. "Is she real or what, Mung? Your Ethel as well – precious, ain't she just." Then he addressed Ethel: "Give over please, mean to say: *application*? *Candidate*? Eth, you're trying to flog this dump – beg pardon if I mis-speak – and I, we, who would not normally even dream of setting a trotter in the land of the haggis-basher and porridge-scoffer but who at this moment in time have pressing reasons of a business hue to be *in absentia* from our usual manor, and who is prepared to make you a serious proposition of the readies kind." He turned to Mungo now. "And she is asking me to..."

Ethel had had enough. "Mr Ashley-Cole...! Cole! Allow me to take the pain out of the form-filling. Righty? Good. Now." She frowned at her clipboard. "Profession?" she said looking over the clipboard sceptically at Dave.

"Dave. Call me Dave, Eth. Profession? Little bit of this. Little bit more of this. Get my meaning?"

[Parenthetically it might appear that Dave is an offensive stereotype that no self-respecting author(s) would offer on paper. But trufe to tell Dave had invented himself in the image of a modern Arfur Dailey for pretty much the same reasons that a Chancellor of the Exchequer would change his name from Gideon to George, or a Shadow Minister of Overseas Development might be seen with a can of Irn Bru in his hand.

Dave (or 'David' as he was known to the authorities) Ashton-Lane was the progeny of a senior civil servant at the Home Office and a member of the BBC Trust (official, like). He had attended London Oratory School on an organ scholarship (no innuendo intended, full stop.). There he had been moderately successful in the usual fields: selling bootleg copies of *The Stones*; photo-shopped pics of the Rt. Hon. Theresa May (Home Sec atow, and most definitely <u>not</u> the Teresa May of *Lesbian Student Nurses* fame (2000, dir. E Vorley; 98.6F); and flogging supposed joints stuffed with a mixture of Old Holborn and ground-down oilseed cake. (Oilseed cake while usually fed to cattle, is not to be scoffed at – well actually if more people scoffed it, we would be a fitter nation. However, if set on fire it should not be inhaled any more than t*bacco should. Or m*rijuana.)

Dave had mixed easily with the scions of the new aristocracy of the professional political class: sons of Ministers, sons of metropolitan journo types and the kind of people who run Channel Four News. He had dined and wined in their homes, had snogged a few of their daughters and sisters and had even burgled a few of their homes, (thereby unwittingly lending weight to Mungo's theory of Class and Criminality, though neither could have known it at the time).

And so, from a life of privilege and not too much excess, 'Dave' as he was known, went in search of the killer deal that would make his name and his fortune. The jury was still out on Dave – as it had been countless times before.

Parenthetically in parenthesis (near enough) – Chelsea did not know about this background above described. She for her part was the real thing. Her role model being the character of *Lisa Locke* (played by Alex Kingston) in *Essex Boys* (2000, dir. T Winsor). In her eyes Dave was *Jason Locke* (played by Sean Bean – another wee fellow wiv big presence on the silver screen). Worth a look for Alex Kingston alone, but in the eyes of these critics, Tom Wilkinson steals the acting plaudits. Rating: 8 out of 10. Available on Netflix).]

Ethel stepped outside the safety of the parenthesis and spoke too loudly to herself as she scribbled, "Self-employed builder, from…" She stopped and looked up to stare at the candidates. "Essex."

"How did you do that? Dave, is that not spooky? She's been to Lourdes as well, bet ya, Dave. How else she do that?"

Ethel almost expectorated: "Nine-hundred years of breeding!"

"And twenty years of *The Sweeney…*" Mungo said in an ill-judged aside.

Ethel would have him for that. In private of course.

"'*Self-employed builder*'," Dave, said slowly, savouring the sound and the image it conjured up. "Look good on the charge sheet. Enough, Eth, I say: stuff the form-filling." He leaped up and snatched the clipboard – and Ethel staggered back and was saved from falling by the bottle of Buckie, to which she clung for a time.

"Mungo, here's the nitty: the old arithmetic. The *bodmas*. Here's how I see it: I'm a man of business; I do the sums. The math. John Public wants a nice piece of Axminster, a shag pile…" Dave looked at Chelsea but patted Ethel's bum at the same time. At the very same time Mungo failed to stifle a laugh and Ethel mentally added this to The Mungo List of Shame and Punishment, just behind the *Sweeney* barb.

"I give a price. John Public gives a price. Dave does sums on piece of paper – add twenty-odd per centum for the chancellor's take, deduct 5 per cent for the blagger; add the number first thought of, and bingo, Mungo, we have the deal. So by my calculation and ready reckoner – you've asked for offers over x; I'm thinking x-squared minus two-pie-r an eels, to keep it round. We arrive at a reasonable sum. We shake hands with the wife's best friend and her dog but one, and we cut out the agent's fee."

During his exposition of the arcana of financial arithmetic, Dave had scribbled furiously on a tatty piece of paper that he now showed to Chelsea before passing it to Ethel. Ethel took it with discernible, almost palpable, if not audible, distaste. Dave tried to force a handshake on a reluctant Mungo. Mungo rose rapidly (for him) and snatched the tatty paper from Ethel. Mungo read it, beamed with delight and extended two hands to heartily shake a right well-satisfied Dave.

"I think this rightly calls for a proper drink," Mungo announced to no one's surprise as he recovered the bottle of Harveys from under the table. He poured one and slugged it off then looked at the paper again.

Dave Ashley had never been nonplussed, bemused or even mildly amazed by anything in his short cynical life, but he was all three now as he watched Mungo wave the paper with his offer on it in the air, hum a samba tune, dance sinuously, and passing Ethel went to grab her. Ethel fought him off with difficulty but easily snatched the paper out of Mungo's hand. She looked at the paper again, poured herself a Buckie, looked again, made as if to pour another but spotting Mungo again at the Harveys, snatched the bottle from him, poured a large one, threw it back, swallowed the air even harder and finally took control of herself.

"There are other candidates, eh viewers. However, shall we say that you have made a strong impression. Very strong."

"Not least on your bum, Eth," Chelsea giggled.

"Quite so, my dear! However, this is a time for calm and reflection. Shall we say, we'll be in touch, perhaps?"

Ethel hung on grimly to the paper offer as a laughing Dave tried to retrieve it from her. "Mungo, please escort our guests to the front gate. By way of the proscenium if you must. But look out for any loose capons."

"Free range. Less rubbery," Mungo tagged as he draped an arm around one candidate's shoulders and just managed to resist placing the other one on the lower waist of the other candidate, as he showed them to the main door of the house that all three felt was about to change hands.

Chapter 11

Oui, nous regrettons beaucoup. (Not Edith Piaf)

Mungo sat in his chair and tried to work-up a wind-chimes effect to get back to the dream of Portugal. He wondered if he should have a drink but rejected the notion, thinking the dream would do it all for him. But then realised that he must be coming down with flu or something that was affecting his ability to think clearly. So he had a small sherry and closed his eyes and waited for the wind chimes.

But it was not to be, for at that moment his wife heavily entered. Very heavily even for her. She staggered to the mantelpiece and propped up the now-crumpled piece of paper – the Ashley-Cole-Cole offer. She gingerly stepped back and tottered to the window. Mungo wondered if she had even noticed his presence.

All of a sudden Mungo felt his heartstrings tug. Ethel seemed so vulnerable at that moment when she was seen but was unaware. He felt a sharp pain in his chest – then realised he had put his rose pruners in his inside pocket and if he tried to move he was in danger of conducting some open-heart surgery.

Taking great care, he repositioned the pruners, and rising slowly made to comfort his wife. Too slowly. Damn it. Ethel turned from the window raising her right hand to halt Mungo's advance and then her left. At first Mungo thought it was the old Floyd Patterson peek-a-boo stance, but then realised that in her southpaw she wielded the Chav's offer which, even as he looked, she swept past him in a cloud of talc and organza that made him sneeze. Happily the pruners were secure and no serious damage was done to his chest. Ethel placed the paper in pride of place on the mantelpiece.

Somehow she managed to convey 'silence', 'contemplation', 'gravity' and 'or else, Mungo!' simultaneously, with her sinister hand.

Mungo cautiously approached the pride of place paper offer, noting also an opening in the uxoriously comforting stakes. Even money, he gave his chances of needing the b*ggy tr*users before the day was over, as Ethel lingered, vulnerable and infinitely engrossed in the Cole-Coles or was it Coles-Cole paper?

Mungo could imagine the torment in his consort's mind as she crunched the numbers, and perhaps even heard the faintest whisper of the wind chimes. But then a frown formed on her visage and Mungo just knew she was having second thoughts. No matter, it was an offer he had no intention of refusing. But first he knew he must play the game, participate in the silent dance with his partner. He slipped his hand onto her waist and began to sway – it was not the sherry, it was the moment. Then their momentum gathered.

Had they been able to, they would have circled the mantelpiece in a full-blown version of the Lakota Ghost Dance, (which is traditionally associated with a state of bliss; but has had a poor press since the Lakota were dancing it just before

Wounded Knee when the perfidious US troops fired on them during the dance).

ANYWAY, the only thing that stopped them was the wall to which the mantelpiece was attached, and Mungo's wounded knee. Had they been on one of the *Location, Location, Location* programmes that choke the airwaves, they could have proposed knocking two great holes in the wall either side of the mantelpiece, and that would allow them to circle the wagons. Instead, they did the next best thing: they swayed from side to side, but never touching each other (to Mungo's chagrin), and never taking their eyes off of the paper on high.

Anyone entering the room now would have sworn that Mr and Mrs Laird were in a trance, the mesmeric force apparently emanating from the central mantelpiece. Eventually the dance ended. Mungo was glad. His bad knee was giving him gip and the other seemed to be on the cusp of welcoming the symmetry by embracing the inchoate osteoarthritis. But no matter: the dance cessation could mean… It could mean… yes! Ethel now stared hard at him. Looking into his eyes for the first time in… in… yonks. He smiled what he hoped was his most becoming smile, hoping like hell that for once she would not treat it as yet another performance of dissembling, masking the lust in his loins. Something of an art form for him. But! Not only had she desisted from the dance, not only had she made genuine eye contact, she was, he was sure, she was about to…

"Mungo, I warn you now – don't take this the wrong way: hold me please."

You ph*ckingreeka! Mungo did not exclaim. Instead he attempted to keep the gleam in his eye down to a vivacious, attractive flicker as he, as smoothly as his good knee would allow, moved to take his beloved in his arms.

Crooning a passable version (to Ethel only) of Stan Getz's: *O Grande Amor* into her left ear (the one with the shampoo in it) he managed to sway her round almost a full circuit before slipping his right hand down to gently cup her left buttock (her best feature, in Mungo's unshared opinion). MISTAKE! That broke the all-too-brief spell.

Ethel removing his hand, then smoothing her skirt, now resumed her lofty position again at the window.

"Oh, Mungo, what have we let ourselves in for? Our home. To even contemplate that type here. Is this what it comes to? Pair of cretins who could buy and sell us? Ugh. *'Knock that wall through; line this one wiv cork veneer. Install atrium for the carp-koi.'* Or was it aquarium? Does no one else see anything amiss about this state of affairs? The injustice of it all?"

She wailed in that way that Mungo found quite provocative, and his mind drifted briefly, inevitably, yet again, to the baggie trousers. But only for an instant, for Ethel was on the move again, in that stately manner that many pachyderms have: it appears slow and leisurely, and there is a graceful sway that gives the impression of simply marking time. But as anyone knows who has been chased by an elephant or a hippo, late on a Friday night or the very early hours of any weekend day, the b*ggars can run, you better believe it.

Now at the window once more, Ethel turned, no longer looking down on the town, to look down on a now-seated husband. Then staring again at the elephant in the room atop the mantelpiece, she went on.

"Is it us, Mungo? Perhaps we are the misfits? Are we going the way of the dinosaurs? In a million years will a team of fossil hunters be poring over what little evidence there is of our existence, and wondering as to what led to our demise? Was it a meteorite? A tsunami? Al Qaeda?"

"Al Gore? Al B. B*ggared?" mumbled Mungo.

Ethel, ignoring him not for the first time, continued, "T'was the competing claims of David and Chelsea Ashley-Cole-Cole and their Essex drug-dealing ilk. *Sic transit gloria*, Mungo."

She sighed a sigh of epic proportions and slumped upon the couch in a posture that it would have taken a Burne-Jones to capture. Mungo waited expecting the pipes to clatter behind the wall in response to the sigh and slump, but in vain. Her request was demanded through a dust cloud.

"Point me south, my love. Place a glass in my hand."

Mungo poured two extra large (purely restorative) tonics of a monkish sort.

Chapter 12

In praise of tonic wine and a
bad year for Saint Émilion.

When the family brewery had failed under Mungo's stewardship and after all of the dust had settled – most of it up Mungo's nose it seemed, because he soon after became rather 'chesty' – Mungo swore to drink no more beer. And so they would have a bottle of a decent wine with their evening meal (they were still eating food with their meals in those days). Ethel had been chesty in a different sense from an early age; but not so early that it would get us into trouble for alluding to it – however no more of that just in case, milud.

Being of a conservative nature by birth and upbringing, for Ethel and Mungo *wine* meant French – not the people of course. Not for them cheap imitations from California, Australia or New Zealand, and certainly not from Chile or Argentina. And as for Jerry wines, well the very thought of them made them feel all-over patriotic each time they disdained a Riesling, a Mosel or a Hock. South African 'wine' was of course not a matter for discussion among consenting adults.

And so the combination of Mungo's chest and their newfound *oenophilia,* led Mungo and Ethel on a tour of the great wine regions of France. At this juncture they thought they still had a substantial pension pot, feeling rather smug that they had narrowly missed placing their savings with Equitable Life. But what financial advisors don't take from you on the swings, they'll get on the chute, the waltzer or even the helter skelter, long before any roundabout.

Everything went swimmingly well. The car, which they had inherited along with the house, was a 1950 Humber *Super Snipe*, and it drew admiring glances, even from the French who watched open-mouthed (*muet d'admiration*) as Mungo got used to driving on the wrong side of the rue.

The only small hitch on the journey south arose as they entered the Bordeaux region, where, at a well-known vineyard, a lecture by a visiting professor of oenology ascended into an extended tasting session. When a few days later Mungo was trying to make sense of what happened, he reasoned that he had learned so much from the lecture that probably too much new information had been crammed into his brain; such that it pushed out vital information needed for everyday functioning. And this was manifested when they had got outside to the car park, where it became rapidly clear to other motorists that he had forgotten how to drive. Anyway, with typical Mungo good fortune, the moat was dry and there was a small mobile crane in the next village.

The only other highlight – and one that would mark a change in their lives – was an incident at Saint-Émilion. Now anyone who has visited this beautiful little historic commune will tell you one thing: the cobbles on the main street (or *grande rue*) that slopes down to really creepy catacombs at an apparently world-famous church built into the side of a cliff, are like glass with a thin smear of Three-in-one oil (*trois-en-une huile*), or WD40 (no trans.). They don't tell you that in the Blue Guide (*Guide Bleu*). You have now been warned.

Anyway, on their descent of that rue, Ethel slipped on her derrière (a*se) and descended like those mad tobogganists on Madeira. Mungo managed to slip her grasp as she tried to take him with her, and he remained standing for a time watching his beloved disappear down the quaint street. Only her pride was injured, but the good thing was she took seven Jerries and four very tall Dutch visitors with her just by the force of her bow wave alone.

By the time Mungo reached the bottom, having stopped off at a little café for a big cognac to steady his nerves, a crowd of concerned by-standers were looking after Ethel who seemed remarkably calm after her experience, as she and they waited on ambulances for the injured tourists. And just at that moment, *timeously,* as Mungo arrived to express his concern, a personage in Benedictine togs appeared and produced from within his habit a restorative tonic wine produced under licence from his home abbey in Devon, (Ingerland ou Angleterre), which did the trick.

And from that moment, from one habit developed another habit. ("*Three small glasses a day, for good health and lively blood"* – a fine example of marketing circa 1890, which says it all. See tasting notes in Appendix 6.)

As to what a Benedictine with a bottle of Buckie was doing in one of the finest wine domains in France, remains a Mystery – a bit like the Trinity. On their return home, they were confronted by another mystery: where had their pension fund gone?

The telephone rang. *Dring-a-dring.* Mungo never thought twice for once. *He* answered that blo*dy phone. Ethel interrupted her appreciation of the subtle flavours of the Buckie and looked in wonderment and suspicion at this rare event as her man spoke into the telephone.

"Laird residence... Val...! The Ashley-Coles. Yes. Yes. Just left. Came, saw, vanquished all did Dave and his dear spouse-come-partner-in-larceny. No, I wouldn't say we undersold it. I think they had made up their mind in advance. What makes me say that? The removal van outside. No, no, Val, just my attempt at levity. I was wondering, did you advertise us in the *Police Gazette?* No, no, nothing like that. No, for a be-muscled and tattooed resident of Essex, perfectly pleasant I thought. Dave was fine as well."

The front doorbell rang. *Dring-dring*. It was a rather refined rendition that presaged an altogether different species of candidate, if candidate it were. Either that or some water from the roof had found its way into the wiring. Mungo looked at Ethel. Ethel looked at Mungo. There was now a duel as to see who could hold out the longest before answering the door. It was in the event, no contest.

"Talk to you soon, Val... yes. I am certain the mugs swung it. Must dash. More candidates, I expect. Candidates aplenty thanks to you, Val. Bye."

Mungo hung up as Ethel struggled up. Mungo went to answer the door as a fairly sober Ethel found her clipboard before slurring after Mungo:

"Mr and Mrs Gurpreet Sartram, I presume."

Chapter 13

Friends from the East – Don't mention c*lour.

Afterwards when he reflected upon it, Mungo made a note of the features that had first struck him about the candidates Sartram. They both, to his trained eye, (the left one), had a professional air about them: he in dark business suit, camel-hair coat with the spiv collar and blue-striped shirt by Hawes and Curtis, set-off with a College of Surgeons of Edinburgh tie. This tie was the one with the '*sun motif*', and Mungo duly noted it because he had a couple of these in a drawer somewhere, that he had picked-up at that superior Oxfam Shop on Byres Road (Glasgow: well worth a visit). In fact in that very same shop he had picked-up the shirt by H&C that was the same as the one Mr Sartram was wearing. He suspected that Mr Sartram had not been shopping in Oxfam or one of their pale imitations.

His eyes were of flashing jet, as was his hair, which was suspiciously shiny and smelled of camphor. And there was something of polished walnut that emanated from him. OK, Mungo's been prevaricating and trying to avoid saying that Mr Sartram's roots were in 'the sub-continent'; though by his accent and his dress sense, they were not from within smelling distance of Kolkata bus station.

Mrs Sartram, like her husband, was in her early thirties and dressed like him, apart from the fact she was not wearing a camel-hair coat with spiv-collar, and in place of the Hawes and Curtis shirt, she wore a well-cut shot silk blouse of the palest peach, that was open at her lovely throat where hung a simple sapphire, mounted on platinum and surrounded by small diamonds, all of it suspended on the finest gold chain (Van Cleef & Arpels, price on request). And while she wore a business suit in charcoal similar to that of her husband, the trousers were gently flared and cut to show the niftiest pair of Nell Calf Leather Ankle Boots (the ones with the gold buckle – a bargain at £275.00 at time of writing from L.K. Bennett: on-line only).

Both the Sartrams were judiciously weighed-down on wrists and fingers by the kind of understated bling (so understated that the noun 'bling' is verging on a singularly single solecism), which the Ashley-Cole-Coles could only dream about or steal. Or dream about stealing.

As well as being an eminent consultant in the expanding field of obesity surgery (*Abdominoplasty*, to give it a medical-sounding name), Mr Gurpreet Sartram (MA (Oxford), MB BChir (Edin.), FRCS (Eng), FRCSEd, FRCS (Plast)) was a junior partner in a company that ran a chain of care homes for the elderly. The senior partner, conveniently enough, was his good lady wife, the Memsahib as he referred to her (when she was not around). But more importantly, he had just recently been elected Vice Captain of his local golf club and that meant at last he had a guaranteed parking spot – he wasn't that bothered about the golf, but saw the club as a good recruiting ground for patients as it was full of fat ba*tards.

But he soon learned that the guaranteed parking spot was in theory only – because despite the LARGE SIGN: *VICE CAPTAIN* marking his spot, there is – as some readers will know – in every golf club one unreconstructed maverick. This person had somehow slipped past the membership screening system and felt that since he (it was always a 'he') paid the same fees as the Captain, the VC, the Club Secretary, the Past Captain, the past VC, the Future Captain, the Lady Captain, the Lady Captain's Present Lover, etc. – he had felt that he was entitled to park wherever the f*ck he chose.

[Actually it was not always the fault of the membership screening system – there were sometimes developmental issues involved: a perfectly decent chap could be welcomed into the fraternity, then over the years a personality change ensued for a variety of reasons: his golf was sh*te; his wife had run off with the most junior greenkeeper – a particularly egregious occurrence and not as uncommon as a chap might suppose. The outcome being that this scoundrel would take it upon himself to park wherever he chose, as has been said above.]

BUT ANYWAY, apart from that little fly in the whatsit, Mr Sartram was now part of the inner sanctum: he had made a generous contribution to the new clubhouse roof fund, and overall was quite pleased with his lot. But not too much so, and he had retained a gentle streak in self-effacement, and even humour, even although he counted Edinburgh University among his *almae matres*. Not only that, he could have been even smugger had he so chosen, because he had married Anita, one of the most beautiful women he (and Mungo) had ever seen. Even his father – the venerable (and alas venereal) Bede Sartram, poet, scholar, warrior and now chief stationmaster of the West Bengal Railway Company – was all for his son's choice and immediately phoned his brother to cancel the arranged marriage between Gurpreet and his first cousin Charu, (beautiful and attractive though she was), on the grounds that there were enough idiots in the family already.

What happened to jilted cousin Charu is the subject of a poem that rivals the *Bhagavad Gita* in its prolixity and subtlety, and, at the time of writing is being made into an eight-and-a-half hour Bollywood musical without any funding from the Film Council of Scotland – as far as can be told from their annual report.

Mrs Sartram, Anita, had qualified in Law (First Class of course – although it was just from Edinburgh– but never mind). After which she had taken a Masters in Accounting and Finance. Despite this being a combination made in hell for the soaking of the poor and the soon-about-to-be-poor, thus far Anita had not displayed any of the traits usually associated with those denizens of the Kingdom of Avarice. Instead she was a caring and compassionate person who could be found marshalling food banks and organizing soup kitchens in George Square or on Clyde Street (both Glasgow and not really worth a visit, unless you are truly and literally starving) on Friday and Saturday nights.

Why, even her chain of care homes seemed to do what it said on the brochure: they cared for their residents – at a price of course, but that is the nature of the beasts. There was no evidence that they skimped on food or medicines or drugged their more recalcitrant occupants, and their staff were reasonably well trained. (All of which begs the question: why the h*ll can the others not be like this?!)

Despite all of these saintly virtues, Anita Sartram did not play golf but was frequently seen on the arm of her consort at strategically chosen functions. Moreover, despite the dead giveaway of the surname, the two Sartrams had somehow made it onto Ethel's clipboard.

Ethel was in her element. Well, in her cups at any rate, and reluctantly after the first visuals, she was beginning to like the cut of the Sartrams' jib (and their clothes). So she was just a little bit tipsy, and why not? It was after ten forty-five, after all, and the day stretched ahead until lights out. And so she swept about the room – Mungo had swept about the room with a brush earlier. Ethel provided an over-rapid running commentary for her candidates, in a rather loud and horsey voice, it should be said. She had decided to get this over with as quickly, if not as decently, as the Race Relations Board would allow, as a restorative and private Buckie was urgently required.

"Doubles as music room. Pianoforte." She banged on the keys and produced what Mungo thought sounded awfully like an *A minor diminished fifth* or possibly an *E flat suspended seventh.*

Mr Sartram was in no doubts whatsoever.

"Ah, Madame Laird is a fan of the incomparable Karlheinz Stockhausen – and you have just played the opening diatonic of the thirteenth bar of his sublime *Aus Den Sieben Tagen.* And most beautifully too, don't you think, my dear?" he said turning to his memsahib. "How does the rest of that passage go? Let me see." And he began to hum most discordantly, which probably means it was a pretty good rendition as far as Mungo was concerned.

At which point the pipes insinuated themselves into the performance, at which point Mungo insinuated himself onto the walls with a hefty kick that brought the piece to a plagal conclusion.

Meantime Ethel was trying to act as if anyone was giving more of a d*mn as to what she was saying than she was.

"Window," she pronounced majestically and caught the sill to steady herself. "What-do-you-call-it: window, bay, naturellement. Original sash. And above we have the whatdjacallit... ceiling. That's the thing. Original Victorian ceiling with classical cornicing and ceiling rose. All original features dating back to 1885 – including myself apparently. Commanding views of whole valley." Then she added a little naughtily as she was digressing from the script written for her by Val, "For what that's worth."

With a flourish she made great play of writing on her clipboard. But she could not get the lid off the pen so she tossed pen and clipboard onto the couch regally before sinking Titanically into it with a great sigh, followed by Ethel giving a little sigh.

Mungo, with his intimate knowledge of his consort, saw the strain she was obviously under, and so, like the man he would like to be, he decided to take up the narrative. He might get into those baggy trousers yet, if he made a good job of this and if Ethel noticed. Which was a big 'if' at this point because she appeared to have fallen asleep – though it could have been that she had simply had a stroke.

He'd read somewhere – possibly *The S*nday P*st* (editorial), for that is where all of his medical expertise came from; or he thought he had read somewhere – that stroke victims sometimes make a snoring sound in the first few minutes, and that it is dangerous to try and revive them at this stage. So he left Ethel *in situ*, all the while the sound of gentle gurglings coming from her person, while a very becoming silvery trail leaked from one corner of her generous mouth and traced a sparkling curve down her chin and under it before disappearing in some nether region. She was definitely better well left.

Of course if it was serious, Mr Sartram, eminent consultant, would have been b*ggar-all use as his speciality was, as previously noted, *abdominoplasty;* and while Ethel might have given the impression of being your average buffalo-wings eater, she was merely *BIG-BONED*. Many women who appear large and grossly overweight are by their nature *BIG-BONED*. This is not a euphemism for *Fat* or any of its synonyms subtle or crass. One would no more speak of an elephant being fat than this type of womanhood. There are no fat elephants: they are *BIG-BONED* like most pachyderms – just one of the several characteristics Ethel shared with this group of non-ruminant mammals, another one being that she was thick-skinned. Oh, and she never forgot a slight (of Mungo's). Oh yes, and she liked buns.

Mungo steeled himself for the spiel, careful not to nudge Ethel in case it was the aforementioned stroke.

Chapter 14

For Peter Sellers, Mungo falls in a buyers' market.

"Yes the view. Quite, quite unique. A clear day one can see Ben Lomond, Dumbarton Rock and the slowly moving queues for methadone at Lloyds Pharmacy on downtown Main Street." (See Appendix 5)

Having confirmed that Ethel was indeed sleeping and there would be no need to call for an ambulance, Mungo introduced himself with his hand outstretched.

"Mungo Laird. You'll take a sherry before the grand tour?" he said, popping the cork – a sound that was music to his left ear.

"Gurpreet Sartram. Thank you no, sir. Mornings only my urine I drink," Gurpreet said with a twinkle in his jet eyes. At this his memsahib choked – probably on a sesame or cardamom seed from last night's Ruby (older readers) or Andy (the rest).

Mungo was taken aback at first but quickly recovered and took the tonic wine from the coal scuttle.

"Then a wee Buckie, mind you will not," he improvised, and not waiting for a reply poured two generous measures – *double jiggers* was the technical term used by the weights and measures specialists that Mungo sometimes socialised with when Ethel was on her monthly pilgrimage to Raymond and Randolph's Tonsorial and Epidermal Unisex Boutique (locally kent as *Salon Shug Two*).

Gurpreet, who as he had previously attested was used to drinking p*sh, slugged the Buckie off in a oner. His jet eyes only briefly flickered then turned red, as did his ears and probably his nether extremities. Memsahib Sartram, glowered very prettily as she was not amused. Why none for her?

Enough of this discrimination and chauvinism and sexism and anti-feminism and that.

Meantime, her husband's colouring had returned to normal for the most part – though if the roof of his mouth could have been projected onto a screen, then it would have been like having the Sistine Chapel Ceiling and the bus shelter at Govan Cross (Glasgow, after the game) all in one in the living room.

"Thank you, sir, most kind you are," he said in a husky voice. And turning to Ethel who had wakened when the Buckie cork had been removed, "Madame, indeed a room most beautiful in its heyday, Madame, of the double aspect and original features as specified in the specifications." And at this, like one of his fakir cousins (a right phac*uer, in Gurpreet's opinion), he produced the Home Report and waved it in the air before continuing.

"As one would hope in a climate of transparency in matters contractual, in a buyer's market according to the *Solicitors Property Selling Gazette* if one puts any trust in that organ, which is not to denigrate it in case it comes to their attention, the libel laws being what they are."

"What?!" Ethel gasped, and looked at Mungo to blame for this nonsense.

"And truly magnificent views. Look, Gurpreet," Mrs Sartram interjected, just to add to Ethel's confusion and Mungo's delight, because Anita Sartram was one of those women who when they speak, feel obliged to squirm a bit as if the pelvis was connected to the vocal chords. Which was fine by Mungo.

"Agree with you more I could not, my sweetness," her husband said, and took her hand and then turned to Mungo. "The direction, sir? In which direction we are looking?"

Mungo looked puzzled, which was not an unusual condition for him when dealing with civilians.

"Direction? Direction? Why..." then he pointed out the window. "That way. Bad day, South Nitshill. Can't say I've ever... ah... you mean the direction, as in boxing the compass? Yes, with you now. Let me see. That's..." and he pointed out one of the sides of the bay window and played for time while his sharp legal mind (courtesy of *The S*nday P*st 'Where Are They Now'* column) searched for the most politic answer. And of course the algorithm that was playing out in his mind came up with the solution.

"East," he said with growing conviction. But not knowing when to stop, when he was sort of ahead, he lathered it on. "Yes, facing east. Mecca's that way. The new one. For Matalan it is handy." He felt he now had a handle on the lingo.

Gurpreet smiled wickedly. "Ah. Bingo, Mungo, if I may partake of a wordplay at your expense?" Then to Ethel with barely a missed beat, "I like very much this room, Madame Laird. You have lived and loved it for years innumerable. Huddling round the fire – is that real fire or Living Flame without living flame? Tinkling the old Joanna Lumley to the sound of sleigh bells and the Jackie Bird bird at Hogmanay."

At which he played the exact same chord that Ethel had earlier.

Despite this, Mungo was not greatly impressed: who does not recognise that bar in Stockhausen, who does not want to sing-along with that chord in the language of der divine Schiller?

Aus Den Sieben Tagen: (SINGEN SIE!): ♫ ♪ ♬♯

(**Note**: as most readers will ken, Karlheinz – or *Karlheinz* to his friends – did not use conventional musical notation, substituting numbers instead. We have transliterated the above for those who are of a less musical bent. Well have you ever tried playing 2.71828^{-3} ? Go on, try it.)

And after a remarkable rendition of that ineffable chord, Mr Sartram, as he was sometimes called – he would have preferred Doctor, but in a perversity of the medical profession in this country, *Mister* signified a consultant (unless it was a hospital janny, of course, but the question rarely arose) – and after a remarkable rendition of that ineffable chord, as remarked before, Mr Sartram addressed the room.

"We are favourable impressed, are we not, Anita, my wife of several years, who is not yet with child but with the hammer and a tong we are going at it, if that is not too expressive a way of revealing our intimacy of relations?"

And at this he took Anita's hand briefly, then glanced at the Home Report in his hand and went back to the window.

"So much land at rear of residential property in most sought-after location. Room for many chickens and not a few goats. Sir Mungo, if I may be so bold to be intimate of name use. The livestock, you do not have, sir? They have been fattened for the Christian festival of Christmas, yes? And a Happy New Year too, to you two too, if that is not a mouthful.

And then lo! The silence of the lambs to steal a metaphor, which is no bad thing given the bluetongue and the foot-in-the-mouth. But perhaps we can see other…" and here he referred to the Home Report again and read:

"'…*capacious dimensions of this prestigious property which has many of the original features and which will be attractive to a perspicacious buyer who will want to realise its potential in the modern idiom.'"*

And with that he looked around the room at his companions as if waiting on a response or perhaps applause.

Ethel reacted quickly and with a hand gesture and a look that somehow simultaneously, instantly signified to Mungo and no one else (Now! Serious!! Private Word!!! Or, else, Mungo!!!!). She then spoke over-politely to the candidates.

"Will you excuse please? I've a bun in the oven. Mungo!" But before she could heave her bosom in the general direction of the door, Gurpreet interjected with concern:

"Oh dear Lady Laird, you must not tire yourself. Lots of rest are this doctor's orders." And he took her hand and looked her up and down as if he was measuring her for a gastric band, subsequent to some severe irrigation of her colon.

Ethel, despite her upbringing, simpered and pulled her hand away and taking Mungo fairly gently by the collar marched him out of the room.

Chapter 15

For Matalan it is handy, or: what do we do now?
(ÇÈ Àã ˜یÇ ˜ÑÊÿ ÀیŸ)

Left alone, for a few moments Gurpreet and Anita avoided each other's eyes; but then their eyes met and they smiled at each other. Then Anita, who had been too quiet for too long (in her opinion), and in an accent that had been born on the white side of the Gangtok Hill Station, polished at a Lake Geneva finishing school in Switzerland and honed and buffed peerless in the cocktail circuit of Eaton Square, Belgravia (OK: she spoke like Baroness Helena Kennedy on one of her better days):

"Drinking urine, Gurpreet. Taking the p*ss you mean. I'm sure the old rogue is beginning to tumble to it. Did you hear him copy you? 'For Matalan it is handy!'"

To which her consort, said, in an accent for which Malcolm Rifkind would kill Roger Moore: "Well, it's what these people expect. Surprised we even got to view it. How many have we expressed an interest in, when suddenly they are no longer on the market? And anyway, they started it. Her bawling in my ear as if I was... Spanish or something. Then him – *Mecca* indeed. Could take them to the Race Relations Board, I'm sure, except

I think I sympathise." He waved his hand at the room. "What do you think? First impressions? Good-to-fair?"

Mrs Sartram had another look about her and went to the window. She hesitated then replied:

"Not quite sure. Do you think they'll let us see the rest of the house. Must say it does not look as bad as the Home Report has it. Strange that. Yes. I like it. Going by this," she indicated the room, "it needs some freshening up. And the plumbing. You heard it for yourself. No problems with freshening up the paint, stripping down the banister to the original. Change a few things. But not in the modern idiom, you modern idiot. Retain the character. I'm not sure about all those samey-looking villas along the road. They're probably full of teachers and social workers. Can we remain aloof? Can we be bothered? Can we carry the shopping up those stairs?" And she turned back to the window.

Gurpreet clapped his hands. "No, Annie. No shopping. No need. Remember the goats?" And he laughed.

"Not to the mention the chickens," his wife responded, and joined in and upped the laughter.

"The chickens! I forgot about the chickens." He laughed even louder.

"I said not to mention the chickens, you modern idiot, Gurpreet!" Anita shrieked, tears on her cheeks awaiting their cue…

And at that her husband began to waddle about the room like Groucho Marx meets Chuck Berry, and flapping his arms by his side like Norman Collier's stage chicken, while singing:

"I feel like chicken tonight, chicken tonight."

At some point during this display, Mungo and Ethel entered unseen by the Sartrams. They stood transfixed and only when the man and wife had collapsed into each other's arms – that is the Sartrams, of course, man and wife: Ethel and Mungo would not collapse into each other's arms in company, except on exceptional occasions – when the Sartrams had collapsed into each other's arms, only then did Mungo and Ethel make their presence known by Ethel coughing dramatically loudly, and Mungo chinking the empties.

At which point there was an embarrassed silence broken only by the sound of the bin lorry struggling to empty Ethel and Mungo's blue boxes. (To be fair, the bin-men never had any problems with their paper sacks.)

Peeling themselves apart, Mr Sartram in hospital consultant mode, fixed his attire and adjusted his trouser front – he found his wife very, very attractive when she was helpless with laughter, and most other times too – coughed politely and went to the mirror above the mantelpiece. After a moment's reflection, he turned and with his serious hospital-rounds face, he said:

"Madame, you have the wind, I note."

Ethel raised an eyebrow that had just that very morning been pencilled in and riposted, "Not so much that polite society would generally comment upon."

"Usually gets away with it," Mungo explained. "Blame Polly. But Polly gone."

"Polygon!" Gurpreet interjected with delight, "'A plane figure having many angles, and consequently many sides'."

"What the hell is he going on about now?" Ethel demanded of Mungo in a weary tone, no longer caring how boorish she might sound to foreigners, especially those with money.

Gurpreet took her hand and pleaded with those liquid jet eyes, "Madame, my apologies. My mind is like the seed that scatters in the wind."

"Not the wind again. Mungo, do something. Say something. And wipe that stupid smirk from your face."

Mungo looked from his wife to Mrs Sartram and striking a pose by the joanna, began to sing:

"'*Pale hands I loved, beside the Shalimar,*

Where are you now, who lies beneath your spell?

(Mungo did have a fine baritone, but he had had to 'let him go' when the lawnmower packed in and the man refused to cut the grass with shears – Wilkinson's best, as well!)

Ethel brought an abrupt end to this sally by slamming the lid of the piano.

Mrs Sartram now took the reins – it was time for the woman's touch, a time to be emollient. "My husband was remarking that it is a nice windy aspect. Do you have the wind turbine? It would be most auspicious on the situation." Then Anita thought, 'God, now *I'm* talking like Peter Sellers'.

"Mungo, you've been out east, Shettleston, Baillieston, Edinburgh, such like," Ethel said. "Do you have the faintest idea of what they are going on about?" Then, turning to Anita, Ethel explained, "I'm sorry, my dear, had quite a day and it is all proving much too much for my nerves." And with that she made to leave, but Mr Sartram was not easily dismissed.

"Oh, dear Lady Laird, the wind turbine, the solar panel. The cheap electricity. The low carbon emissions. Save the planet, dear lady and sir."

"Environment, my dear," Mungo translated for his wife in a thespian whisper. "Green nut job. India's full of them. Drink their own… you know what."

Ethel was suddenly revived at this. The environment was one of her pet hobbyhorses she was determined to break.

"The environment?! Oh we don't have that here. Don't have time for such nonsense. The Environment. Passing fad. Mark my words: few years, hear no more about it. It's doomed. That right, Mungo!"

Mungo took up the theme for his wife and explained to the candidates:

"We're old enough to remember when AIDS was what they scared us with." And at that he badly mimed chiselling a tombstone epitaph while he intoned, "'*You're doomed you shower of reprobates*', courtesy of HM Government. We never shared our needles, did we dear?"

"Far too late for us. Had two children by then. Fat lot of good that. Where are they when we need them?" Then to the Sartrams, in a tone of resignation, she said as if signalling defeat for the moment, "Suppose you'll want to see the rest?"

Mr and Mrs Sartram exchanged swift glances that meant god knows what. Then they took each other's hand and Anita it was who sweetly trilled, "If that is not too much trouble, Lady Laird. Already the favourable impression has been formed, and now to consolidate it."

With that Ethel led the Sartrams out of the room and Mungo collapsed onto the couch and tried to have a blackout, merely succeeding in having a grey-out courtesy of the augmented dustbowl around the couch.

The next thing Mungo knew was that he was quite sober and dozing comfortably and at that juncture did not have a care in the world. Then reality kicked-in the form of a kick on his shins. Ethel was standing above him, glaring and moving her head in that attractive way she had when there was shampoo (or too much wax) in her ear and she could not shift it. Mungo straightened up and rose unsteadily to his feet. At times like this one, he would take his handkerchief – a clean one kept in his right-hand pocket just for such emergencies – and wet the end of it with his tongue, twirl the dampened end into a little pointy thing, and go to work on Ethel's ear. He had tried once to use his tongue to this effect, but a reflex action from Ethel meant that he had been unable to walk in an upright position for a fortnight.

This time it was not the ear problem with Ethel. The Sartrams were standing behind him and waiting expectantly. For a moment there was silence broken only by the bin lorry doing a second collection for the blue boxes (a special arrangement for the 'Laird' street in which it was not only the greenery that was lush all the year round).

Then Mrs Sartram could contain herself no longer. "Oh, Lady Laird, I can contain myself no longer. This house is just what I've always dreamed of. Gurpreet: we must make an offer. Please, my love." And with that she took her husband's two hands in hers and simpered outrageously.

It worked on Mungo but, as he moved to join the huddle, Ethel put out a drayman's arm and almost knocked him over the piano ('joanna' or '*keyboard in a box*', as some perspicacious readers might know it by now).

"Really?" Ethel boomed. "An offer?! Steady on. We are not in any sort of rush, you know. Don't want you to be disappointed. Others to interview; more candidates and so on. Big decision. Biggest of your life. Wouldn't want to be thought of as exploiting the zeitgeist. This house tends to do that –

mess about with the emotions. B*ggered him up over the years," she finished, indicating Mungo.

"My dear Mrs Sartram," Mungo began and tried to get round his wife for the huddle, "did you say an offer?" Then to Ethel, "Well, my dear, this calls for a wee celebration. I'm sure there is a pen somewhere." And the moment was lost because he could not choose between looking for a pen or opening the bottle.

"Mungo! Sit down. You're p*ssed, " his wife h*ssed.

Mr Sartram freed one hand from his lovely wife and looked at his watch – a Patek Philippe, by the way; there's brass in fat. (*A Patek Philippe is far more than a means of telling the time; it is a unique, personal object steeped in precious memories.*)

"And perhaps, since it is past midday, by way of celebrating this epiphanous revelation, we could have that other little drink, the proper libation to seal the bargain, if that is not too bold?" the bold Sartram said boldly.

Ethel put on a shocked face. "Thought you people didn't drink?" Then turning to Anita and adopting that conspiratorial woman-to-woman tone, as if she viewed Anita as an equal, said, "If that is the way he holds his urine, you are nurturing a problem for the future, my dear." Then to her own problem of the present she said, "Mungo: the door for our visitors. Been most interesting. We'll call you, should you make it on to the final list. Thank you. Mungo!"

Looking puzzled, even a little bit hurt, Mr Gurpreet Sartram (Fellow of this and that), tried to work up a sense of outrage at the offhand dismissal – except so mild-mannered were they (it comes from the scents of the Shalimar) that they allowed Mungo to hustle, quasi-huckle them even, out the door.

A few moments later they were standing on the top steps wondering how the perfumed hair oil they were going to get down those old stairs that did not seem to have any handholds. Mr Sartram looked at Anita and said something along the lines of: ںیہ ا کـــرتے یاب ہم ک (transliterated as: ab hum kya karte hain).

Chapter 16

To civilized behaviour.

After the Sartrams had taken their leave with good grace, Mungo watched them admire the view for an inordinate amount of time. So much so that on returning to the drawing room/music room, Ethel was already a half-jigger ahead of him and in grim determination (which he would pay for later, he knew) he wrestled the bottle of Buckie from her hand, and in a trice had moved a whole half-jigger ahead of his beloved. Then he flopped on the couch and dreamed of *The Golden Road to Samarkand* for a moment. He often got his dreams wrong. He was really looking for *Shalimar Bagh* which is not a river as it might seem and is not in India. Mungo never let small details get in the way of his overarching vision of how he would like his world to be.

"That's all we need," Ethel sighed resignedly. "An offer that can't be refused from people like that." She drained her jigger. "Drinking urine, indeed."

Mungo knew an opportunity when he saw one – he leapt to his feet (poetic licence) and re-filled his beloved's schooner and then his own. Ethel gave a weak smile – it could have been a grimace such was the lighting in the room – then she raised her glass to her soul mate.

"Mungo: To civilized behaviour."

"To civilized behaviour." Then *he* looked in the mirror and after a moment's reflection (repeated motif) he murmured, "Goats and chickens, indeed. Piss-off the neighbours, really it would."

"That thought, do I like," Ethel said and chinked her glass against Mungo's.

Chapter 17

G'day, it's a ripper.

It had been a long day and it was going to be longer as Mungo glanced at Ethel's clipboard while she snoozed on his chair. Two down – Dave and the lovely Chelsea and the svelte Sartrams: Gurpreet and the even lovelier Anita. Mungo topped up his glass and thought about things and how they had come to this pretty, pretty ugly pass.

It was all the fault of the roof. Welsh blue slate, thank you very much. And the garden. Now if he could just get a new roof he could sell-off the buckets. And with the money from the buckets, if he could put it on a winner at decent odds, he could probably hire a gardener. The garden was a problem. It had always been too big, but that had been resolved by the roof – each year that they needed to spend money on the roof they sold-off a sliver of land. But that had led to two consequences: ordinary people (plebeians) had been able to buy the houses on the several slivers of land that had been sold off to builders. The more houses that were built on formerly Lairdland, the lower the value of the big house. That in turn meant when they resorted to re-mortgaging, equity release or whatever, they could raise smaller amounts each year. So they had to sell off more slivers of land. And now they were left with just enough for about six goats and ten chickens. But that had been a disaster.

Mungo kept a Purdey 12 gauge (*sidelock ejector*) that Uncle Brodie had given him as an eleventh birthday present. Uncle Brodie was not the best person to show him how to shoot – he was blind in one eye and the other was completely useless. ANYWAY: Mungo having been badly taught decided that as a bonding exercise he would teach Ethel. Goodbye goats and chickens and hello still surviving fox, who never even said goodbye or thanks for missing me and had had the temerity to set up home in a corner of the garden with Mrs F and their three little f*ckers. Who needs Animal Welfare?

MEANTIME, BACK TO THE PRESENT, (near enough), Mungo decided he would take advantage of Ethel being in – what trade unionists call – *the recumbent position*. And so he got some tea, and his paper – now a couple of days old because of events, dear boy, events. Skilfully, as if he had done it all his life – which it felt like he had – he quietly dragged a side table with his foot, placed the cup on it and sank into his other chair. With a deep well of pleasure washing over him, he opened his paper quietly, lifted his cup to his lips and the ph*cquing doorbell rang. *Dring-dring.*

"B*llocks!" he expostulated (quietly). He waited to see if a servant would get the door then remembered there were no servants. He was *chef de cabinet*, *maître d', non-cook and bottle drinker*, etc., etc...

He tossed his paper down carelessly, not giving a toss now if Ethel awoke – his peace was disturbed and his day was already heading towards an express train crash (well an electric Blue Line one). The bell rang again – a strangely, but melodiously effete tinkling sound, as if it was someone else's doorbell or the finger on the knob was of delicate disposition.

Tinkle, tinkle.

He rose heavily and, accidentally on purpose, kicked Ethel's outstretched leg. She did not stir, so he gave her another tap then hobbled nimbly away and out the room.

The bell rang again – this time more persistent and demanding: masculine in its *Urgency*! *Dring, dring, dring*! That was more like the thing, Mungo thought.

"Yes, yes, I know. I know. Coming, coming. Hold your water."

He took a last look in the mirror of the coat-stand in the hall – to make sure there were no tell-tale dribbles, and to see if his eyes still had that steely-blue sheen that exuded a man of quality who had never had to do a hand's turn to earn his bread: they didn't.

[TO THE TELL-TALE DRIBBLES: Mungo had learned over the years that if one dribbled Buckie while asleep (but not when upright), it left a little silver track as if a tiny snail had slithered out of the corner of the mouth and had reached under the chin by a circuitous route. In a certain light it could look as if a string of translucent pearls was attached to the lower face and neck, reminiscent of the practice of some of the older and rebellious Bayakan grannies, who had the good sense (and wherewithal to be fair) to substitute Jungle Juice for Buckie.]

ANYWAY: Face unadorned by ersatz snail-slime, Mungo opened the door and was faced by two of the tallest, broadest, handsomest, hunkiest, dishiest (male) gods he had ever had the... privilege to cower before. Mungo thought he must be dreaming and had gone to hell.

"Mr Laird? Mr Mungo Laird. G'day. Dirk Hutton and may I present Brucie Cameron." And the speaker, a tall, athletic-looking athlete of about thirty-six-and-one-half, weighing in at 170 lbs and wearing Calvin Klein CK IN2U HIM, and X-Brand Denims held around those divine hips by an X-Brand belt in black crocodile skin (killed for scientific and humanitarian purposes), with a buckle of Toledo silver, and boots of Spanish Leather, smiled like one of a pair of Mormons (no offence, but two of them and what about those teeth! – no real man). Brucie was dressed the same.

Mungo processed all of this information in the time between two heartbeats – which for Mungo was quite long for a man of his age and non-defibrillated condition.

And in that time Mungo suddenly felt small. Tinier than small and insignificant in the scheme of things. Here he was, a man entering what people who should have known better but didn't have a scooby as to what they were talking about, called his *best years*. Hah! When he saw these two divine beings, he realised what it was that Cortez felt on that peak on Darien; what Armstrong must have felt when he took that giant step for mankind (if indeed he did – there had been a story in *The S*nday P*st* –Sceptic Readers Page – in which some rational people had offered a different view of that 'event'); and finally, Mungo felt as insignificant as the time he looked up at the night sky, on his back from on top of a hawthorn bush and, after struggling to get out of it, he gave up and pondered the stars.

For the first time in memory – or that day – he felt deeply depressed and contemplated ending it all. And he thought of his Purdey 12 gauge (*sidelock ejector*) – but rejected the notion as he decided that these two cobbers were not worth a cartridge between them let alone two.

Dirk (or was it Brucie) held out a shovel of a hand and enveloped Mungo's in his. To the untrained observer, Mungo was speechless and tongue-tied. But if you could have seen his vocal chords strain to produce a sensible sound other than gibberish, while at the same time you could have measured the electrical currents that flow between them and the speech centre of the brain, you would instantly recognize that Mungo was in the throes of a (hopefully) temporary Broca's aphasia.

[Strictly speaking or to be pedantic, an electrical current does not flow – it excites the *neurons* (electrically excitable cells) that turn to their neighbour neuron and say: *pass it on*, whatever information the brain is transmitting. An easy way to grasp this concept is to imagine that each cell has a pair of elbows – which of course means they must have arms as well, but that is immaterial to the argument. When one cell is excited by something – say a particular Bach cantata (*Soli Deo Gloria*), or a *Victoria's Secret* ad. (take your pick – they are all superb) – then it elbows the cells on either side of it and says: *what about that then? Eh?!* And these cells become excited in turn, and eventually the message gets back to the brain and the bit dealing with emotions or whatever. There you have in simple form the entirety of neurology, or to give it a scientific sounding name, *neuroscience*. Now that was not that difficult, was it?]

To add to his feeling of utter helplessness and insignificance in this or any other universe, Dirk's companion, (or was it Brucie's?) held out his hand and for a moment all three hands were as one until Mungo pulled his away with horror.

"We could stand looking at this view all day, Mr Laird," one or other of the b*ggars said.

“We’re here about the house. To view?” the other b*ggar said. Then they looked at each other in puzzlement at Mungo’s seeming paralysis of speech and thought.

“You think he’s full cobber, Dirk?” Brucie said in what passes for a whisper in downtown Earls Court (older readers) or Shepherd’s Bush (younger readers) (or *Fosters* adverts – younger readers still).

Mungo exhibited some vital signs by looking at one of them then at the other.

Brucie (or it could have been Dirk) said with what was a good impression of concern:

“Have we come at an inconvenient moment?” With which he pulled a sheet of paper from inside his superbly cut and hand-stitched denim jacket. (*Jean Shop*; £295 atow.)

“It’s just that is says here, you know, we were to attend for the viewing today at…” He indicated his watch. (*Tag Heuer Aquaracer. Excellent visibility in the dark or underwater.* And it tells the time.)

“Oh,” Mungo said. “Ah.” He was beginning to catch the drift, the old vocal chords were beginning to respond to the little pulses of electricity that were stimulating the elbows of those neurons who were passing the message on. “Candidates. Ethel’s clipboard. These must be the idiots that came all the way from Australia or was it New Zealand.” Mungo might have said it aloud – he certainly thought it aloud.

“Of course. Had a little wobble there – clocks changing and that.” And that set Mungo off on a diatribe on the iniquities of the clocks being pushed back or was it forwards for the poor ph*cquing farmers, who anyway didn’t give a c*w’s t*rd because they had all the electric lights they needed and no one had noticed at the Whitehall Department that was in charge of clocks. Then taking a grip of himself, Mungo remembered his manners. "Don't stand there, come away in then."

As he stood aside for his guests to enter, Dirk, or the other one, he noticed, held a bouquet of flowers and as they passed, Mungo got a distinct whiff of jasmine, cedar wood (or was it sandalwood – he always got those two mixed up) and just a hint of English plum that a bird has just pecked in the last days of September.

Of course he could have been completely wrong – but even so it was encouraging that he had formed such a complex model of the olfactory sensations because what is happening in the *piriform cortex* (a bit of the brain that processes signals from the *olfactory bulb*), is a pretty good indicator of whether or not an elderly person is going, or is likely to go, doolally. Mungo knew all this from *The S*nday P* st*, (Doc's Column: every week; worth a read), and it cheered him up to know that he was still as sharp as a pin. *Oleo ergo sum* he might have declared, had he not been forced to take dumb subjects like chemistry and physics and French at St Kentigern's.

(That one decision taken by that school put paid to any hopes Mungo might have entertained in the future as to the Leadership of the Conservative Party; for by depriving him of the human right to sweat over Latin, they deprived him of ever being able to bandy Latin aphorisms with the likes of B*ris J*hnson or George (*né* Gideon) Osborne. Of course he could still have become the leader of the Tories in Scotland, or for that matter the 'Scottish' Labour Party who always seem to be on the lookout for a leader.)

“We were just saying before you came, Mr Laird – may we call you Mungo? Much better. The view. We could’ve stood all day and admired it,” one of the b*ggars said.

“Up to my wife, you would have. This way, chaps.”

Chapter 18

A little later that same g' and ripper day.

He led them to the living room where Ethel was still sprawled in his chair. Had she been vertically arranged, at this moment, she would have called to mind *Aphrodite at the Waterhole* (T Hancock, 1961; *Stookie on chicken wire with Ready-mix Concrete 2" slump. The Rebel,* dir. Robert Day.).

"Darling, our visitors. They've come a long way by the sounds."

Ethel stirred and began to focus. The music of the samba faded and the warm Mediterranean breeze that had been causing the beaded partition to gently sway, died away. With a shake of her great head she returned to reality.

Meantime, to show they had a modicum of good manners – one never let-on one had seen such a sight – they looked away, but not before a look passed between them, which Mungo also caught and did not like one *anna*. However, as a man of acumen, he was prepared to overlook it for the moment. And he too pretended he had not seen his wife in that state of... vulnerability.

"We didn't actually come directly from Down Under," one of the b*ggars said, to which the other interposed waspishly:

"Oh don't be so literal, Dirk, always so literal. They're all like that from Touraq by way of Redfern," the b*ggar said, not without another glance at Ethel who was rolling-up her stocking over her corned-beef outer calf – the one closest by habit to the fire, in the days they could afford the two bars.

"We've got them like that. Milngavie by way of Bearsden. Schools I blame," Mungo riposted, having made a full recovery. Then he made to seize the flowers that one of the b*ggars held.

"Oh, for me. You shouldn't have." At which moment the great consort pushed him aside with a playful but smarting shove, and took the bouquet and held them to her face. This had the advantage of hiding that silvery snail-like trail that traced its way from the corner of her mouth, down under her chin and thereafter into the deepest recesses of her décolletage, at which point we will draw a veil over where it might have ended up.

"How thoughtful. You shouldn't have. What a nice touch. I like that," she said and took the flowers away from her face, with some effort, as some of them had stuck to the aforementioned silvery trail.

"Allow me to make the introductions," Mungo harrumphed. "My good lady wife, Mrs Laird. Or Ethel as she is sometimes called. Darling, this is..."

"I'm Bruce and this is Dirk," one of the b*ggars said ignoring Mungo, having sensed that easy lay her head with or without a crown.

And so there was the ritual of hand-shaking – Mungo shook Ethel's a couple of times in the scrum and found it quite by far the most manly of the lot – not excluding his own.

Ethel once again held the flowers to her face, then said, "I'll put these in water." At which she handed them to Mungo. "Put these in water, Mungo darling," and before he could preen himself at her calling him *darling* she added, "and don't slouch so."

"My husband, not usual self – pressures of contemplating giving up this much loved family home," Ethel pronounced and swept the room majestically with the same forearm she had used to shift the piano the once.

Mungo's head appeared at the hatch. "With spectacular views over the Cathkin Braes and the eastern stretch of the Clyde Valley, not to mention..." Then he trailed off as Ethel accidentally slammed the hatch doors with her a*se as she wobbled past en route to the mantelpiece, with the intention of propping herself thereon as she had suddenly had an attack of the gillespies. In another display of sensitivity – that is, pretending they had not seen the little spat between husband and wife – the two b*ggars had gone to the window.

"Oh god, Dirk, another view to die for. I expect you get visitors telling you all the time, Mrs Laird. And the ceilings – Dirk, look at the rose, the cornicing. Did you ever? Mrs Laird, may I say..."

"You must call me Ethel. I insist." Ethel insisted and simpered at the same time. Not easy.

"*Ethel*," One of the b*ggars said, savouring the name as if it were something really savourable. "A name to grace this wonderful example of post-neo-Palladian splendour. And what a wrench it must be to even contemplate leaving this, if I may be so bold?" the emboldened b*ggar made boldly.

The other b*ggar sidled up to Ethel having made sure the hatch was secure and that Mungo was not out in the hall listening.

"All the more reason to be careful as to whom you deal with," this b*ggar said quietly, with a grave look of concern on his sculpted visage.

As Ethel gazed into those nut-brown eyes, she recalled a time long, long ago when she had gazed into Mungo's and had felt the earth move beneath her feet. Though that time it had been the bulldozers demolishing the tenement next to their bijou apartment in Upper Shawlands. Still, it's the thought that counts.

Chapter 19

What else looks good on paper?

Bruce (né Clement) and Dirk (né Desmond) were not strictly speaking antipodean since neither was born actually in the Pacific Ocean. According to his CV, Bruce first surfaced in Joondalup to the north of Metropolitan Perth, and is a graduate of Edith Cowan University (BA, Hospitality and Tourism) with a PG Certificate in Communications. (Nevertheless this is a fine university in a fine town and although it is about sixteen miles from the centre of Perth, graduates of Hospitality and Tourism can be in that city within thirty minutes by train and another thirty minutes to get to Perth Airport (Terminal 1) and another twenty-odd non-stop hours to reach London if in a *hurry,* which Bruce had been some years previously.)

Dirk on the other hand was born just outside Guildford, Surrey (England) and was educated at his local comprehensive, where he did not draw much attention to himself. After which he attended a technical college where he took a certificate in practical print technology. On moving to London he worked as copy boy in a national newspaper and earned some extra cash by doing some 'modelling' work – mainly for tired Parliamentarians who had acquired an interest in cinematography, as a means of warding off boredom occasioned by the late-night sittings and the absence of their spouses. And while we have seen previously that Chelsea Cole-Cole sometimes described herself as a 'photographic model', it is not known if Dirk and Chelsea ever '*met on the mat*', as it is known in the trade (or *profession*, if you prefer).

Then fate took a hand. One day Dirk was walking aimlessly in Shepherd's Bush when he took himself into the *Walkabout* (honestly – it's called that; worse than Irish themed bars, if you can believe that is possible). And there he met Bruce. A few doovalackies later and they were bosom cobbers (or something similar like *pectoral*).

It was in historical terms not quite on the same level as when Crick met Watson, or Simon met that other geezer, (no, not Garfunkel, older readers) but it was certainly on par with Mike and Bernie Winters (older readers still). And so they became partners and like good partners they pooled their resources. Before you could say 'dunny rats' they had acquired very impressive additions to their CVs. And before you could say 'dunny rats' twice, they had obtained lecturing jobs at two of the newer Scottish Universities, who were very pleased to have such highly qualified colonials on their staff rosters, especially since they had invented doctorates in their respective, invented fields of... Actually the print quality was not quite up to scratch as to what their doctorates were in, suffice it to say they were able to lecture in Economics when no one else would touch it with a Taswegian's tallywhacker.

(Should be pointed out that Dirk's first degree certificate was pretty similar to that of Brucie, and he had acquired a very affable Australian accent – nothing suspicious at all in that fact: just like dogs that begin to look like their owners, so some people that spend a lot of time together – say in the kitchen or at play or in bed or the garden – begin to display similar traits. Psychologists have an impressive name for this behaviour that can explain absolutely everything and nothing, so we won't bother you with it.)

Anyway, in the nature of such occupations, they found themselves with lots of time on their hands – and that is when they started to move into property 'development' as a side-line to educating the youth of Scotland; well those who bothered to turn up at lectures – which anyway, as is well known, are pedagogically and existentially a complete waste of time. And truth be told, the two heroes were completely useless at it – so tallywhackers all round.

The charming young men from Australia or New Zealand or Earls Court or Shepherd's Bush, need not have worried about Mungo at this point since he had taken the opportunity to go to the lavatory and lock himself in with his paper and a fresh cup of tea. The great thing about this lavatory – this is not estate agent hard sell – is that you can sit on the throne – real wood (mahogany as it so happens) so no chilly b*m even on the coldest day. (The closest you can get to it in modern manufacture is the *Imperial Westminster Close Coupled Pan and Cistern,* £544 atow. But beware of fakes.)

WE SAY, the great thing about this lavatory is that you can sit on the throne, read a paper (or a book if you are the literary type), vacate your bowels if you so choose, and look down on one-third of the town spread out below. (Some of Mungo's ancestors would not have hesitated to d*efecate on the townspeople from such a lofty position, but had to settle for metaphorically doing so due to some obscure laws.) This act always gave Mungo a sense of the democratic nature that runs deep even when there are strong class divisions in life as we know it, and for which we give qualified thanks: for thanks to the invention of the fireclay pipe and the *low-back siphon toilet bowl and mechanism* (sometimes wrongly attributed to Thomas Crapper), all the peoples of this great little town were united in that their jo*bies ended up on the same 'sl*dge boat' that sailed from Erskine and dumped its caked cargo somewhere in the Firth of Clyde (nuclear fleet and weather permitting).

[Editor's note: this is an unfortunate anachronism since the boat (the k*ech barge) no longer sails. However, the principle of democracy is still enshrined as long as the people's sh*te flows to the same end, whether it be a sludge boat (k*ech barge again) or… where do j*bbies go if they are not dumped in the Clyde today?]

We will leave Mungo there for the moment in peace and return to the drawing room, or whatever Ethel is calling it today, and listen-in to what is transpiring between Ethel and the two didgeridoo repairmen.

"Exactly my sentiments, dear boy," Ethel said to one of them. Then turned to the other. "Been trying to tell Mungo. He never listens. Discriminate, discernment. Taste for quality. Appreciation for the other, shall we call them, spiritual dimensions of life?"

"Stop!" one of the b*ggars said in a dramatic and loud whisper – not too loud, just loud enough still to be described as whisper-ish. "Don't anyone move. Feel that, Dirk."

"Oh yes, Bruce." At which both of them stood in the centre of the room – actually it was difficult to stand in the centre: for furnitorial reasons the centre of the room was occupied by the ph*ucquing great tiger's head on the ph*ucquing great tiger rug which used to be a f*cking greater tiger, and there was the aspidistra in the cast iron plant pot on the fairly central occasional table.

ANYHOW, centre or not, the two b*ggars stood like a pair of Japanese Oh Noh contestants or celebrants, with their hands spread wide above their heads and fingertips, not for the first time, touching.

"That's the strongest yet," one of the b*ggars said.

"The energy. A positive vortex. The vibrations," the other b*ggar said. There was silence apart from the vibrations, which it has to be admitted were quite pronounced.

Ethel remained mid-stride – she had got cramp, but was not prepared to surrender to the pain – and whispered, "What is it?"

"The pipes are calling," said Mungo, who had entered unseen and had immediately identified the phenomena.

Bruce or the other b*ggar chose to ignore this attempt at soiling the moment. "*Feng shui.* Don't you just feel yourself immersed in it?" Apparently he was not alluding to the cargo of the ke*ch boat for he added, "Oh, this is good. This is the strongest, most beneficent we've ever felt. Wouldn't you say so, Dirk?"

"Easily, Bruce. And what about the bush?"

"I say, steady on, you only just met the wife."

Not for the first and not for the last time, the two b*ggars chose to act as if Mungo did not exist. Which is par for Mungo's course.

Chapter 20

Kith and Kin and blind tasting.

Bruce (or the other b*ggar) put his arm around Ethel – which will give you some idea of how big he was – a BIG b*ggar – and drew her towards the window.

"Before we go another step, Ethel, you must tell us the name of that divine bush." And he pointed out the window. "Are we right in thinking that it is from the *Apocynaceous* family? It is so reminiscent of one we saw in Bali last year, Dirk. Or was that the year before in Bangkok? No matter, it lends a nice touch of the exotic, which one imagines will be most welcome as it flares up in late September, October, yes?"

Ethel almost swooned – luckily she didn't because even the BIG b*ggar might not have been able to stop her head splitting the solid oak floorboards.

"So discerning you are: *Variegated oleander. A rosebay hybrid.* And you boys, but you're alone? Your wives trust you?" she laughed girlishly. "I mean, not with me, with the decision as to the house. Trust. I mean. Oh, you've got me coming all over coy." She trailed off, becoming all over coy.

Mungo was almost sick in the tiger's mouth at this.

"Wives?" one of the b*ggars laughed girlishly. Then took the other b*ggar's hand. "Oh, sorry, for any confusion, Ethel. Dirk and I are partners. Seven years now."

"Ah, that's the way of the world today. Especially in post-Salmond Scotland – it's everywhere. Business, business, business. Can't say I wholly agree. Mungo tried his hand at it once. Family brewery. Complete disaster. Had a businessman call at the door yesterday, huh! Little Irish fellow. Heard the house was for sale and wanted to buy it on the spot. Time was, all tinkers, the Irish. Now call themselves businessmen. Though he could have been from South Ayrshire – they're a bit like that. Can't understand a word they say. Country's full of foreigners. Time to move abroad. Not that we count you boys as foreigners – kith and kin, eh?"

"Knock the buggar down and build..." Mungo began, having had enough of this p*sh and having had the temerity to light a small, cheap and very nasty cigar – though he did have the good judgement to stick his head out the window to meet the hand that held the thing.

"Heavens no, Mungo," one of the b*ggars said, acknowledging for a time Mungo's existence. "I may call you Mungo – feel we know you already. Good. No, should we decide to buy, and may I say, we are already positively inclined, yes, Dirk?" And Dirk nodded and inclined his head thoughtfully, while Brucie continued.

"We would want to preserve the essential post-neoclassical features of the building. What we have in mind is to tastefully sub-divide into four, at most five, self-contained service flats, which will be aimed at what used to be called, *retired gentlefolk of means*. People like your good selves, people of taste, of background, of well... maybe we shouldn't say this, but we do not want *hoi polloi* here," this to Ethel, "do you? Of course you don't." And Ethel nodded vigorously.

"Not many of us left," Mungo said expansively having exhaled outside the window. "That's the whole trouble. A class thing. I like that in a man: honest prejudice. Discrimination."

Mungo haughtily lifted the clipboard and pretended to write, then holding it out to Brucie said, "Sign here." To which Ethel snarled, "Mungo!"

At which Mungo once again assumed his role with a sigh and said to the candidates, "Anyway, expect you want the grand tour, but before which, just a few questions for our scientific survey?" He pretended to read the clipboard.

"Mungo! Put that silly clipboard down!" Ethel snapped, taking it from him and almost sending him over the sill to join the stub of his half-smoked cigar.

"Please ignore my husband. Delusions of past grandeur. Clipboards and questionnaires indeed!" With which Ethel gave a shrill laugh. "Sherry, boys, to fortify you for the great adventure ahead?" With which she went to the brass coal box by the fireplace and extracted a fresh bottle of *Harveys' Very Special Reserve: Limited Edition* (5,000,000 bottles and counting) *Sherry Extra Sweet and Dry.*

Giving the two b*ggars a very generous measure – by Mungo's scale this was *circa* jigger-and-quarter – she ignored Mungo and clinked glasses with both the b*ggars.

"*Kith and kin*," Ethel proposed.

"*Kith and kin*," the two b*ggars replied with a knowing glance between them that said they were right in here.

Ethel downed hers. The b*ggars sipped at first but under the beady eye of Ethel, they both took a deep breath and tossed the sherry over with a passable panache, while Mungo stood by with a passable ash pan (just in case, like).

Ethel then took the sherry glasses from her boys, deposited them with Mungo, once again answering that existential question that was always at the back of his mind at such times, both regarding Ethel and the b*ggars.

Ethel struck a pose of statuesque proportions – always a sign that the sherry was kicking-in nicely with the Buckie.

"Well, *informality* being our credo in Maison Laird – a value you Australians esteem above all others I understand... and all credit to you and your thrusting nation if you allow me the Old Country observation. Anyway, why don't you take a gentle *informal* wander *sans chaperone* around our abode. Please take all the time you require. Any questions we can deal with over some canapés back here – or as we say: *amuse bouches*." And with a flourish of her arm that knocked over the long-redundant humidor and nearly took Mungo with it, Ethel ushered a bemused Bruce and a relieved Dirk out of the room.

She closed the door firmly and immediately flopped on the couch, not realising that Mungo was already there. For less than one of those really short nano-seconds he thought he had won a prize – but with a careless shrug of her shoulder he ended up on the carpet, narrowly missing the open jaws of the tiger.

When he realised he had on his invisibility cloak he took the opportunity to take a slug from both the Harveys' and the Buckie's. He did it 'blindfold' after rotating the bottles several times. Not a blind bit of difference.

After a decent interval Ethel arose majestically and moved steadily to the door by a circuitous route. Upon reaching which, she opened it – having at first thought you pushed instead of pulled the thing – and sticking her fizzug out into the hall she needlessly called in a gravelly stentorian voice that would have done justice to the epithet 'Churchillian' after his twelfth Cuban-beauty thigh-rolled *Romeo y Julieta* (no relation) of the day:

"Make yourselves at home! Take all the time you need!! But do appreciate the unique carmine Carrara marble in the third loo!!!" Then she steadily – by a circuitous route (but not the same one) – made her way back to the couch and beadily eyed her spouse who had a gleam in his eye of his own. But it turned out it was the light reflecting off the silver (remember the slug slime path?) trail from one corner of her mouth down under her chin, down further into her décolletage and further still at which point we draw the same (now used) veil as previously over the next course of the snail of lust.

Ethel flopped on the couch; Mungo meanwhile, thinking she was as blind as he was at that point, took the opportunity to take a slug at the Harveys Reserve and the Buckie. However, the competitive element in Ethel as usual in such cases of discriminatory libation, came to the fore and she sprung-up (well some hyperbole is allowed for) and catching him by the throat with one bottle at his lips, she easily relieved him of both (bottles not lips) and slugged deeply of them in turn. 'Turn' being normally and tastefully determined best by respective ascending alcoholic content. That determines that Buckie is the former bevvy but is outweighed by the fact that you can taste *nothing* within fifteen seconds of a mouthful of Buckie unless you are connoisseurs like the Lairds.

"Well?" one of them said.

"Decidedly," the other replied.

"Hooked?" One of them said carelessly.

"Can take it or leave it." At which Mungo rose relatively steadily. "Prefer to take it. No harm in it."

Ethel gently (by her standards) separated Mungo from the one bottle he had managed to reach. "Mungo. I speak of the charming boys upstairs. What a pretty pass it has come to when it all resolves on this," She said, waving the bottle above her head. Mungo had never see her look so desirable – or so sober, at this time of the day.

"Oh, that," Mungo said with little enthusiasm. The whole process had lasted almost a day and he felt exhausted and needed either a snooze or a Buckie-me-up.

"Hooked indeed. If not now, then the pink streaks in the marble toilet bowl should swing it, by the looks of them." This was said more to himself than with any expectation that Ethel would have a clue as to what he alluded.

And indeed Ethel was not listening. "I feel it. In my water. They are *destined* to live here. Charming, erudite, civilised."

"Australian?"

Ethel hauled herself up and shuffled over to the door and stuck her head into the hallway and listened, before returning having closed the door quietly.

"Mungo!" she whispered conspiratorially. "We should agree as they suggested to me – when you so rudely shut yourself away in the lavatory, oh yes I did observe – they sensibly suggested that I, that is we, take the house off the market, and they would match the offer of the Ashley-Cole-Coles's. Can't wait to remove that hideous green sign of your precious Val. A travesty outside our family home. Yes! That's what we'll do. Mungo! We are agreed on this, right! Though as usual, being the one who must assume control of business matters, before any major decision such as this, I shall sleep on it for a little. Don't want them to think we are desperate. Would not do." And this was not now a question for discussion.

"Whatever makes you happy, dearest, tickles me plumb to death. I'll drink to that," (which was all he was really interested in by this stage). At which point he tried to grab the bottle.

But Ethel was made of sterner stuff – which he really should have known. "The hell you will," she drawled and made to pull a gun. And with that she emptied the last of the bottle down her throat.

Chapter 21

An (*sic*) Collector Calls.

A few days and no more candidates later, Mungo was striking a pose with a cigar as he thought Ethel was still indisposed. At the open drawing room window he puffed contentedly, fastidious in ushering the curling smoke and rebellious ash outside. When, as was happening too much during this period, the doorbell went: *dring-dring*, but not too insistently. He wondered who it could be as he did not recognise the tonality.

Mungo took one last luxurious puff and threw his cigar stub out of the window, with an élan that was redolent of days spent at the *E&O* in Penang, *Raffles* in Singapore or the *Algonquin* in New York. Pity he had never visited these places. Meantime, he popped his head out to check where it had landed. He wished he had the strength to toss it as far as his closest neighbour's 'guy' – the provocative s*ds always started building their guy and bonfire at the end of February: probably trying for a sighting by cosmonauts returning on the fifth of November. Mungo hummed and sambaed towards the door and with a flourish that went unnoticed, exited.

With another flourish that matched this mid-morning *joie de vivre*, he threw the front door open and almost fell over as Meg Dalgliesh entered and brushed past him still speaking into a mobile phone lodged between one collar bone and an ear, while skilfully opening a slim document case as she moved down the hallway towards the drawing room.

Mungo caught up with her as she reached the room and began to speak, but she waved him away with a flick of one long talon-like finger and continued to speak quietly but determinedly into her mobile.

Mungo would have torn his hair had he had any spare – though he did contemplate pulling it from his ears, nose and the back of one hand where there was a surfeit of the stuff. He took the path of least resistance and closed the door quietly and sat and, making the best of it, began to fantasize about Meg while half-listening to her on the phone.

"No, James, you don't accept that from the old s* and s*," Meg was saying. "Listen, and listen well: you keep your voice even – get that tremor out of it, you're a big boy now – and you say quietly, '*I'm disappointed that we can't reach an agreement. It means that our recovery specialists become involved. If that happens it reflects badly on me'*, meaning you, James – then you say, '*and quite frankly, I don't approve of their methods. They're a bit unconventional. These guys have no interest in procedural niceties. You know the type'*, you say, '*part-time cops who know just what they can get away with'*. Have you got that, James? All of it? Well the gist of it? Christ, go away and practise in front of a mirror. Think John Travolta in *Get Shorty*. What?! No, James, wrong movie: don't ask the old dear to dance. Get the DVD and study it. And James, I'll be very disappointed if you disappoint me."

And with that she hung-up on James – poor b*ggar whoever he was – then quickly searched through her texts. After dashing off a few replies – two fingers twirling like dervishes on decent acid or something stronger than was usual for that repressed minority who have had a bad press in the imperialist writing of history, she eased herself onto the couch beside Mungo. She crossed one elegant leg over the other – did we say she was wearing a very smart charcoal black jacket with matching skirt, (*Nooshin,* Savile Row, available from *Pinstripe and Pearls*; £455.00 atow). The skirt was just the business side of decent and there was the presumption on Mungo's part that those lovely legs sheathed as they were in dark nylon, were also bearing those little attachment things that come with suspenders. One thing he knew for sure was that he would never know for sure.

We have previously discussed the characteristics of the Buckie dribble – remember the silvery trail from the corner of the mouth to… Of course you do.

Well Mungo was close to actually foaming at the proximity of Meg and he heard a disembodied moan from somewhere in the room, then realised it had come from himself, when she patted his knee and let her hand rest there just a little bit longer than was proper for a man of his sensibilities and imagination and lack of plumping of the recent variety. She was talking to him now, but he did not have a scooby as to what she was saying. He was in Paradise – or next door to it and standing on a wheelbarrow and looking over the hedge and just getting a tantalising glimpse of it – when the wheelbarrow rolled away and tipped him in the man*re pile.

Meg Dalgliesh was the third and last child of two parents that seemed to care for each other, even after more than thirty years of marriage. And they had cared for their children in turn – going so far to as to move house to be in the catchment area of a good (state) primary school, before sending each of the siblings in turn to the 'best' fee-paying school in the city. Meg had been the brightest of the three, and was the star of her year at H*tchie (H*tchesons Grammar, Gl*sgow). But still she felt the need to bully others – sometimes girls, but mostly boys. And she liked to manipulate those around her including the staff. But she was going to be *Dux* and she was a young lady with a real future – she was president of the Politics Society and there was already talk that she would be the future leader of the Conservative and Unionist Party in Scotland. Or even the 'Scottish' Labour Party, if things did not work out with her first preference (which was highly unlikely for bountiful reasons – the reasons being bountiful unlike the candidates).

ANYWAY, she went on to university – and the manipulating continued. She was late with coursework and other assignments, and even managed to fail an exam or two in her first year. But then she made a life-style choice. With the help of the Student Advisory Office, a case was made that she had extenuating circumstances: she felt isolated because she had two parents who were still married to each other, still lived together and were not abusive to each other, to her siblings or to Meg herself. And to make matters worse, they were not in any sort of chemical dependency situation. This damaged her self-esteem as she could not identify with her fellow students. And so some allowances were made for her – the default position was the 'deadlines' did not actually mean what they said. And that was without any suggestion that a lecturer had formed an inappropriate attachment to her – and anyway that had merely been a backup strategy.

But still there was the whole boring thing of having to take exams like the others. In her second year she made another life-style choice and diagnosed herself with *Medium Term*

Late-onset Asperger-Autistic-Dyslexia – a then-unrecognised condition that did not appear in the *DSM-IV* (*Diagnostic Statistical Manual of Mental Disorders),* published by the American Psychiatric Association. A couple of things you should know about this publication: firstly, it is the ambition of every practising and ambition-driven psychiatrist or psychologist to identify and have recognised by the *DSM* a previously unrecognised mental disorder. Then the fees charged can go through the stratosphere, which is how progress in psychiatry is measured. Secondly, if it appears in the *DSM*, you can be sure that there will be an outbreak of the disorder in Britain (and the Republic of Ireland and France) within a twelvemonth.

Fortunately for the rest of us, there is a substantial gap between editions of the *DSM*; so whatever you think you've got, if it's not in the *DSM*, you should not worry about it until the next edition is out, upon which you can quickly check it out. (A bit like checking the obituaries to ascertain whether you are dead.) In the case of Meg Dalgliesh's diagnosis, happily it does not appear in the revised *DSM-5,* published in 2013. (Note the switch from Roman numerals. Does this say something about the mental health of American Psychiatry?)

ANYWAY: This got Meg extra time for assignments and exams, as well as a reader for her exam papers and a scribe to take down her answers. Oh, and an exam room to herself. To be fair to Meg, she did have to turn up on the day.

And after four years, Meg graduated with the First that everyone had predicted for her from way back when. In her own unique way, she had worked for this moment.

At her first job interview, her interviewer raised the issue of her dyslexia, which apparently some idiot of an academic referee had mentioned in her references. She snatched the offending document from the interviewer's grasp, rapidly read it (she was a speed-reader of extraordinary powers – she knew *War and Peace* was *more than* just 'about Russia'), noted for future action the name of the academic who had signed this, then ripped it up and tossed it in the nearest bin.

"I'm cured," she said.

She was offered the job which paid a ridiculous salary for such menial work, but turned it down when she was offered the position of Revenue Procurement Executive with First Hammerhead Consolidated Securities. And she loved it.

Fortunately her learning difficulties condition disappeared – well if whatsisname yon Ernst Saunders (Iron Cross and Bar) the former CEO of Distillers can recover from Alzheimer's anything is possible, no?

And now she was with Mungo for reasons that will be revealed, Dear Reader. She looked at him with that smile that both melted and chilled him, but mostly chilled him at this time.

He stuttered, "Meg, my dear. How good to see you, but..." And he made to rise but she held his thigh in a vice-like grip that in different circumstances would be beyond his wildest reveries. He trailed off with: "Not exactly convenient... time and all that." He looked at his watch but quickly reasoned that it must still be with Cash Convertors courtesy of Ethel.

Meg bounced up on to her lovely p*ns and for a moment Mungo thought she might be leaving. But instead she took-off her jacket, folded it neatly and placed it over the back of the couch. Then in her lustrous silk peach blouse (*Nordstrom*, $198 atow, excluding shipping) she moved over to one of Mungo's chairs and sat down with her elbows on her thighs, a sweet, questioning smile on her lips and a twinkle in her eye as she gazed at Mungo.

Despite his confused state of mind, Mungo was not that far gone as to miss the opportunity to try and see up between her legs; but today Meg was in knee-clenching mood and he gave up and waited for whatever it was she had planned for him.

"A drink, you say, Mungo? How kind. Why not?" Meg said, barely moving her lovely lips.

Once again Mungo resorted to the look-at-bare-wrist-ploy. "Well no, actually. I mean of course. Just that..." He rose and went to the window where he peered anxiously out with his back to Meg. He took a deep breath and went and stood in front of Meg.

"Well, thing is, I thought we had a sort of agreement. You know sort of thing: no need for... you know... house call? Don't want to bother you."

"Words, Mungo, but I don't hear the clink of glass?" Meg said, taking her document holder and unzipping it provocatively in Mungo's view, and just briefly he was transported to the banks of the Shalimar – except it is not a river! No! That one was for Mrs Sartram. No matter, the moment was lost and he returned to earth.

"Clink of...? Ah, drink. Of course... do forgive. Senior moment."

He went to the table and taking two glasses wiped each in turn with the handkerchief that he used on Ethel's ear. Held them up to the light and satisfied that there was little-to-no evidence of shampoo or ear wax, poured two jiggers of the best that Harveys could do.

Taking the glass from Mungo, Meg rose and walked to the window where she took a sip, then going to the mantelpiece she placed her glass down and faced Mungo. Her arm swept the room (which Mungo had already swept, as previously noted – pay attention Dear Reader… sorry… that was another morning, Authors).

"And so, Mungo. This is what it's all about – selling the family silver. *Passé*, Mungo, these places. Dodo-land. Extinct. Oh, do sit down, you almost make me nervous. First Thursday of the month? Correct? Mrs Laird's hair, nail and facial? Correct? Four hours minimum? Correct? Relax, Mungo. She won't return until she's fully made over. Credit me with some professionalism, please. I won't embarrass you until I have to." She went up close to Mungo and added, "You were saying?"

Mungo shrunk away from Meg who began to circle him – making due allowance for the aspidistra and the tiger rug with head attached and gaping jaw.

"The thing is, Meg. May I call you Meg? Please feel free to call me Mungo. Or for that matter anything you fancy, don't want to be too stuffy, what? Anyway… It's just that I thought we had a… well an agreement – you know, agreed – keep it our little secret – no need to call here?"

"Mungo, think of it as a courtesy call – I was in the area and thought I'd just pop-in on my most favourite new client. And surprise." She waved a document before his face – actually flicked him playfully on the nose with it – Mungo was sure she did not intend to bring tears to his eyes, and anyway that could just have been his dry-eye syndrome kicking in. "By sheer coincidence, the agreement that matters to hand. Would you like to see it again, Mungo? Check your signature? Check Ethel's signature? You know, confirm that at least one of them is not a forgery?"

Chapter 22

If it's a crime to steal a trillion dollars then I'm guilty (Mr Burns, *The Simpsons*).

Mungo recoiled in horror at this less than gentle reminder. Then he cast his mind back to his readings of *The S*nday P*st* legal column, and tried to recall a piece that made a nice argument that forgery was not always a crime. But for once his fine legal brain failed him and he collapsed onto the couch with his hands covering his face, and rocking back and forth and moaning, he peeked through his fingers and the dust cloud to see if it was working with Meg.

But she just stood before him with that hard little smile playing at the corner of her lips. So. He peeked instead at her skirt-encased thighs, which he only had to reach out and touch, which of course he didn't, but his spirits were raised when he saw what he was sure was the outline of one of those little clasp things that snap on to the suspender things. This was the best thing that had happened to him that day.

Then the spell was broken as Meg went to the side table and poured another generous dollop of the Harveys (Not So Special Un-Limited Edition – very few sold and counting has stopped) and forced him to take it. Mungo smiled and took a tentative sip – probably for the first time ever – and found that there was actually quite a pleasant taste to the stuff. It was not all effect. At which he took another small sip. Yummee. Must try and remember to do this again with Ethel. Maybe even get her to try it.

"Mungo. What are your playing at!" Meg said sharply. "You can do better than that. Go for it. Toss it over like a man in a hurry. A man who is not frightened to make decisions. Big ones. You know, like the way you went for your place in the sun. What was it you said to me: *when I saw it, I knew I just had to have it – damn the consequences*, you said."

And with that Mungo did as he was told and slugged-off the sherry with a dash of élan, as was his usual style – which involves basically holding the drinking elbow out level with, and at a right angle to, the shoulder (the same shoulder).

Meg produced a handkerchief from somewhere – not Ethel's ear-cleaning one – and dabbed at the corners of Mungo's mouth.

"Feel better now, Mungo? Good."

Once again she got him to join her on the couch and when he was comfortable (sort-of) she patted his knee.

"Feeling better, Mungo? The booze, it does help. Despite what those doom-mongers in government say."

"Actually, now you mention, yes, indeed. Much better. Most kind. In fact might just add a little splash." And with that Mungo made to rise only for Meg to flatten him against the couch with the back of her arm.

"Mungo, there is just one little matter. Those consequences, which you so cavalierly damned? They bring us together, don't they? Yes? You know of what I speak? Tell me Mungo what I want to hear. Go on, whisper in this ear."

With that Meg leaned against Mungo, putting her delicate pink ear up to his mouth. But Mungo seemed to have been struck dumb. Meg looked at him quizzically.

"I'm not hearing you, Mungo. Lose your tongue? No, that would be a last resort. A small digit only... for starters... Come on, Mungo, string some words together – I'll rearrange them for you. You know that word game – word association? Yes you do. Someone says a word and the other person says the first word that comes into their mind? Yes? Good. You start, Mungo."

"Drink?" he managed to squeeze out tentatively.

Meg shook her head. For a game in which there were no wrong answers, Mungo had managed to find one. He must try harder. Enter into the spirit of the moment. Then in a flash it came to him – brilliant!

"Money," he said with forced aplomb.

"Loan," came the rejoinder.

"Payment," Mungo shot back, gaining in confidence and beginning to quite enjoy the intellectual challenge.

"Due."

"Already?" (This with fake disbelief.)

"Overdue." (This with cold steel.)

"Jesus!" (This with a frantic call of nature looming.)

"Saves... with Hammerhead Bank. The thing is, Mungo, it must have rang some bells."

(Mungo noted the jarring class shibboleth, but Prudence had struck him from a faraway and strange place so he said nothing. It was not a time for correcting elementary past-tense grammar. But he made a mental note to dash off a piece on the failures of the private school system in Scotland.)

"You had trawled all the banks and other possible sources of finance, We, Hammerhead, were the only ones that didn't blink an eye. You asked for x, we offered you two-x-plus-y." She waved the paper in front of his face. "There it is. Yes? And whose name do we have here? One *Mungo Ballantyne Usher Laird* of these parts. And here, what does that say? Ah yes, a little bit indistinct, as if the signatory was a little bit unsteady, unsure, at the time – but definitely, one *Ethel Sharpe McNiven Laird*."

Mungo thought he heard a beat – or was it a heavy, short interval of silence that carried menace?

"Mungo: where's my money?"

Mungo weighed his options and was found wanting. So in lieu of same options, he gave a big sigh and straightened up as far as the sagging couch would allow him, to force his shoulders back.

"Right. Meg! Truth be told – I don't have it. Here." He held out an arm followed by a leg – which was quite a feat given the state of the couch and his joints.

"These must be worth something. You know: black-market in body parts. Bound to be a rich terrorist Afghan amputee cleric somewhere in West London, who'd give his right arm for one of these." And with that he tapped his leg.

Meg laughed – though it was a matter of judgement whether there was an iota of humour in it. Then she stood and began to pace the room. Much like Chelsea had, but without the tape measure and the fake tan. When she spoke it was as if the last remaining spark of compassion in her body was confounding her brain.

"Mungo, oh Mungo, what am I going to do with you?" She remained silent for a further moment and the mad moment in which sympathy had almost taken over, passed, and she felt so much better, once again clear-headed and calculating.

"You know what this means, of course? You were on our *preferential rate*, now I have to put you on our *preferential-plus rate*."

Mungo bounced off the couch (after two previous attempts), ignored the dust cloud, smiled and held his hand out to Meg.

"Well, now we've got that out of the way, let's have that little something."

She ignored the outstretched hand and he went and poured some fresh drinks. Meg refused hers – not in an obviously hostile way – and Mungo thought to himself: *all the more for yours truly*. He was beginning to feel much better. The booze does help; there were no two-ways about it.

When he had taken a generous slug, he accepted the pen from Meg and, without hesitation, made his mark on the fresh document where she indicated. With a flourish he offered the pen back, but she smiled and shook her head and pointed to another part of the document.

"Now, now, Mungo, you're coming close to chancing your arm. And a leg. Your other signature, remember. Your other half."

"Oh what the hell? In for a penny in for..." and with another flourish he simulated his lady-wife's mark. Meg took the document, checked it briefly and put it back into her document case.

At which moment Ethel entered the room and did not at first see Meg.

Chapter 23

Bad hair (and face) day.

"Mungo, assistance please," Ethel said, trying to remove her moulting beaver-lamb coat.

Mungo looked at her in horror and Meg in amazement. Ethel was a fright-fest: it was a toss-up as to what won the prize: hair or face. In his haste to hold Ethel – no to birl her round so that she would not see Meg, or would think Meg was part of the aspidistra given her slimness of form – Mungo fell over the riot of shopping bags.

"Mungo. Look out. Oh get up and just shove them under the table, Mungo. I could kill for a large sherry. That is *if* there's any left. Started early I detect. Scottish Government has much to answer for: shops now concealing the Buckie behind the *Pampers*. Would you believe?!"

All of this while she smiled happily in the mirror above the fireplace (has that not been sold? Must see if *Cash Convertors* would take it, Ethel mused to the vision before her.). "Not as bad as I feared," she said aloud to the mirror.

(But it was worse, Dear Reader. Much worse.)

"Nary a nail touched, covered in foundation cream, half-way through my first blow dry, and the electricity people decide to cut-off Francois over some trivial…" Then she screamed –

she had spotted a creature in the mirror who most certainly did not belong here. Slowly Ethel turned – this was not for effect; it was the effect of her corset having rucked-up under her oxter.

Meantime, Meg had taken to pacing the room and tapping the walls and writing little notes in a pretty little black-covered notepad.

Ethel fled the room.

"Mungo. Explanation!" Ethel demanded some fifteen minutes later, and indicated with a disdainful paw somewhere in the general direction of Meg.

"And you must be, Mrs Laird, so good to meet you. Mungo has – I mean Mr Laird – has told me so much about you." Meg said advancing while putting away her notepad.

Ethel looked askance at Mungo, then equally askance at Meg. "He has? Mungo, what have you been saying about me!?" Ethel said sharply.

"Allow me to explain – may I call you Ethel? I'm Meg. Meg Dalgliesh of Alban Associates. This was a little surprise he was keeping up his sleeve for you. You know how our men, like to, well, like to think they can... you know." With which she handed Ethel a business card.

"MC Dalgliesh?" Ethel peered, squinted, frowned, grimaced and read with difficulty (vain, remember?).

"And your reason for being here?" Ethel was not easily charmed. Especially not by the kind of brazen hussy that could melt Mungo. Ethel was made of sterner stuff. She turned her back to put on her specs (One pound from The Pound Shop. Good value; 3x) and carefully read the card, her lips barely moving. "And all those letters, after your name..." Ethel did not hide her suspicion. "University of… what? One of those upstart colleges I expect, dear."

"Edinburgh, actually. But I like to treat everyone as if they were equal just the same." At which she struggled round Ethel and snatched the card back.

"Edinburgh, indeed. In those heels?" (*St Laurent, Paris Heart Print*, £440 atow) Ethel riposted, not giving any ground and slipping her specs up her sleeve before turning to sneer.

"Real estate management," Meg said sweetly. "Consultant to various local, central government bodies – I won't bore you with details. Just to say that this property scores in the high nineties on the *Aschenbach Scale.*" Meg airily waved a hand to indicate the room. "You doubtless know what that means in terms of a potential sale to a local authority? We, I mean your Local Social Services Estates Division, will definitely want to progress this beyond the exploratory stages, taking it forward. I can see my clients, wanting to make a positive offer. Even over the odds, given the priority to the disadvantaged." Then, in an attempt to be inclusive, she said to Mungo, "Doesn't it just give you a warm glow all over?"

"That'll be the sherry," Mungo said sadly, noting that the Harveys was now being drained by Ethel who was not slugging out of the neck as the previous description might lead one to infer. Ethel was draining the remnants into a glass that she had wiped clean with the hem of her dress, at which point Mungo tried to get a glimpse but was too late. Speaking of which, of late he had been slowing down in his reactions to such opportunities that arose. This was a cause for some immediate concern.

Now Ethel took a generous slug (from the glass) and smacked her lips in a way that made Mungo melt with love, as

Ethel now swaggered up and down on top of the tiger skin rug, managing neatly to miss putting her foot in its gaping jaw. That swagger – which in truth had elements of a stagger in it – spoke volumes for Mungo: his lady had taken control of the situation.

"Let me see my dear, *Meg*? If I have this right? You are here as some sort of... what... surveyor? Assessor? Correct? Your client being the Local Social Work Department? Correct? And what the devil would they propose to use this place for? *Danse du thé for the Single Mothers of Addicts and Vulnerable Two-Year-Olds*? I think not. The very thought of people like that..." (If *shudder* were spelled *shugger,* Ethel would have added an extra 'ug' here.)

A pained expression passed fleetingly across Meg's face. "Actually, Ethel, I'm sorry that you can't empathise with the less fortunate." She began to pack away her documents. Donning her jacket she continued smoothly. "Frankly, Mungo had told me so much that was to your credit – your sensitivity, your compassion, your... your... Would you begrudge others less fortunate than yourselves the opportunity to... well it's not for me to judge, but, look around you, Ethel." And Meg's arms indicated the room. "This would make such a wonderful, temporary shelter for those who need a wonderful temporary shelter. And the name of Ethel Laird would go down to posterity in the ranks of... Brother Francis, Mother Theresa and every single one of The Little Sisters of the Poor." Meg moved to the door and paused. "I'll see myself out," she said, while with her eyes she made it very clear to Mungo that he had better accompany her. At which both left Ethel to her thoughts.

Ethel looked about the room and suddenly all the beauty that was in her face drained away. (Think hyper-nano seconds.) When she spoke, it was to the walls.

"Oh that these walls could speak – my god, they would scream in protest at the indignities that might be heaped upon them. Tempted to take a match to the whole thing right now and end it. Wonder if Mungo paid the insurance? A *refuge* indeed. What about my place of refuge? Yes, can just see it, the feckless to rule the earth. Vulnerable two-year-olds indeed. Well, spirit of the old house, gird your loins, for what may be about to befall you: battered wives in our basement. Battered husbands in our attic. All seated in our kitchen being served battered haddock. And who the f*ck is Brother Francis?!"

Chapter 24

Decisions, decisions, decisions, or: in praise of discrimination.

Mungo as usual was first to rise. He dressed to suit the balmy spring temperature: his old favourite and only dressing gown, his second best skinny woollen scarf, and his best jaunty bunnet. Absentmindedly scratching his crot*h, and pleased with having achieved another safe descent of the ever steepening stairs, he strained to bend to lift the *Telegraph* lying on the hall mat. Damp – the paper and the mat. No need to read the Anglo-centred generic weather forecast, he thought.

A quick brew later he had just settled down in his corner of the living room to gingerly peel open his newspaper, when Ethel entered, wearing her homely housecoat and carrying her clipboard. She propped it on the mantelpiece where once had stood a Greek Thomson Church in the shape of a clock. (*Visitors Welcome.*) Ethel, shivering, positioned herself strategically in front of the one-bar electric fire – which had replaced the Living Flame-with-no-living-flame-and with two chilled hands shrucked up the back of her housecoat to heat her numb b*m.

"Times like this wish I was a man. Something tangible to scratch in the morning," she rasped.

"Keep taking the steroids, dear. Voice is getting there," Mungo said from the depths of the still-damp field at Wincanton. Then, tossing aside his paper to intimate that he was interested, he said:

"Well, my dear, having slept on it *again,* any final conclusions?"

"Mungo, you know I never sleep. My jumpy legs see to that. Anyway, decision stands."

"But we have nothing in writing. First we have to wait for expressions of interest. Then to see if these turn into concrete offers," Mungo offered reasonably.

"Hogw*sh. Who would not make an offer? Those awful chavs did. Chelsea said it was '*the Study what done it'* for her. What are people like that going to study? Casing a bank as we speak, doubtless. I refuse to even contemplate selling to that type. Anyway, there's no rush, is there? Well is there?"

Mungo swallowed, audible in the silence. He shuffled in his chair, managing to wobble his teacup on his little table. He grabbed it just in time. The table. The cup was another matter. No matter must be one left. Somewhere. His mind jumped back to the bigger crisis. The biggest crisis that he must keep from Ethel. At all costs. Chiefly his own. He adopted his very best whine that almost whinged in resonance.

"Well, there's that little detail of which we hardly ever speak? A rather large deposit on our place in the sun is costing interest as we mull. I propose that we..."

"Mungo, the loan, we're not in any sort of... you know? You wouldn't hide anything from me, would you?" Ethel stared for as long as it took for Mungo to raise his head and look his now looming wife in the eye. It was a long time. "No, you wouldn't,"

Ethel stated. She was convinced. That was until Mungo in a decidedly unconvincing tone went on.

"Yes, dear. Just thinking: would be less of a bother all round, take first *written legal offer* that meets our needs. Chavs or Ethnics or Your Two Boys. Get the business over with? Mmh? Yes?"

"And you could live with yourself if those god-awful Ashley-Cole-Coles were to install themselves here? Can't you just see them?" Ethel put her fullest bosom fully into her shudder.

The pipes were silent behind the walls and Mungo wondered if this was the pretty pass that things had come to – where even the pipes had given up the ghost.

"Very well, Ethel: whom have you anointed?" Mungo sighed a sigh that knew the answer to his question. He was no general, despite a two-year stint in the school's Officer Cadet Corps, and eighteen months National Service as a filing clerk (lance corporal by the way) in Malaya. He knew when he was beaten. Mungo did not require a Sioux arrow through the b*lls.

"I don't think there is any question, the people of class, and I never thought I'd see the day when I'd associate that word with colonials…" Ethel began airily.

"I quite liked the ethnics," Mungo interrupted. "If he only had a sense of humour, he would have been quite likeable. That's the difference between us and the Asiatics – no sense of humour. Awfully sensitive to criticism. Everything's racism with them. The old race card – wish we could play it. All stacked against us: white, middle-aged, middle class. Decent with it."

"*Adriatics*, Mungo. They're the ones without humour. I blame the mothers – *Tony's agoodaboy. He noameantamachinegunthesucker*," Ethel said, in an uncharacteristic display of stereotyping perspicacity, and for a moment she and Mungo wondered what had brought that on. Then she recovered.

"The ethnics, yes." Ethel mulled over this possibility that she had not admitted even to herself. "I did quite find myself empathising with the female – probably because we have so much in common. Looks, intelligence, she even refused to enter into a forced marriage. Girls from these families have it really hard, you know. Parents probably Taliban as well."

"She's white?!" Mungo screamed silently, astute enough to realise his wicket was sticky enough as it was. He let Ethel ramble on.

"... decent university despite parental disapproval. Works at Debenhams, manages the Edinburgh Crystal department. Full of spunk, that girl."

"Not surprising: trying for a family for ages: Mr Thingie said it himself '*going at it with the hammer and a tong*', and I quote," Mungo quoted.

Ethel chose to ignore this insertion of vulgar carnality into the discussion. "Sad. Just not our type, Mungo. Simple as that. No, it has to be Brucie and Dirk. I liked that proposition they made. And I, that is we, shall keep our side of the albeit silent verbal bargain I made. We shall indeed take the house off the market. Makes sense. Speed things up. That should please a man who seems to be in a curious hurry." And she eyed Mungo with a steely glint with this last pointed remark.

"But..." was as far as Mungo got.

"I've been thinking, Mungo: we'll have them to dinner. Close the deal, as they say. There, does that please you?"

“You think that’s wise, dear? This is not meant to be a criticism; it’s just that last time we entertained, your sherry trifle caused our guests to go blind.”

“What b*lls you speak, Mungo Laird!” Ethel exploded. “Aunt Muriel had a temporary loss of her sight. Eyes were never her strongest feature. Uncle Brodie was mostly blind anyway before we started. And as for the cousins, admittedly they did experience some blurring of their vision. I put it all down to an hysterical over-reaction to the fuss made by Aunt Muriel.” She plumped some cushions as was her want at times of emotional turbulence, then closed this subject with: “And anyway, we got them down to their car without serious incident. And we heard no more about it.”

“Heard no more of them,” Mungo muttered under his breath before resuming his normal whine when ‘negotiating’ with Ethel. “I was just thinking of you, dear. More time you spend in the kitchen, less time to charm our guests.”

“You do have a point. For once, Mungo. Let me think about this. I suppose we could replace the sherry trifle with…”

Ethel’s musing was cut short by the front doorbell. (*Dring, dring*, in a sort of humble tone.)

“Mungo, get that please. And if it is the postman claiming again that the letterbox has rusted up, then I swear I’ll go straight to Her Majesty.”

Ethel’s due consideration of alternative, appropriate puddings was rudely interrupted by her husband’s return and question.

“Ethel. Another couple! Do you have your list? A Mr and Mrs Walters?”

"Nonsense. I know the list by heart. And *the house is off the market* as of five minutes hence. Send them off with a flea in their ear."

"Too late, dear. I've asked them to wait in the hall."

Chapter 25

Picafor v Pollensa: a contest. (Alcudia was eliminated in an earlier round.)

Before Ethel could b*llock Mungo, two heads keeked around the door. One female then one male. One cheery, one down in the mouth. When the rest of their bodies slowly entered, Ethel instantly knew these were not serious candidates. She could just tell. *Time wasters*, in the language of that paragon of honesty, the estate agent fraternity (if that last word is still allowed). Nosey. And working class. Impertinent to boot. Uninvited. No introduction…

"As we speak, my dearest, the eponymous Mr and Mrs Walters. My very good lady, Ethel."

"Sorry for turning up like this," the man, (Tim) spoke. "We just got back from C'an Picafor last night. The plane was late. You know what like *Flybe* is." He paused in the face of Ethel's face. He swallowed and blurted, "Well maybe you don't. Anyway. The plane was a day late – apparently the crew at Bergerac… you're no' really interested in this are you? Naw."

His wife (Idris) came to the rescue. She had to. This was all her idea. "C'an Picafor. We were at C'an Picafor. That's the one that's a better class than… than Alcudia. Much, much better. So it is, sure it is, Tim?"

"That's right, Idris." Tim smiled drily. "Better than Alcudia. Admittedly no quite as classy as Puerto Pollensa, but there you go. You can't have everything, can you? Some day though we'll…"

"Puerto Pollensa! That is class. Intit, Tim? Full of teachers without the weans. I mean kids. We've two ourselves, so we appreciate that sort of thing. No having them, I mean." Idris seemed to suddenly dry up. Probably in the face of Ethel's face.

"Fascinating," said Mungo, who as quite frequently happened was comfitttted by Ethel's discomfiture.

"I'm sorry, but we're not hiring staff," said Ethel, not sounding in the least bit *désolé*.

"No, no. We're here to look at the house, ma man explained to your man. At the door. You know," Idris Walters explained patiently. She had lived with Tim for a long time and had had to develop that virtue. It had been touch and go a few times, but a vow is a vow, Idris had explained to her daughter, Melissa.

"I'm sorry Mrs… eh… Watters?" Ethel said.

"That's Walters, Mrs Laird. But don't worry, we get that a' the time. Easily done," Idris said, her eyes sweeping the room (it would save Mungo doing it later).

Ethel nodded her great head in sympathy – how many times had she been called Mrs Baird and worse. And much worse. The latter all behind her considerable back. But enough feminine empathy.

"There's been perhaps a misunderstanding. We, that is *Villa Laird*, are not part of East Renfrewshire's '*Open up your house and garden to any old stranger*' initiative. Ludicrous idea. Stately, as our Home is, the house is for *sale*. No *not* for sale…" Ethel concentrated harder. She needed *Buckieing* up, badly. "Or *was* for sale… as it is now off the market and anyway only candidates who had expressed and registered an interest with our estate agent prior to today and who have or had, anyway… whatever… *met* certain minimum but quite stringent criteria have made it on to my list… that is no longer current." And with that Ethel lifted her clipboard from the mantelpiece and waved it majestically. "And have already been granted an interview."

She pretended to scrutinise the clipboard. "And no, no Watters here, I beg pardon: no *Walters* here. You do not appear to be on said list under either name. So sorry, but you've wasted your time. Mungo, if you would? Thank you for your interest." And Ethel made a passing good attempt at a sweet, though with a hint of condescension, smile, and indicated the direction of egress for Idris.

"I told you, Idris, we should have done it official before the holiday. Sorry to bother you, and that. Thanks for your time." And Tim limped towards the door like a mildly chastised cur, (in Idris's eyes who was used to this from her husband of many years and who could no longer go at it with the hammer and a tong. Apart from that, he was basically decent.).

Idris, with the genetic instincts inbred in women (according to the S*nday P*ost), knew instinctively who the soft touch was and turned from Ethel's Mount Rushmore (with capillaries, remember?) face to the much kinder one of Mungo.

"You see the thing is, we were up the hill here, wi' the Ramblers Association – I'm not a member, I hasten to add," she hastened to add. "I've got three jobs. Tim is always ramblin' on. He's got lots of spare time. Invalidity. So anyways, we seen the sign but it was the day before we flew off to C'an Picafor."

"C'an Picafor. That's the one that's..." Mungo liked this woman. (Let's face it Mungo liked women.)

He began to scan her with his barcode eyes. Idris Walters (*née* Watters) was about half his age, with a slender, athletic-looking figure that was probably due, not to the mindless pursuit of some ideal body image in the gym, but the aforementioned three jobs. She probably had to dart between these with little time to lie on the couch with a tub of Buffalo Wings (this always puzzled Mungo: when did buffalo sprout wings?) and a gallon of some gut-rotting and rotting-gut sugary drink. Yes. He already admired her. He wondered if she ever considered using sussies? Her hair was cheaply dyed blonde with the dark roots showing at the nape of her beautiful neck, where a strand or two had come loose from the factory-style chignon which gave such women, in Mungo's eyes, a chaste but tarty look. He expected that in her chase between jobs, her unblemished skin would be coated in a golden sheen of... something like sweat but not as vulgar and much more tasty. Whatever the Queen had before she grew out of it. Today, Idris was wearing...

"Mungo! You're dribbling." Ethel jabbed him in the ribs.

"Yes, yes. C'an Picafor. That's the one that's better than Al..." His steel-trap mind formed the thought that would levitate the moment and was joined in it by Tim Walters in perfect harmony.

"Al Qaeda," they both said.

Mungo liked this man. (And Mungo liked few men.)

Idris let the male sniggers fizzle out – she had brothers.

"Anyway," she began emphatically – she was not going until there was nothing else for it, "we wondered what it would be like. The big hoose. We've always looked up here with, you know, whit's the word?"

"'*Awe*' would be apt," Ethel suggested with just a hint of saccharin.

"Aye, as in '*aw, ah wish ah could afford to live up there'*," Tim said, rather boldly for him, Idris thought with some admiration. Getting a word out of him in recent years had been like getting something that is really, really hard to get, like a stone out of the blood of a kidney.

"Aw, aye?" Mungo was enjoying this.

"Precisely my point. Mungo, if you would, please?" Ethel spoke over Mungo not for the first time, and again waved a hand airily towards the door.

"Well thanks anyway for your time, Lady Laird." Idris seemed genuinely disappointed – but don't be fooled yet; we said she would go only when there was no other choice. "So sorry to have troubled you." She turned to her man. "Well Tim, we can always boast that we saw inside this place. Magic, so it is. Wait till ah tell oor Melissa. She'll no believe it."

She turned back to Ethel, but then more quickly to Mungo. "An' if you should ever need any catering, ah'm available for the purvey. You know, golden wedding, funeral an' the likes. Ah've got a card somewhere." She fumbled in her huge fawn handbag. "An' cleaning." She looked about the room. "Your cleaner is no exactly... there ah go again, speaking oot o' turn."

Mungo silently mimed to Ethel, 'Come on. Why not?' Ethel sighed and sank on the couch, reached for the Buckie before nodding her reluctant assent through the stoor.

“Seems such a pity,” Mungo said, “that our visitors having made the effort – the climb and what-not. Perhaps you would like a quick tour?”

“That would be just pure brilliant.” Idris’s sudden beam almost lit up the large room. No mean feat.

“Would it be all right if I just sat here?” Tim asked the Lairds and pointed to his right knee. “I’ll no touch the silverware.”

“Tim’s got a knee. And a heart. It’s just a murmur. Ye can hardly hear it.”

“Well we certainly don’t want you tipping over on us. B*ggar of a job getting coffin out of here. Mungo, you keep Mr Walters company.” Ethel turned fully to Idris. “He only gets in the way.”

“Aye, Tim’s a bit like that. They’re all like that, when you think about it.”

The women abruptly left their two men.

“’Spect you’ve heard it lots of time: that’s some view.” Tim turned from the window to survey the room. “And that plasterwork – the cornicing, the ceiling rose. That is *craftsmanship*. You don’t get that these days.”

The pipes clattered, seemingly in accord with Tim’s finer appreciation.

Mungo’s atavistic loud cough and jog to kick the usual spot on the wall was appreciated by Tim. The pipes stopped instantly.

“You do know what that is?” Tim said matter-of-factly.

“What?!” Mungo did not really ask through an even louder cough. “Never heard a thing. These old houses play tricks on the imagination. You were saying?”

“Was I… oh… aye, the views and the house. Aye, some place you’ve got. You look at this, the hill, and you ask yourself: how did they manage to build it in those days, what, hundred and thirty-odd years ago? I mean, no cranes and the likes. Must have cost a packet as well."

"Never give it a thought. Always in the family. Needs some work, though. B*ggar to heat. Don't tell the lady wife I said so. Anyway, I can tell you. No harm in that."

"Aye, I'm really sorry about this. It's Idris. She's done this before you know: taking us to view houses we haven't a hope in hell of ever buying. Can be really embarrassing. Her psychiatrist said it's a harmless trait that's on the increase. He blamed the telly. I told her that, but she had to have a psychiatrist say it, make it official like. All our neighbours have got some sort of support professional. Social worker, substance-abuse counsellor, probation officer, independent financial advisor and the likes. Idris felt left out: she wanted someone to make her feel part of the dependency society. As far as I'm concerned, that's a real social disease. You can keep your gonorrhoeas and your chlamydias. Anyway, there you have it. I'm afraid we are the classic time-wasters."

"No shame in that. World's full of them today." Mungo was really warming to this stocky little chap with the endearing limp. He had a mind to adopt that particular gait the next time Ethel asked him to go down to the street. It's the little details that make the difference.

Chapter 26

Oh Danny Boy.

The pipes gave a discreet warning rumble, as if politely inviting the audience to settle down, then they charged straight into the opening bars of *Also Sprach Zarathustra* (without going into detail, just think of the opening scene in *2001: A Space Odyssey*, dir. S Kubrick – but without the sunrise). Mungo briefly thought of conducting them, but instead forsaking all semblance of a cough simply leaped and booted the wall soundly. They shuddered to quiet, and night fell and The Sentinel was discovered on the Moon.

Tim was evidently not a great fan of Richard Strauss (or Nietzsche or Kubrick). "That's your pipes. I could fix that for you. It's my trade. It wid take jist a couple of minutes. Have you got a washer?"

"Did have, but paid her off some years back. Oh, you mean the little round thing with the hole. Don't believe I have, old boy."

"Old boot?"

"No, can't see her having one."

"It's wellies, I'm talking aboot. Any old rubber boot'll do. I'll cut a washer from it."

"Ah. With you. You know, Tim, we had green wellies before they became fashion items for gangsters and garagistes. But that's the way of the world. Wouldn't concern yourself with the plumbing. Leave it to the next lot to worry about. So, you say you are from the old town?"

"The Bottom Scheme, aye. Ah used to look up here when ah was a wean and dream of someday being up among the stars. The impossible dream. There was a time it could have been said I was from the wrong side of the track. 'Cept the ar*eholes, pardon the vernacular, dug the track up and built a skateboard arena. Really handy that turned out – everybody dumps their rubbish there now. Me myself, I'm on the invalidity. Ma knee. And ma heart, you know. Doc said to take up gardenin'. For the most part ah spend all my time in the nursery."

"Nursery?" Mungo paused. "Children? Vegetables?"

"No, no, they're fairly normal. Fact, one of them is quite bright. The other wan is doing media studies."

"We've got ones like that. Caught VSO at an early age. Incurable optimists."

An exhausted Ethel and an animated Idris came back just at this.

"VSO!?" Idris exclaimed. "Aw naw. Mad cow disease. How awful for baith of youse."

"Mad cow? What are you going on about now, Mungo?"

"Mad cow in a fashion. VSO. Variant strain: sufferers have delusions they can work their b*llocks off for benighted savages and their leaders will stop stealing from them. Not always fatal, but leaves permanent brain damage."

But Idris had had enough of the philosophy and jerked the *craic* back to a more prosaic level. "You should see the house,

Tim, you missed yourself. It's pure magical. An' a' they rooms jeest for the two o' you." Idris as many before her was drawn to the window of the drawing room.

"Oh look, Tim. You can look down on the whole toon." That was not Ethel speaking, though she shared the sentiment as she spoke now.

"Always liked doing that. But they ignore us now. What with all those little chalets nibbling away at the space. Time to move on." She trailed off with something between a sob and a sigh – a sibh – and sank into the couch in a little puff of stoor that caught Idris's professional interest.

"Wis always green and country when I looked up here as a boy," Tim said. "Pity they built all those houses round about you. Ah wis sure it was greenbelt or something."

"Indeed it was – managed to get that changed. Those days we had influence. The council you know," Ethel said.

"You got it changed?!" Idris was still high. "You would need to be mad tae... I mean... well..."

"Had to, my dear." Mungo smiled. "No head for business, apparently. Still, when I poured Laird's Lager down the stank, it was a blow on behalf of the drinking classes. Was all p*sh and wind. All forgotten." He turned to Ethel, still smiling. "Right, dear? Anyway. Needed to sell off little plots. We have to live. We are the dark side of social mobility. *On the chute*, as those dreadful French would say. Meritocracy? What hope for me in that? And then there is the roof – always the roof. Might never have bothered for all the good it's done: still leaks. Bl*ody W*lsh slate. And the nails. The nails... " He was just building up a good head of steam when:

"Mungo!" Ethel shrieked.

"If this was mine I would have kept it all," Idris interjected. "Kept a' the fields and the trees an' that. I just dream of having no neighbours. Being able to look down on people. Ah would love no having Alsatians next door. Ah would love tae huv a big garden." She paused. "Some chickens..."

"Oh C*rist! More chickens..." Mungo swivelled to Idris. "Forgive the language, my dear, inexcusable in front of a lady. Just that... well it's not how it appears from down below. Not paradise. Not magical. Unless you're on something stronger than sherry. In truth it's god-awful, it's a constant battle with the Welsh—"

"Mungo! Control yourself!"

"Please. Say no more. Tim. We've got to put an offer in." Idris ignored the splutters of both Mungo and Tim, but especially Ethel.

"We can do it." Earnestness was all over her fine work-sculpted face. Mungo's heart filled as he watched her continue.

"I'm working continental shifts. I can squeeze in another job. When you've got three jobs you would never notice a fourth. Tim has a limp sum for his lump – naw, the ither way aboot: a lump sum from his limp. It's due and we can borrow on it, sure you huv? The motor goes. And there's those people – what they called, Tim? – aye, Hammerhead Securities or something. They'll give us a two, or wis it a five-hundred percent mortgage on our own house withoot asking questions? Look: I just want to live somewhere where there are no junkies, no pit bulls, no social workers, no more dugs – you've no idea, honest: see they dugs – excuse ma language – they're fuckin' (******g) animals. Some o' them are nearly as bad as the people. Naw! You can't stop us putting an offer in. There's no law that says you can."

Ethel had to act. "That's precisely where you are wrong, Idris, dear. It's not as if you're ethnic, or think you are a man, or disabled, or too old. We can frankly tell you to b*ggar off, and we don't need to give a reason. You don't count, my dear. Simply do not count. In fact: you're just like us."

(Ethel on reflection hoped that no one had heard that last phrase. If it was thrown in her face, she would deny ever having said it. The very thought! Not that the Walters were not decent, even likeable-in-a-mildly-condescending, no *not* patronising, way. It was just the cl*ss thing overriding any notions of a shared humanity. So there!)

"But doesn't that no' mean you can't turn down an offer from any of that other lot you just mentioned?" Tim asked.

"Oh don't be silly," Ethel snapped, reverting to type momentarily, before recovering what passes for manners among her type, and smiling sweetly added, "Naïve, shall we say? Of course we can turn down offers, as long as we do not do so on any grounds covered by the Discrimination Act. We may be dinosaurs, but we're not entirely permafrosted when it comes down to playing the system."

"Well I think it's wrong, discrimination. It shouldn't be allowed." Idris looked both angry and sad.

Mungo looked sad for her. "'Shouldn't be allowed?' Human nature, my dear. We cannot survive without the instinct to discriminate. I go into a room full of people, see a chap with two heads. I avoid him. Maybe later I'll speak to one of him if the rest turn out to be immensely dull… or two-faced. That's discrimination. We each favour people we perceive as being like us – skin colour, age, language, accent, background. It all makes sense. Darwinian. Has served us well for millennia. A man says he does not discriminate? Liar or lunatic." Then realising he had revealed more of himself than he had intended, Mungo sought to bring matters back to the mundane, the reason they were having this conversation. He shrugged apologetically. "I'm so sorry, this house is just not for you." Then as if to banish the pain that appeared on Idris's work-smoothed brow, he added, "Believe me. We're doing you a favour. Did I mention the W*lsh slate?"

Idris appeared crestfallen, and Mungo felt he had been a brute to her and wondered how he could make it all up and whether she had ever been to Crieff (with Tim). But she quickly perked up.

"Oh well, there's always the purvey. You'll no forget noo? Ah've no' got a card wi' me, but here's ma number." Idris pulled a piece of paper and a pen from the jumble in her big bag, and wrote out her phone number. She deposited the paper on the mantelpiece, smoothing it out before turning smartly.

"Right Tim, aff yer a*se. Time we were off. Wance he sits doon there's nae movin' him, so there is'nae." She turned to Ethel. "Yours like that as well? Thought so. You're right, Mrs Laird. You're just like me. We've mair in common than ah thought before ah came here. You live and some of us learn."

Chapter 27

Let there be dark.

That night, when Mungo was still trying to get a third word correct in the *Telegraph* cryptic crossword (his record was nine), Ethel in a foul mood brushed past as the telephone rang. It kept ringing. He did not need to look up – he could sense her mood by the weight of her tread (the tiger's jaw snapped shut) and anyway she always answered the ph*cquing thing. He did doorbells. She did phone bells. It was how marriages survived. Sharing. Sharing chores: sharing bells; sharing bins; sharing buckets. He looked up to be met with the back page of *Scottish Field* with its A4-sized bottle of some obscure and decidedly appealing single malt.

Mungo dramatically struggled up, dramatically chucked the *Telegraph* to the floor, dramatically and noisily shook his head (his jowls impressively taut and not slapping together so much so that a stranger might notice, he thought). All to no avail. He non-dramatically lifted the telephone, but answered it dramatically loudly.

"Madame Laird's butler speaking..." then he spluttered and choked. "What!?" Mungo walked as far away from Ethel as the old phone cord would permit. He lowered his voice, conscious that he was on the wrong side of Ethel (not for the first time that day – this time it meant the side with her good ear).

"No, eh… I mean…" Now he whispered, "Meg said what? She says you've to what? 'Give me a reminder'? Well just put it in the post, I suggest… Tonight? Yes we'll be in. No! I mean we're about to go out. Called away suddenly. C'an Picafor, that's the one that's…" He assumed a bad foreign accent, someway between *Te reo Māori* and *Yupik*. Take your pick. "So sorry wrong number!"

He hung up the phone as if it was on fire, stared at it then looked up to see Ethel peering round her magazine at him. She watched him return with two torches. She reluctantly took a torch from him and watched him turn off the lights. She threw the magazine out into the darkness, trusting that it would cause him some damage.

"Mungo! The devil you playing at?! Who was that on the telephone? And stop playing silly b*ggars and put the lights back on!"

"Sorry, dear, forgot to mention. They called earlier today. N-power. That was them just reminding us just now. N-power. 'N' as in, eh… 'nae' power for a couple of hours this evening."

Mungo sat and with his torch cast *Batman*'s symbol on the walls and ceiling. He'd forgotten what fun that could be and for a moment his mind drifted to *Citizen Kane* (1941, dir. O Welles. Still worth a look for the camera angles and lighting), and contemplated that his last words on his deathbed would be: '*fetch me my Batman torch*'. (The baggy trousers would be of no use then.)

Ethel tried to read her magazine, but the *Hopalong Cassidy* image cast on the pages was quite distracting. And so she fumed and in a fit of unseemly curiosity demanded:

"Remind us of what, Mungo?"

"Electricity johnnies. Testing some new system – upgrading something or other. Everyone to conserve power for an hour or two. National interest and all that. You heard them on the phone yourself."

"Damned inconvenient. What if I had been in the bath? Attached to an iron lung or something? At least give me the decent torch." They exchanged torches and nothing was said of the relative importance in contemporary culture of *Batman* and *Hopalong*. (An easy pub quiz question is: Name *Hopalong Cassidy's* horse. Answer given in Appendix 9 of de luxe edition.)

Mungo was on a roll. Eight words nearly correct. The penumbra seemed good for the senescent brain. Ethel's gentle (for her) snoring seemed to congratulate him on a successful ploy. She was completely in the dark for Mungo had gently switched-off her *Batman* while muffling (can you muffle light? Answers only by Morse telegram please) his *Hopalong* one with an old sock of Ethel's that he had found down the side of the couch.

The doorbell rang. *Dring-an-ef*ing-dring-dring-dring-dring-dring!*

Ethel started. Mungo switched off his torch. The doorbell rang again, longer.

"Mungo. Where are you? What's happened?"

Mungo quickly tried an impersonation of a stage hypnotist (he had only ever seen one – a very bad one). "Shush, my dear. I'm here. You are asleep. Sleep. Sleep. You are having a bad dream. Sleep, sleep, your eyes are feeling heavy, heavy, heavier and you want to go to sleep, it's all a dream…"

"Mungo! Stop that nonsense!"

“Ethel, shut your mouth! I’ll apologise later for that, but just do it.”

The bell rang again, more insistently this time and with many asterisks, and never seemed to stop, this time. *Dring – ****-dring***** dring- dring-dring-∞*

Now the door was obviously battered, now it appeared as if they were being broken into. A deep male voice boomed:

“Answer the door! We know you’re in there. We just want to talk. Discuss a few details. Come on. Hurry up!”

There were more louder and louder breaking-in type noises.

“Mr Laird! Mungo!” A second male, a lighter more refined voice. “It’s Henry. Henry from Hammerhead. Remember? Spoke to you on the phone an hour ago. Meg sent us. Asked us to call on you. Courtesy call, like. Now just come to the door and be a good lad. And don’t give us any more sh*te.”

“Look, Mungo,” it was the first one again. “What is your problem, mate? If you have a problem then we want to help you out. That’s what we’re here for. So, come on, don’t p*ss about. Answer the door!”

“Come on we’ve no’ got all night.” Henry again.

There followed more serious noises of the attempted breaking-in nature. Then some desultory half-heard exchanges and curses along the lines of ‘these old doors are a b*stard to smash’. And ‘told ye tae bring the sledgehammer, ya t*sser’. Then the first male spoke directly again.

“Open the door you old… distressed gentlefolk. We know you’re in there. If we’ve got to knock this down you’ll pay for this, ya old pair o’ b*sta… eh, people of a certain age…”

Henry helped him out, adding, “Youth disadvantaged!”

The racket and shouts suddenly ceased.

"Mungo, is there something you want to tell me?" Ethel whispered entering into the spirit of the occasion.

"Shush, Ethel. Could be a trick."

"Mungo," Ethel whispered. "What the devil is going on? Why are they…?"

"Shut up and listen for once in your life."

"To what? Listen to what? Can't hear a thing?"

"They've gone. Must have. Well, my dear, seems a lot of fuss over nothing. Must have been the wrong number. Call Centre in India, probably. Or Hull. Happens all the time." Mungo lit his torch and pretended to resume the crossword. "'Spect you want to get back to your little snooze, my dear. And, sorry if I was just a little bit brusque there. Strain you know. House and all that."

"Mungo, enough of this evasion. Time you told me what the h*ll is going on. *Hammerhead*. He distinctly said *Hammerhead*. That's not the same people who…"

"Shush, my love." Mungo put out his torch. "Heard something again. Did you hear it? Listen."

"Mungo, don't think for another moment you can pull…"

"Ethel! Listen. There it is again. They're back!"

The doorbell rang *Dring-dring etc.-dring*. The letter box rattled. There were raised voices. Different. Good G*d, Mungo thought, they've sent a gang this time.

"Come on, open up. Mr Laird!" some woman shouted. A woman! Was this especially to deal with Ethel? Ethel the co-signatory to the loan?!

"I'm thure I saw a light at the front when we came up the stairth. Try the window!"

A male voice. Bl*ody h*ll, Mungo thought, they've thent Mike Tyson.

The door was thumped and banged again.

Ethel had had enough. She grabbed Mungo's torch and stomped to the hallway:

"F*ck off! We'll call the police!"

"Madame, we are the police," the female said. "We've had calls from neighbours about the noise earlier tonight. A general disturbance. Please open the door. At once please."

Ethel raised her voice. "Mungo, fetch the Purdey (sidelock ejector)! Let's give these b*stards a taste of lead! Think they can fool us?"

Mungo was now at the widow. "My dear, tiny possibility they're telling the truth. Police car down on street."

"Taste of lead is it?! Then we'll jutht call in the armed rethponthe team..."

"And the helicopter!" the female added.

"Mungo, you got us into this. Answer the door and tell them to wipe their feet. And put the damned lights on!"

Mungo sheepishly returned to Ethel followed by two uniformed police. One female police constable (WPC), and one male police constable (PC). (We realise by assigning gender to them we are in breach of several ordinances, but there you go.)

Chapter 28

What's all the fuss about and what's the fuzz all about? Eh?

"Mungo, have you checked their identities?"

The WPC ignored this. "Would you care to explain what is going on, sir, madam?"

The PC elaborated. "In addition to thith evening'th reported dithurbanth…"

"Disturbances." The small WPC was obviously the lead in this double act. Probably because she could articulate her Ss Mungo thought (sought) then switched to thinking about tiny Hylda Baker and her extra tall stooge as she took over the script.

"There's been a number of complaints made over the last few days, about certain activities relating to comings and goings at this address."

Ethel wasn't having this. "This address? Complaints? Never! Against us?! By whom? I demand to know. I've a right to know."

"We'll come to that later, Mrs… Laird, is it? And you, sir. Are you related to madam?"

"Don't know about that – she let's me work in the garden in summer months, few odd jobs here and there. Get to share a bed with her. Once every equinox."

"Married. Right." This from the female. "The thing is neighbours – not just one, but several – have been reporting strange behaviour here over the last few days culminating in a reported disturbance this evening."

"Disturbance!? Are you mad, young lady?" Ethel spat. "It was you who caused the disturbance! Five minutes ago."

Mungo quickly moved behind Ethel and mimed the tippling sign to the two cops. The WPC had produced a small black notebook. She riffled some pages then read in her courtroom voice, "*Suspicion of drug dealing, of holding unlicensed séances, suspicion of running a house of ill-repute...* and maybe we'll need to add 'holder of unlicensed firearm'?"

Ethel spluttered while Mungo's twinkle suggested a little bit of being chuffed at the very idea of some of this.

It was the PC's turn. The tall cop had what must have been once a rather pretty face, but was now a bit askew as if he had recently had his jaw smashed in a car chase – well they drive a bit too fast – or with a sledgehammer. And apart from his distinctive sigmatism, he had appropriately a very thick bottom lip that reminded the sporting minded observers of the one-and only Miiiiiiiiiiiike ('Iron Mike') Tyyyyyyyyyyyyson in the blue corner. Except he was a foot (30 cms) too tall and was a pasty shade of greyish white.

"Do you admit that over the latht few dayth – after yearth of being almotht..." he pawthed and thtuttered. "Reclutheth..."

"Recluses. With few visitors." The WPC took command. Her given name was Emma and she had developed a sort of protective sufferance for her partner in crime-fighting (and crime), Big John. Despite the brain damage – he could have been a contender for the Police National Boxing Championships – he was still more than great at the muscle end of things. The problem was it was impossible for punters to take him seriously these days if he opened his mouth (not mouse). Not until his mouth mended, if it ever would. But he would try despite her gentle hints. Pride and that. But Emma tried to take control of dealing with Joe and Josephine Public. So she ignored Big John and continued with her court-side manner.

"And all of a sudden people – usually and invariably couples, but usually of varied ages, genders and ethnicity – have been coming and going from this address."

Mungo laughed and smiled at this attractive policewoman. He swept away a vision of bed sheets, truncheon and handcuffs as he spoke to her.

"Of course we don't deny it. Trying to sell the house. What else do you expect, but coming and going. Bloody idiots – not you of course. The complainants. Morons. We're surrounded by a herd of small-minded pygmies who couldn't get on a sports management course at the local poly. Cretins. *House of ill repute*? I wish."

"If you don't mind, thir. That word." Big John shook his head disapprovingly at Mungo and tutted thoftly.

"Word. What word? Cretins?"

"Thath' a no-no, thir. Our Cretan community might take offenth."

"What?! But they're two different things, man, cretins and Cretans."

"I know that, thir, and you know that, but the Cretanth don't." Big John paused then added, "Not very bright, thir."

Emma took her cue. "And the other one, sir. 'Pygmies'."

"Pygmies, who on God's earth could possibly…?"

"Our Bayakan community. We have a small though very engaged Bayakan community. They have a strong sense of self-esteem. And community. We would not want to upset them, would we, sir? Engaged yes. Enraged no…"

"Bayakans?" Mungo queried and bent to mime 'low height', to which Big John really bent to mime 'even lower'.

Emma made a mental note to praise Big John later. Mime could be his new thing.

Mungo felt it was his thing as he mimed a blow pipe, blew into it, clasped his neck and collapsed on the couch to enquire:

"Don't want to lower their self-esteem? Bayakans? Which begs the question: what the blazes are these… little b*ggars doing here? Apart from raising average height? Cultural exchange?"

"Have a problem, sir, with issues of ethnic diversity?" Emma asked Mungo. "We have this diversity training programme which might just be what you need. Help you come to terms with your problem. I can recommend it. Big… Constable Herd here went through it. Didn't you?" She made the mistake of turning to Big John.

"Yeth. You thee, I would go about beating up trannioth for no real reason."

"Trannieth?" Mungo had to athk. He looked at Ethel who shook her head and had a rather glazed look about her. Mungo sometimes found this quite attractive, but this was not the time. He looked at the WPC and repeated, "Trannieth?"

Emma whispered in Mungo's ear, "You know, Mr Laird, men that look like Mrs Laird there."

"Ah, trannieth. Trannies. Transvestites!" And Mungo looked at Ethel with a new interest.

"The thing ith I would beat them up for no apparent reathon. But to be fair to mythelf, I'd then feel guilty afterwardth. Tho they offered me this diverthity training programme."

"It was either that or the bullet, wasn't it, Constable?" Emma cut in. John would go on about that bloody programme of his all night. She tried to cut to the chase as she went on, "And cheerio pension and ta-ta cushy retirement at fifty!"

"Oh, it wathn't tho bad – actually it wath quite interethting. They delve into your innermotht being. Helpth you underthtand why you do thuch a thing. They take you right back to the beginning."

Ever eager to learn about the depths of human frailty, Mungo sought to encourage the poor thod (s*d). "Ah. Freudian slippage. Your childhood, relations with your mother. That thort, thorry, *sort* of thing."

"Further back, Mungo. Thorry, Mr Laird."

"The womb?"

"Further. The cave."

Mungo nodded thagely. "The cave. The dark night of the soul; the drip, drip, drip in the pitch blackness; the snuffling of the unseen beasts in the dark; the stentorian breathing of the heavy-browed mate."

"Sounds all too familiar," Ethel said drily.

"Still if it works…" Mungo slowed.

"It cured Big John," Emma interjected. Then slowly enunciating each word as if it was a sentence, "No. Two. Ways. About it." She slowed even more as she folded her hands behind her back, stretching up on her toes. "You…

see... Mun... go... If *Big*... John... were... to... *beat up...* someone the night... for example, he wouldn't feel the... least bit guilty. Would you, John? Don't answer that."

Mungo got the message and smiled weakly. For a moment he thought he might try standing on one leg as a prelude to constructing an insanity plea somewhere down the line. Then, before he could decide on which leg to raise, the WPC spoke.

"We can issue you both with an ASBO right now and that would be one of the conditions of your remission. But we don't really want to do that – lots of paper work, and we can't be ars*d. But you've caused us some grief the night and justice cannot be seen to be blind."

"Ossifer, my husband sometimes gets a little overwrought." Ethel now made her version of the tippling sign. "The point is, the reason you are here? Yes? Quite simple: this house is for sale and the comings and goings are related to that. You must have seen the sign?"

"Sign's gone, dear. Must have slipped your memory." Mungo now made the tippling sign. He had removed the *For Sale* sign earlier that evening – it was to have been a lovely and pleasant start to Ethel's next morning as she drew the bedroom curtains. He was recovering remarkably quickly given that he had not had one drop for ages. "Brucie and Derek probably flogged it to our Bayakan neighbours. Build a community centre for the whole tribe... or a raft upon which to repatriate to Africa. Or Bearsden."

"For thale? Ah, that makes a bit of thenthe..."

"But does not excuse the foul language you used against us, madam. Nor the clear indications of ethnic hostility from your husband. Not to mention the shotgun threat. Can we see it? Do you have a licence?"

"Of course he has a licence. Show them your licence, Mungo."

"Not sure the driving licence is what they have in mind. And anyway, it's expired. Supposed to reapply at seventy. I can show you the gun. A beautiful Purdey..." Mungo made to rise but Emma shook her head.

"No. Second thoughts, just lead to a lot of paperwork, and we can't be ars*d with that." She turned and looked up at Big John. "Maybe we should have a look around while we're here?"

"Yeth."

"May as well. Bloody freezing outside."

The two officers left to case the joint then returned some fifteen minutes later. Just as they had done as they had left the drawing room, they spoke to each other as if the house owners were not there.

Emma came in, in mid-flow to a trailing Big John. "...Some house. Loads of potential. High ceilings. It's dead like that old red wallpaper, from yon Nicole Kidman movie, you know the one, in Paris. What a cracker she is by the way, suspenders and that. She's this French tart wi' a bad cough. And all those rooms." She suddenly turned to Mungo and demanded, "How many rooms, Mungo?! Not including bathrooms, pantries and kitchens? Eight? Nine?"

"About that. Val would know. Our estate agent. And what is your assessment – with regard to security, burglars and the likes?"

WPC Emma was aghast. "Oh. You want us to do that?! We were just having a look. Seeing as it's for sale." She turned and grinned up at Big John and asked him in an aside that

Mungo could hear perfectly, "Would make a great knocking shop, eh?"

Big John replied, "I am thhocked." Then laughed through his lop-sided grin. "Jutht what I was thinking. Only problem I thee is the parking. No room down below."

"No problem that. Patrol cars. In an emergency, taxis. The sarge in Triple X Division runs a fleet in his spare time. I know his wife, Ailsa, she's the controller. An ex-cop and a bit of all right too. She used to do the run for the Aquarius up Park Circus."

"Thame they shut the Aquariuth. Bloody councillorth. Artheholth the lot of them."

"Ideal for the nightshift, so it was. Kept the r*ndy b*stards paws off me I can tell you. Aye the Aquarius. Top-class establishment. Better not say to the inspector about this place. He'll want in. Mind you, he's got the capital." Emma spun to look at Mungo who had sidled to the window side of the couch to hear. "How much are you looking for?"

Ethel answered for Mungo as normal in matters financial.

"Well actually there is an offer in. And we have taken it off the market. Just this evening as it happens."

"You don't want to worry about that. There's always ways and means round everything. Forget your estate agent. Shower of crooks, estate agents. And if you need a bridging loan, we can put you in touch with a very reliable firm of financial advisors: *Hammerhead*, heard of them? They're on the telly. We do some work for them. Part-time. Consultancy. Financial recovery." Emma's hands were behind her back again as she stretched on her tiptoes. "Know... What... I... Mean?"

"Mind how you go, thir." However hard he tried, Big John, despite his accident-altered appearance, was just not good at *verbal* menace.

And with that they left.

Chapter 29

Mungo's very, very long and good day out (plus one night).

On the morning of June 25th 1876, Chief Sitting Bull looked up at the sky and, turning to Crazy Horse, said in the language of the Lakota, "It's a good day to die." In the event neither of them would die that day.

Mungo looked up and thought: it's a good day for a funeral. The dark skies, the intermittent gale-driven drizzle, peppered with sleet and the bitter cold, high country air that could only have been improved for effect by some *Sturm und Drang*. He pulled his faithful charcoal Crombie (original: red lining '*a touch of the dandy that reflects the wearer's personality*': £895.00 atow) about his thin but erect shoulders, and raised the collar against the cold wet slaps of rain that splattered against the back of his neck, where the brim of his equally faithful black homburg (Christys' and Co: £125 atow) offered little protection. He couldn't have cared less. Not about the wind and rain and the sleet, nor the cold seeping into his feet, despite his semi-brogue Oxfords (*Crockett and Jones of Northampton* £209 atow) that had been reserved for just such days since he was entering manhood.

And in his unique way this day, Mungo was a happy man. He stood alone behind the highest point of the dry-stone dyke looking down into this small, time-scarred country graveyard, barely catching the gusting snatches of voices that blew on the wind towards him. For a fleeting moment inchoate words swirled about his head then were tugged away to who-knows-where. He had been afraid that he would be late, but the one train, the two buses and finally the brief taxi journey, had all flowed together seamlessly and so he was here on the spot appointed for himself, by himself. He took some satisfaction on reflecting on all of this – that his organisational ability was not always as bad as others, among them his dear wife Ethel, had claimed in the past.

And yet there was a sense of disappointment too. For when at the lowest point in his life some years back, he had sworn that there would be several days like this one; and that these special days would bring the sweet taste of satisfaction that would make all of the suffering worthwhile; would banish all the bitter aftertaste of failure, and, most satisfying of all, would erase his self-pitying, sterile sense of victimhood. And not for one moment had he imagined how it would really turn out. Yet in that very disappointment, there was too, that satisfaction he had thought he had craved; but it was the satisfaction of learning that he had come out the other end of the process and was still the better man. Better than the others.

Despite the cold and the rain, Mungo now, though briefly, removed his hat and bowed his head before looking up just in time to see the casket being carefully lowered into its resting place by the six black-clad cord-bearers, all of them male. And he slowly walked down the mud-streaked grassy slope towards the group of mourners.

And so the last man on Mungo's list was returned to the clay from which our proto-ancestor was formed.

When Mungo turned sixty he did not make a '*Bucket List*' – a term, had he been familiar with, he would have found both vulgar and apposite. No, Mungo prepared what could have been termed a '*Kick The Bucket List*'. A list and a vow to personally attend the funeral of all the b*stards who had shafted him and screwed his family brewery and him into administration, liquidation and genteel poverty. He wanted to make sure that not only were they dead but also buried or burned.

His preference was for burials. No curtains to hide behind. Yes burials were more definite. And while cremation – Mungo preferred to think of it as '*incineration*', a word that had more edge to it – was probably bad for the environment, this carried no weight with Mungo, for he had not become a closet-environmentalist. It was just that good old-fashioned earth-to-earth was just as it said on the label.

On his list – kept inside his head – were, in no particular order: the company's finance director who had failed to keep the cash flow flowing; the purchasing director who had tied the company into onerous barley contracts with a multi-millionaire grain baron in Norfolk and who, in lieu of credit, had taken securities against the brewery. And not satisfied with that, this expensively educated (Fettes and Oxford) n*mpty had persuaded Mungo that the way ahead was for 'green' beer (for that read *ecologically sound*, then read *expensive*); and that could only mean New Zealand hops!

(In some of this there might be small clues to Mungo's antipathy to antipodeans, and his indifference to environmental issues that he shared with Ethel. But that is a separate issue, and this is not the place to pursue these themes and those interested in so doing can have a gander at DSM-5.)

On his list alongside the purchasing director and finance director, Mungo included his marketing director, who, in a mirror image of the purchasing director's business acumen, had sealed contracts to supply one of the largest supermarket chains on the globe. Thus they devoted the bulk of their output and crafted their product. The beer itself was 'crafted'; as was its packaging – shifting from nice cheapish kegs for the pubs and hotels, and even cheaper cans for the Licensed G's and other outlets of that kind, to expensive and bespoke bottles and labels. And all of this to meet the requirements of this golden goose. After which the supermarket chain decided that the price would need to be re-negotiated. At which point Mungo thought it was time to resort to the Vino Collapso as his company imploded.

Was it his fault, as Ethel had more than on occasion more than hinted at? If you take the Branson view of corporate success (and its opposite), then yes. For he had chosen the men (all men) who had done for him. But that reflection only came later, much later. Meantime, he had set-up his list and waited for them one-by-one to fall over into the abyss, at which juncture, Mungo's several days would have come.

Today's was the last. Today it had been the turn of the marketing director. And this would turn out like the others, of that he was certain, for Mungo had come to know himself for the better through these rituals. As he approached the open grave, and as the family and other mourners began to move away having let drop little wet fingerfuls of dirt that were held out to them on a board by the funeral director, a woman in late middle age, tall and slim, prosperous-looking and rather attractive in black, moved towards Mungo and waited as he too stared into the gaping wound in the wet earth and let fall a token of clay. As he stepped back and turned she held out her hand to him and he took it. Behind her two tall young men stood, and each nodded to him respectfully as his eyes briefly met theirs.

The woman spoke, her words almost torn away in the gusting squall.

"Mungo, Hilton would have been so pleased to know you came." She hesitated for a moment then drew Mungo aside and away from her sons.

"You know, he always blamed himself. For what happened. For the... the company. He thought you blamed him too. But I told him you were not that kind of person. That you were bigger than that." She looked at Mungo almost pleading for confirmation. There were tears in her eyes, but that could have been the effect of the cold wind. And this woman could just as easily have been the wife of the other two whose funerals he had attended with the intention of gloating and giving what is vulgarly known as 'the finger'. And this sentiment of Hilton Park's wife and the anxious faces of his two handsome sons, was just another part of the ritual that he had come to be familiar with. As was how Mungo would respond.

Mungo took her hand in his again. "Nonsense. Could've happened to anyone. Was bound to happen some day. Confluence of market forces. That sort of thing. He was a good man, your husband. The best of men." He heard himself say the words that should have been like bile to him. And in saying them – he had pretty much said the same thing to the wives of the others on his list – he began to believe them. Good men, but incompetent. *Sic transit gloria Mungo*, indeed, as Ethel would say.

After a few more dissembling words and handshakes with her sons, Mungo moved away, and when he was out of earshot he let explode, "B*stards! They've done it again to me. B*stards! All of them."

He took a deep breath and looked up at the sky where patches of blue were mottling the grey and… but look! There! Over there, the sun was beginning to burn through and the wind had died away taking with it the chill squalls. And he, Mungo Laird was alive and the other bastards [we left it: respect! The authors] were no more. He suddenly felt hungry, and not for the first time, thought how a morning burial certainly sharpened the appetite for lunch. And another realisation suddenly came over him: he was struck by the feeling that the increased fear of dying induced by the proximate death of others was more than compensated for by lessening the fear of living.

And he turned to Crazy Horse and said, "It's a good day for living." And on that he turned his pony towards the cemetery gates and cantered off scattering the mourners before him.

Mungo was still musing, as his taxi passed the trickle of mourners making their way on foot to the nearby small country hotel – surely glad the dreich burial was over and no doubt looking forward to a dry purvey. They were already smiling, some laughing, pausing to light cigarettes. They had already begun to forget whatsisname.

'Purvey'! Mungo shouted out. The startled taxi driver turned as Mungo mumbled his apologies.

Chapter 30

The Hustler and the colour of money.

He had had an exhausting, though in many ways satisfactory, day and it was not yet finished. The funeral had gone well and the widow had looked lovely and had held his hand for longer, it seemed to him, than the statutory time, whatever that was, for the occasion. And yes, with that lingering touch and the glint of a tear in her lovely eyes, Mungo's resolve had left him and the dead man had been left in peace without the contumely that Mungo had planned to heap on his little box of pine.

But he, Mungo Laird of the parish, was alive. The cold sleet had been banished by a burst of sunshine whose warmth had sucked out some of the nagging pain in his knee. And so it was with a new sense of optimism that he had approached the lunch date with Val – a date that had in it a *frisson,* for Ethel did not know of his plans in this respect; a necessary little subterfuge if he was to claw back some semblance of a say in the destiny of *Villa Laird* and enhance their prospects of some sort of place in the sun in the autumn of their years.

When he had proposed that they meet, Val had tried to wriggle out of it, putting imaginary and sometimes real obstacles in his path. The usual stuff from that type who believe the g*ff on Channel Four about *working hard and* *playing hard* – and these were the geeks at school! The ones that in the words of more than a few grannies of the old school, '*had never done a haun's turn in their life*'. And still they thought solipsistically about the world that revolved around *them*.

But Mungo was as determined as he had ever been, and eventually Val had acquiesced. To listen to her in the early days, it was as if 'their' estate agent was ready on the eve of battle to address the troops on behalf of Ethel and Mungo. It almost brought a tear to Mungo's eye, the thought of Val in sussies declaiming over Villa Laird: *This blessed plot, this earth, this realm, this England.* (Scrub the last phrase.)

And so after the funeral they had a late lunch of sorts (food included which was a bit of a shock to Mungo's gastric system). Fat Eddy's was the only French restaurant (as the name suggests) in another small town that could have been twinned with Borrfoot, and had been chosen by Val, presumably to inconvenience Mungo. But on this day, nothing could upset his equilibrium, his sense of purpose and control. (He often had days like these and was usually wrong on all three counts; but hey-ho, if the jar was more than half-full, well he could soon fix that, provided he could get the lid off.)

They had hardly sat down when Val's mobile went and she had to step outside – *I just have to take this call.* (Otherwise the world would stop spinning on its axis – around her.) Mungo looked about the bistrette and at every table. There was only about ten covers in the place, and at each the diners were talking into mobiles. It looked as if they were phoning each other across the crockery and silverware and glass and the polka-dot paper table covers. It's good to talk. (Mungo had once received a mobile for Christmas from his son Mongo. But he couldn't find where to insert the money, so he binned it.)

Mungo ordered some drinks, but nothing for Val as he was from the old school that never presumed to tell a lady what to drink. He settled down content to wait, and watched the young waitresses go about their business efficiently but with an *hauteur* that suggested they were indeed French – the kind from around *Île-de-France* – or doing politics at Glasgow Uni.

"But surely Mungo you can see my ethical dilemma – Ethel is as much my client as you are. The property is jointly owned – not that that matters in Scots law," Val said with a slightly pained look of concern etched on her small features. She delicately spooned a small chunk of tiramisu towards her tiny mouth. "I can't really act behind her back, now, can I? It's what the police call *a domestic*. Something you need to settle between your two good selves… Professional ethics, Mungo." And she took a sip of still water, after which she dabbed at the corner of her mouth with her serviette. Mungo would have offered his, but it was already in his pocket – he would have a need for it later.

"Yes, of course. Ethical dilemma. You chaps have something like the medics business – the old Hippocrates oath? Good to know. Reassuring." He slugged off a glass of a passable Malbec that he had ordered while Val had been away taking another call. He had asked for an imported Buckie, but the supplier had failed Fat Eddy this month. Eddy, a lugubrious-looking individual in a dark suit, collar and tie, stalked the tables like Paul Newman in *The Hustler* lining-up a shot (1961, dir. R Rossen; 9/10 (men only)), had dealt personally with this query. With a perspicacity redolent of someone who knew the nuances of booze, Fat Eddy suggested that the Argentinian Malbec had some of the qualities of the Buckie. And so it had come to pass. Mungo dabbed at the corner of his mouth with the table cover. Eddy had been right.

"Code of Ethics. Oh, yes," Val enthused. "Estate agents – we call ourselves *realtors* now – have the highest ethical codes along with bankers, lawyers and plastic surgeons."

Mungo choked on a hairball at this, and on recovering ordered another Malbec to wash it back down, then while waiting for it, dried his eyes on another corner of the cover.

"Well here's the thing, Val. I overheard a snatch of a little conversation between the lovely Mrs Sartram and her charming other half. The gist being our Home Report seriously undersells the property. They have had some property development experience and... well... you catch my drift." Mungo raised another finger to Fat Eddy who was what Americans call, *a quick study.*

"But Mungo." Val took his hand across the table. Mungo would normally have liked this tactile little gesture, because despite her profession, she was a tidy little thing who always looked as if she had stepped straight out of the shower into her business dudes: a nicely-cut black jacket and matching skirt, with a pale blouse of cream or the palest peach or blue. (It was the pale blue today – extremely nice.) And on any other day he would have speculated on whether it was sussies that held up those sheer black stockings on her slender legs. But today? Well actually he did still wonder about the sussies, but with a great mental effort, shoved it to a corner of his mind where it would be recalled next time she got up to take a call on her mobile.

"But, Mungo, they're amateurs and our surveyor..."

"Your surveyor, Val. Yes, I was coming to him. Curious thing, heard the two antipodeans mention his name in a conversation I shouldn't really have overheard. The old house has these strange acoustics. The pipes and things – you know the old bell-pull runnels concealed behind the walls."

Mungo sat back and toyed with his glass and was shocked to find it was empty. Val motioned to Fat Eddy who was hovering (actually he could have been doing with Hoovering – Mungo tended to spill his bread crumbs, but never his drink), and he appeared at Mungo's working elbow and topped him up with the ersatz Buckie from the pampas.

Val began to stutter some sort of explanation but was cut-off before she could really begin. "Thing is, Val, those two lovely chaps." He paused as Val's eyes took on a dreamy look, and Mungo wondered what the female equivalent of baggy trousers was, but then returned to his purpose. "Yes, those two nice boys have charmed Ethel and have persuaded her to take the house off the market. And would you believe my dear wife was so naughty as to show them the piece of paper that the Ashley-Cole-Coles made their offer on? The boys promised to match it. So? No contest. My wife still has a residual snobbery in her bones, even though we can't really afford it."

Val seemed relieved that there was no blame being laid at her door, and the business with the surveyor seemed to have slipped the old s*d's mind. She took another sip of water and Mungo leaned across and with her napkin wiped the corner of her mouth.

"That is of course your – or rather Mrs Laird's prerogative. To choose to whomsoever she wishes to sell," Val said, her eyes glittering, her tiny perfect teeth glistening, her lovely shell-like ear not really listening.

"Yes. Of course. Why didn't this old s*d think of that?" Mungo leaned back and did something totally out of character – he shook his head at Fat Eddy who made to top-up his glass. "Tell you what, Val. There's something I want you to do for me.

Do this and... let me see... what can I do for you as a sort of *quid pro quo*? I've got it!"

He now took a slug of the Malbec – and in truth it was beginning to make a passable impersonation of the Buckie. "Yes. You do this little favour for me and we'll say no more – for the time being – about your surveyor and possible conflict of interests and codes of ethics and disciplinary sanctions of the RICS and what is your professional body called?" Mungo pretended to search his memory for the answer to this question he had posed, but he didn't have a scooby and anyway he saw from Val's face that she would do his bidding.

So he leaned across and told her briefly what he wanted – and it had nothing to do with sussies as he was not that sort of blackmailer, although on the train back into the city he wondered if it would have worked and regretted his ingrained timidity.

Mungo called for the bill and was most gratified when Val brushed his offer aside and settled with a smile as plastic as her payment mode. He thought then of asking if she could see her way clear to include a cairry-oot (he of course did not use that vulgar phrase – we have provided it as a guide to what he had in mind), but decided against it.

Yes, it had turned out a good day after all. And the day had not ended, for in a rare burst of *vim* (not the drain cleaner – Mungo never touched that stuff; he had standards, although *Fairy Liquid* diluted to fairly liquid was another kettle of cod and much more civilised than quondam enemas), Mungo had decided to go the whole hog and make a rare visit to his club.

Chapter 31

If anyone is looking for me they will find me at my club. Or not.

The Explorers Club (Division 2, North) was located in an anonymous-looking building that was indistinguishable from all those around it and those in the surrounding streets. Mungo rarely visited it, one of the reasons being it was located in an anonymous-looking building that was indistinguishable from all those around it and those in the surrounding streets, and he had difficulty finding the bl*sted place.

This had been deliberately so chosen by the founding fathers a century or less ago, to test the mettle of aspirants for membership. These pilgrims were a cabal of men in hairy undershirts and brown corduroys that were as ribbed as the roof on a Nissan hut, who tucked the bottom of these trousers into stout shoes. Attired thus, these giants of the past had the propensity to clamber up the north face of some bl*ody great mountain on the backs of quaint, sturdy little natives. These native chaps were assumed to appreciate the honour bestowed on them as well as the weight of the fetid lumps on their shoulders. As a variation on north-face-ism, these same stout chaps would navigate rivers in godforsaken swamps such as those that had caused Pissarro or was it Aguirre?

(*Wrath of God* – Herzog, 1972; good one unless you are a Spanish RC zealot) to shake his heads and say (in Spanish): *Puta*: or *f*ck this for a game of sojers*, before turning about and slaughtering a few thousand Inca, Mayans or similarly handy natives because he was now in a right bad mood.

The second reason Mungo rarely visited *The Explorers Club* (Division 2, North) was more prosaic. Mungo felt that since he had joined (when he came back from National Service having been conscripted in early 1960, as one of the last bunch – how bad was his luck!?), standards had declined abominably. The august elite whose founding aims seemed at this distance distinctly lost somewhere up a Big Mountain (like Mallory who never even got on the club's blackball list – just not the right sort, those elbow patches, all wrong) or down a deep suppurating swamp.

The founding fathers (or *stupid old s*ds* as some referred to them) had they been alive today, apart from being record-breakingly old and well beyond the reach of NHS 24, would surely have frowned on a big wimp like Mungo. Sure Mungo himself had only made it by the skin of his teeth – he had successfully instructed a lump of a Kuala Lumpian taxi-driver in how to get him from Chow Kit Market to the Pan Pacific Hotel and from there to the Coliseum Café, in total a distance of about one mile. (Don't bother Google Earthing Chow Kit or the Coliseum; the former was bulldozed and the occupants turfed out as were the street sleepers for whom nothing changed. The latter no more flash-sizzles huge steaks in butter in front of your (white) fizzug – they put a barber's gown over you first, should you worry about the mess.)

BUT HAVING SAID that, standards for entry to the *The Explorers* (Division 2, North) had sadly declined, one only needs to scope the type of 'exploits' or 'achievements' in the world of exploration that were littering the club. All of these were mentioned in a list that was displayed behind a glass cabinet that only the secretary had access to. There had been three keys but the other two (that of the President and the Keeper of the Great Map – of Glasgow Underground) had been lost by their holders.

On searching that evening for the building where the club was located, Mungo had resorted to asking a passing Chinaman if he happened to know where he could find the club. Whereon the Chinaman said 'yes' and had walked on without further ado. But somehow he had made it, and now as Mungo entered the hallway (or *lobby* if you prefer) his eyes alighted on the glass cabinet of honour (*Cabinet d'Honneur*).

And there it was: the name of the latest member to be inducted: Archie McIndoe-Woodrow, for finding and mapping the source of the *River Bevvy*.

Mungo had to admit this was an achievement of sorts – The Bevvy flowed through the town of Borrfoot and after merging with the Cart flowed into the Clyde near where the j*bbie boat used to sale from. But the source of The Bevvy, had never knowingly been pinpointed. Archie McIndoe-Woodrow spent seven years following it. At first he had thought it had come from a high-up, leaking, horse trough on an abandoned farm to the south of the town that had been the hideout of a gang of drug-dealers or a (very legitimate) taxi-company owner. But that was soon refuted when the very legitimate taxi-company owner blasted the trough with a Mac-10 sub-machine gun when he saw Archie studying it and taking notes. And when after a few months, The Bevvy continued to flow through Borrfoot and environs, Archie M-Woodrow had his application turned down.

But being full of s*unk (like Mrs Sartram according to her husband), Archie, taking as his model Sir Ranulph somebody-else, pressed on. At one stage, like his hero Sir Ranulph somebody-or-other, Archie had thought he might need to hack his foot off to escape entanglement with a T*sco trolley on the river bed, but as he only had a pencil sharpener to hand, he resorted to dragging the trolley with him. And eventually – just when the club was in danger of going under – *mission accomplished.*

Archie demonstrated irrefutably (in the proper sense of that word and not the way BBC broadcasters, journos and politicians use it), that the source of The Bevvy was an overflow pipe in a decrepit mansion to the east of Dunlop (the village, not the tyre, not the man) whose ballcock had ceased to function correctly because of an exceptionally warm summer circa 1932. He proved this by a series of maps, historical records of the Met Office and with diagrams from the *Plumbers' Mate Handbook* – a volume that, despite the questionable apostrophe, is in its own way on par with the *Diagnostic Statistical Manual of the American Psychiatric Association* (for who has not gone at least temporarily insane over a toilet that will not flush?).

In the event, Sir Archie M-W, on gaining membership never attended as he built up a global empire on shopping-trolley recovery and recycling.

Mungo, on reading this encomium, did not know whether to weep or turn about and leave. But good sense prevailed when he realised he would never find his way back to the station in the gloaming. And so he signed-in and was greeted by the weasel-faced steward who turned his back on him, perhaps symbolic of the fact that even the steward thought standards had declined. But a moment later, Nellie the waitress gave him her huge smile and he felt cured and human once more and he thought about asking her whether she had ever been to Crieff, but decided against it. It would be just like the thing for her to agree to meet him in aforementioned town (worth a visit with our without Nellie) and for Mungo not to be able to find it.

And so, producing from his pocket the napkin from Fat Eddy's, he draped this over the back of his favoured rattan chair as his own antimacassar, and settled down – the skelfs from this chair, incidentally, never failed to make a lasting impression on his a*se. Content with life, Mungo accepted a schooner of sherry from Nellie. His suggestion that the club stock-up on Buckie, had been supported in principle by the bar committee, but as usual the meeting was inquorate (not the village in Sana'a, Yemen) as not enough members could find the club that night.

To be fair to them, the scheduled night for the committee meeting had seen a pall of mist from some river or other – apparently someone mentioned the Cl*de but was laughed down as the sensible majority knew that flowed into the Water of Leith in Ed*nburgh. This mist had had a disorientating effect on the committee members, especially when coupled with the orange street lights that people over a certain age find less than useless for navigation, especially around about the festive season. To make matters worse, as it had been a Friday, there were chip pans on fire throughout the city of Glasgow. One lungful of the evening air was as nutritious as a deep-fried special fish supper. So no Buckie was the outcome. But all of that was in the past.

In the morning Mungo felt refreshed and after removing the skelfs, set-out at a brisk pace with determination written across his forehead – this had been a prank of the weasel-faced steward when Mungo had been snoring comfortably on the rattan chair; and by the time he found the station, the mid-morning rain had washed it away and he was set fair for Villa Laird and the battle a few days ahead for which he had girded his loins. Well, he had grilled chops for breakfast.

Chapter 32

Mungo Mingles.

When he had risen that morning, Mungo just knew it was going to be a day different from all others, though it had begun in the usual fashion. About mid-morning (generously interpreted), they had ceased to huddle together for warmth under the old patchwork quilt and Mungo rose with a helping nudge from Ethel.

Quickly donning his old dressing gown (cordless – not for any self-harm prevention reasons, but because the cord was now helping support the pulley in the scullery); cardigan (to hold the dressing gown together); bunnet – 8-piece herringbone (*Dunn and Company*, 1886-1996) and slippers (*Primark*: 3 for one pound – not pairs), he went down to the kitchen. There he quickly produced his signature dish: tea and toast for himself and Ethel. Sometimes they would have banana on toast – if there was a banana and if there was any bread. This morning it was plain toast that he carried back upstairs to the bedroom where Ethel now appeared to be wearing the patchwork quilt as she lay propped against the dark oak headboard. If that headboard could speak of that it had witnessed, it would have remained silent.

They both savoured these moments – it was after all the main meal of the day. And they nibbled away at the toast and slurped the tea, not obviously in a way that showed there was a race on to consume the most of the bread. After which they would rest propped together and sated, and for the most part in silence. It was too early in the day to speak, and words at such moments were otiose, and anyway Mungo would have preferred a good cigar and Ethel a better Buckie. And there our two heroes half-lay gazing out the window and down on the huddled masses below them in the town, and picking the crumbs from their belly buttons.

From time to time the cold morning air in the room would be ruffled by a sigh, or bedspring, as one or other of them shifted with a half-hearted intention to rise and face the day. Inevitably their innermost thoughts would turn to what lay ahead and when it would be a decent time to have their first tonic. At which juncture they both bounded up and raced to get to the lavatory on this floor. For a BIG-BONED woman, Ethel could be remarkably nimble when it counted, and apart from the speed thing, Mungo was giving away about two stone *avoirdupois*. Sporting types will recognise this as what used to be called a 'catch-weight contest' (or slaughter) in boxing, and so he settled for one of the downstairs latrines (military-speak).

And so time drifted by as the day wore on and after dressing in the usual fashion, they came together again in the drawing room. Since this was likely to be a long day, they both resolved to be relatively abstemious, even if warning signs of dangerous side effects should emerge, in which case they would refresh their goals (and the goalposts) for the day. To which end they had double-jiggers of their tonic-of-the-day: Buckie with two fingers of essence of vanilla (*Nielsen-Massey*, blends well and has its own little alcohol element; thus no danger of an oil-and-water effect). The vanilla was a nice little touch as it was not needed for the dinner party since this was in the hands of the purveyors hired for the occasion.

At some point in the day – it could have been evening – the purveyors appeared in the shape of Idris and Tim her helper. They quickly scoped the condition of their employers and rustled together a simple but healthy light supper with strong tea. After they had dined in the kitchen they served the same fare to Mungo and Ethel, who were unsure about eating during the day and were frankly nervous about consuming so much tea, which they knew had harmful ingredients like caffeine and other carcinogens (*S*nday P*st*). Nevertheless, to remain on the good side of their servants, they went along with them and even took a snooze in the drawing room at Idris's behest while she got the purvey ready for the dinner party.

[This compulsion to keep the servants happy is, as many readers will know from their own experience, a common phenomenon in the master-servant relationship. See for example, *The Servant*, Pinter's 1963 film version of Robin Maugham's original story based upon Hegel, *Phänomenologie des Geistes* (1807) translated from the Jerry. Available on NetFlix. The film, that is, not Hegel.]

But now that was all in the past, and the dreams Mungo had enjoyed by the two-bar fire – Tim had fixed the other bar and had made noises about resuscitating the Living Flame – were as chaff in the wind that came down the chimney. Useful chap, Tim, Mungo decided. And likeable with it. And now Mungo was awake and at his most febrile (loosely defined) and his razor-sharp senses (even more loosely defined) homed-in on the conversation Bruce and Dirk were having over Ethel's simpering, fawning gasps of delight and admiration – sounds that passed for telling contributions to the topic of discourse of the moment.

Like a demented speed-reader, (*War and Peace* 'takes place in Russia', to quote a cynic of the art), Mungo only needed to hear a few key words and he could summarize the gist of the whole discourse on any topic in which these key words (or *totems* to use this word in the wrong sense) arose within his hearing. And within a few seconds of tuning in to Ethel and the two macho Ozzies who had made him seem smaller than was possible at the molecular level (minimum condition for organic potential), he heard the sort of t*sh (sh*te) he expected. Without apparently drawing breath between them – exclude Ethel in this as she was panting with delight – the following tripped from their lips, teeth and tip of the tongue:

Empowerment
Inclusiveness
Multi-cultural
Positive discrimination
Bio-degradable
Eco-friendly
Gaia – WHAT!?
Global warming
Parallel universes
String theory
Chief Medical Officer
'Units' of alcohol
Progressing this going forward

Renewables

Guano

Fish… What?! No that was Mungo talking to himself. He fancied a wee bit of white fish – haddock preferably in a beer batter with (small) new potatoes (note spelling, Dan Quale) washed and not peeled, some peas and a couple of slices of WHITE bread and FULL-FAT AND SALTED butter. All washed down with… something different, say, a Hock. M&S used to do a decent one, but it's all gone to pot since Twiggy stopped doing the buying. Now if *Primark* move into the wines… the stuff that dreams are made on.

As suspected – what a load of b*llocks Mungo affirmed as he pretended to listen to Ethel and the two Ozzie b*ggars and pretended *not* to look at his watch. Waste of bloody time. It was long pawned (or '*pledged*' as Ethel would prefer to term it. The lower orders 'pawned' their baubles.).

Late or too late thoughts were much worse now than his early morning heebie-jeebies some call paranoia. And despite his opposition to the very idea of a dinner party for Ethel's two chosen 'candidates', Mungo now fervently wished that the Sartrams would come soon and even Chas and Dave (he was beginning to get a bit befuddled, but we know who he meant in this case). He wished that any of them would appear now and break up this nauseating love-in. Then they could get down to the business and agenda that he had planned, that Ethel knew nothing of and maybe even then, Idris would let him have a drink.

Where the bl*zes were they? It must be nearly half past seven. For a while (well a minute or so), Mungo practised standing on one-leg while keeping his eyes fixed in what he imagined was a look that would seem as if he was interested.

Then he changed legs and managed twenty-five seconds. There was no way of knowing if this was a new record, because he had never done this before. He had never ever been so bored as to have even contemplated it before.

But of course that was a mistake – the standing on one leg – because one of the big b*ggars alluded to the Zoroastrian belief that the *one-legged dance of Yü* traces the stars of the *Big Dipper*. Mungo thought for a moment he had alluded to *The Big Bopper* and fleetingly was interested, because he had his own ideas as to who was flying the plane that fatal night when the dreams of so many died near Clear Lake, Iowa. In fact he had thought of a title for a song: *The Day the Mucus Died*, but then dumped it as too euphonically, punningly trite. He had faith that History's judgement would prove him once again not fit for purpose.

Returning to the present and Zoroastrian philosophy, Mungo thought about riposting that the *one-legged dance* was a misnomer as it was in reality a '*limping dance*'. But then he thought: *ph*cque' it – let him stew in his ignorance*. At which Mungo limped away (his standing leg was in a cramp) and in that posture he began to try to mingle. Except there was no one with whom to mingle. But just then he was saved.

Chapter 33

You just can't get the staff or the stuff these days.

Idris opened the serving hatch and he immediately understood that she was taking pity on him, and advantage of Ethel's being busy with the Ozzies. She placed a cup on the sill and indicated to Mungo it was for him. Crafty folk, but salt of the earth, Mungo thought of the working class, in an atavistic reference to class relations of an older era. And winking at Idris he took the cup (no saucer supplied, a quaint reminder of their differing backgrounds), and keeping his other eye on Ethel, he drained the amber liquid in one.

The shock almost did for him – tea! Ph*cquing tea? And cold with it! What a mean, ungrateful bunch the lower orders could be. Idris looked shocked. Her face disappeared from the hatch and seconds later she was helping him through into the kitchen where she sat him on a chair by the range which was burning brightly, (the range not the... you know). Mungo had forgotten about this thing when they had run out of trees and old wardrobes to burn, but at the moment he was not in a condition to notice or comment in any rational fashion as strange things were happening inside his insides.

"Quick, Tim," she said. "See what it says on the label." She handed her husband a small dark bottle with a yellow label and went to the sink where she filled a glass with *water* and stood over Mungo while he drank it *raw and undiluted.*

Tim put on his reading glasses (*Instore:* £2.99 case included) and peered at the label.

"*'For greener leaves and vibrant colours*'," he said.

"Give me that," Idris snapped and grabbed the bottle. "Dae everythin' for maself." She looked at the label. "Disnae tell ye much." She opened the little bottle and sniffed it then poured a drop on her hand and said to Tim, "See what you think. Taste it."

Tim licked Idris's hand (in itself a treat and, despite the strange feeling in his stomach, Mungo wished that she had held it out to him to lick). Tim then took the bottle, sniffed it as Idris had done before him:

"Smells like Marmite." He took a gentle sip, savoured it and looked at the ceiling then finished the bottle off. He wiped his mouth with the back of his hand and nodded to Idris:

"No' bad." Then to Mungo said, "You'll be all right. It's just Marmite watered down."

"Thank God for that," Idris exclaimed then shook Mungo by the shoulders. "Whit were ye thinkin' aboot. Drinking *Baby bio.* Yae ken that Ethel said ye had tae feed yon big plant in there." Then turning away from him, the harshness gone from her voice, she murmured, "Daft auld galloot."

Tim made a face at Mungo that only men dominated by their women can fully understand. That look said more than ten thousand words could about the affinity of their experience at the hands and tongue of such women as Idris and Ethel and Princess Katherine (never *Kate*). That face men make to each other behind a woman's back – somewhere between a guilty smirk and a grimace of pain – spoke of their shared vision of womanhood and what they might reasonably expect, and how they would come to be disappointed and in turn disappoint.

[That look between real men such as Tim and Mungo and Prince whatsisname, is the equivalent of all the hugging that goes on whenever modern men, *metro-men*, the kind of men who appear on Channel Four, meet having not seen each other for a whole twenty minutes. *When did we become a nation of huggers*? An important question for historians of the future, because that point in time, when the hug replaced manly handshakes, was the moment that this great country went into terminal decline. Nauseating does not describe it. Still, a few words might have said it all.]

When he was fully recovered from his near-Marmite experience – with the help it must be said of a nip of a genuine goldie (40%, blend) sneaked to him by Tim while Idris pretended not to be able to see out the back of her head – Mungo went back into the drawing room and addressed the plant as it was by far, in his opinion, the most interesting conversationalist available. There is no record of what he said but it certainly grabbed the attention of Ethel, Brucie and Dirk who fell silent while Ethel after a time inspected the ceiling.

There is no scientific proof that aspidistra cannot hear or, if hear, cannot understand English. But on the basis that a possible if not putative, future king of England had averred to talking to weeds (garden variety, not equerries nor Old Etonians and the likes), then on such authority one can imagine what that aspidistra heard. Not to mention what it thought of Mungo scoffing its jigger *of Baby-bio*.

Mungo's instinct, formed over many years, was not to trust his instinct when it came to what was termed by The Night Soil Association Quarterly, *interpersonal relations and first impressionism*. In an outbreak of subversive neo-liberalism, that publication had carried a few articles that offered the view that it was possible that not all Australians and proto-Australians were on the make. The context is not important here; suffice to say it was concerned with speculation as to where and on whom the Australians were dumping their Blue Mountains of *gunang*. (Note: not to be confused with *Gunang Weed* which is a herb used against Apolu Fever. Get them mixed up and you'll wish you had Apolu Fever.)

These articles made a strong impression on Mungo whose instinct was not to trust anything published by that publication unless it was in relation to a matter he had written on. And though he had spoken a lot of '*gunang*' in the past, this was not the case in this instance. And so, perhaps in an obscure allusion to his knowledge of things Zoroastrian, he now regarded these two b*ggars in a dark light. And he felt guilty by his amused inaction for he had stood idly by, had been complicit by his silence, and had had an anticipated sense of *schadenfreude* – as these two had easily talked Ethel into taking the house off the market if they matched the Ashley-Cole-Coles' generous offer.

Mungo just knew he should have put his foot down. But when did he last do that? The time just before the kids left, just before the hobbling dash to A&E to check out the blurring (and bruising) of his right eye? Probably.

They said they would match the Ashley-Cole-Coles' offer if the Lairds obliged them. 'So much more civilised.' And should the Sartrams persist, then the old 'kith-and-kin' pitch would get round the 'chicken and goats' prejudice and take care of the Race Relations Act at the same time, Bruce and Dirk had reassured Ethel. And Ethel, who did not have a single prejudiced bone in her body, was delighted all the same by this get-out clause. Clever boys. And pretty too.

Chapter 34

Neuron elbows giving it laldy.

The doorbell rang. *Dring-dring-a-dring-dring – dringdring*. Sounded like the Ashley-Cole-Coles, Mungo thought, and his heart skipped a beat. That would be the *Baby-bio* kicking-in, or the *Marmite*. No harm done. Mungo made his excuses to the aspidistra and quickly exited, leaving Ethel's involuntary curse and apology behind.

"Who the blo*dy he*l?! Oh, I do so apologise, boys... Mungo, I forbid you to allow anyone entry. And don't linger. I am about to instruct the staff to serve the *hors d'oeuvres...*" She trailed off as Mungo trailed off, and we will leave her behind as we trail Mungo to the front door or *portico* as Ethel had recently taken to calling it – which architecturally is simply wrong. But since there is no *haute* term for front door, it is understandable and we can sympathise with her on this for as long as it took Mungo to grab the handle and swing the door open.

And there, under the *portico* (correct usage) bathed in the brown light of a forty-watt bulb and a sheen of sweat from the steps, was what at first Mungo took for a pulvinated frieze of erotic aspect. Then Dave took his tongue out of the furthest reaches of Chels's pharynx – on a good day he could tickle her epiglottis – and greeted Mungo. Meantime Chels deftly replaced her *soutien gorge* as she had come to call her br* after an 'audition' with a 'French' film 'producer' while all the time Dave had looked on with 'interest'.

Those neurons were elbowing each other like highly excited electrically charged cells.

Mungo, after another palpitation, beamed with pleasure as he anticipated the reaction of Ethel and, more deliciously, that of Brucie and Derek to this unexpected visitation *on them.*

"So, Mung, old son," Dave began as he strode past Mungo not bothering to wait for his consort. Chelsea tottered skilfully in his wake on six-inch heels and wearing what looked like a vinyl pelmet encasing about eight inches in depth of the sensitive area of her lower torso. In some circumstances her mode of dress might have seemed a touch inappropriate. But since Dave was wearing a US naval officer's Dress Whites, a remnant from An Officer and a Gentlemen Theme (Swingers only) Party, the young-ish couple could have been taking a stroll down Burgos Street, in the Makati district of Manila, having fortuitously encountered each other and having been instantly smitten. For an hour at least and at regular rates.

"Mung, you've had more than the chance to study our offer. Am more than a bit many disappointed, old son, that we've been blanked by your briefs," Dave said over his shoulder as he entered the drawing room.

And he prattled on in this vein for a bit while Mungo tried to think where his old Y-fronts (*M&S*, though *Primark* making inroads on price and quality) came into the business. Then Dave opened a small travel bag that no one had noticed (including us authors) until this moment (it had been over his shoulder), and looking around furtively let Mungo peer into its shallow depths. And there Mungo saw the trove of inhalers that Dave had insisted he 'take off his – Mungo's – hands' when they had been together in the mistress bedroom during the viewing tour. Mungo looked from the bag to Dave with some sympathy, for until that moment he had not realized that the poor fellow was asthmatic.

He need not have worried for as he followed Dave and Chels, he abolished all rational thought as he looked *in wonder and despair* on Chelsea's buns (repeated motif), *almost boundless and bare,* (stanzas rearranged for dramatic effect) and with a *frown and wrinkled lip* he tried to summon *a sneer of cold command.* To no effect. Dave and Chels were mingling with Ethel and Bruce and Derek, and only the aspidistra remained aloof it seemed, having not had a drink all day.

Mungo left them to it and wandered about the company and wondered about the company and wondered if Idris had any back up for the Baby-bio.

At some point in the evening, Dave had turned to Mung and in his version of a stage whisper cracked:

"Time for the old Salbutamol distribution, Mung?" And not waiting for a reply produced an Evohaler from his pocket, took a couple of quick snokes (alt. *snoak*) then began to spray it about the assembled company aided by the divine Chelsea who had come up against a brick wall in the shape of the two boys from Oz. One thing about Chels was that she could tell when she was onto plums, and so she entered with gusto into the dousing of the room in Salbutamol.

Bruce and Dirk, who had been whispering to Ethel who stood between them by the piano, looked on with fascination and horror. As a sort of diversion, Bruce or it could have been Dirk, lifted the lid of the box that contained the keyboard (aka piano) and had played a decent rendition of snatches from Chopin's *Fantasy in F Minor* that had impressed Ethel. Mungo sneered inwardly and thought about saying: well if Jack Nicholson can play it on the back of a truck doing eighty-five in a built up area, is that so great? Though to be fair to Jack, it was for Karen Black (*Five Easy Pieces*, 1970; dir. B Rafelson; 8.5 out of 10; available on Netflix – worth it for Karen Black's strabismus).

MEANTIME, during the Salbutamol spraying, the breeding of the boys came to the fore and they made a good fist of pretending that Dave was not behaving like an absolute m*ron. And Chelsea ditto. This made no impression on Dave, sensitive soul that he could be at times. When Chels called on Dave to pass another inhaler as she had finished her own, he chucked it so skilfully that it hit her nose but did not break the skin, and for a moment it was trapped in one of her eyelashes before she wrestled it free and gave herself a quick dose.

[Warning: it has to be the blue inhaler – it does not work with either the brown one or the purple one, though the latter looks as if it should.]

From another pocket Dave produced more of these inhalers and swiftly distributed them (chucked them) to the others. Ethel and Bruce and Dirk, seemed to huddle together and move away about the room as a group of huddlers, though they were limited in this respect that they kept coming up against a wall. Just like Chelsea had experienced with her attempt to 'entice' Bruce and Dirk to enter into little touchy-feely games as a sort of *ice-breaker* (management-speak).

And later, just when the only sound that could be heard was that of Dave and Chels snoking vigorously, and Mungo wheezing with what might have been restrained mad laughter

– though it could have been an asthma attack, the two being indistinguishable except by experts in pulmonology, and some of them are duff – the doorbell split the otherwise silence.

Chapter 35

Send not to ask for whom the bell *dring-drings.*

Dring-dring, the bell it burbled.

Hope that's the Sartrams, thought Mungo with relief, only for Ethel to riposte, "Mungo, why the h*ll do you hope that?!"

He had been thinking aloud again. No matter.

"I'll get it," he said or thought, as he rose, just as Idris entered with the eponymous couple and introduced them to the room.

"Doctor and Mrs Sartram," Idris announced, taking their outer garments from them. (Mr Sartram is wearing a *Dolce and Gabbana* two-piece, *the suit that screams centre of attention; suitable for work, party or dinner with friends*. £645 atow. Mrs Sartram has dressed down as well and is in a black jacquard prom dress.) (*Jenny Packham,* £125 atow.)

MEANTIME while the others were taking in all the details above regarding the Sartrams sartorial ensembles, Mister Sartram was trying to explain to Idris that while he was a doctor, his title was *Mister*.

Idris folded his overcoat (*Canali*, slim-fit, velvet collar, £970 atow) over her arm, listened patiently and when he had finished she said:

"Suit yerself," and passed his and Mrs Sartram's coats through the hatch to where the Master of the Wardrobe was waiting to take them.

Then Idris led him by the hand to a seat next to Chelsea, changed her mind as Chels's eyes had lit up, and seated him beside Mungo on the old couch. Dave can be ignored for the moment because he was in a corner of the room staring at both his hands which were shaking violently – one of the possible side effects listed. His nose had not yet begun to run, nor had death ensued.

Meantime, Anita, wife of several years who is not yet with child of Mister Sartram, had been ushered by Mungo to a chair that was not within two arms' lengths of Dave, when Idris announced that dinner would be served presently, while she went to join her sous-chef (and coat-check boy) in the kitchen.

Mr Sartram spotted Ethel partially hidden by the aspidistra, and with a smile of apology to Mungo he bounded up and taking at first one of the leaves as Ethel's hand – a mistake seamlessly corrected – he said:

"Ah, Madame Laird and of course Mister Mungo, most accommodating and most gracious apology accepted by both my wife Anita and I via the estate agency of McGregor, Campbell and Glencoe through the efficient and effective auspices of Ms Valerie Kilner of course. It is with the utmost and humble pleasure we partake of your invitation to properly bid for the first, and it must be said with no suspicion of admonishment, only occasion this evening for your renowned not to say esteemed establishment, and..."

"No apology required, dear boy," Mungo quickly interjected, not sure if this piece of information was yet in the public (Ethel's) domain. "Always glad to have you. And your good lady wife."

And with that Mungo leaned across and took Anita's hand, raised it to his lips and planted a delicate kiss on the back of his own hand. But it was well intentioned and he had read somewhere (S*nday P*st) that among the Junker class in Jerryland (well Prussia, to be accurate), this was how they did it. Possibly because they were wearing poor quality monocles? Mungo mused.

No matter, Anita Sartram seemed quite taken with his chivalric gesture (much preferring it to Mungo's previous chauvinistic behaviour during her last visit) and might have been about to say something in this vein, when Dave slid in on the other side of her and offered a snoke of his Evohaler. She recoiled in well-judged distaste and almost fell into Mungo's lap before recovering.

"Suit yourself, luv," Dave said cheerfully. "If it's something a little stronger then..." He made a lewd gesture with his head (which is quite a feat in itself), went behind Chelsea and whispered something as lewd as his head gesture into her ear – having first carefully pulled aside a couple of her large hoop earrings. Dave had to be careful with this move since once before in a similar social situation, he got his head stuck in one of those fings. But now Dave and Chels both stared at Anita Sartram and Chelsea blushed, simpered, then gave a little sigh of acquiescence and said coyly:

"Yeah, suppose so. Thought you said Mung had promised. Does that mean Eth's a no-goer?"

At which the company en masse turned and stared at Ethel.

At which Idris de-iced the frozen living room tableau by her perfectly timed...

Chapter 36

Dinner's served'n that.

"Dinner's served'n that!"

And they as one rose to follow Ethel who followed Idris – and no one was more puzzled than John (one of the authors) and Mungo, that there was another room in which they were to dine.

Down a corridor that Mungo vaguely remembered, they trooped until they came to an open door by which Idris stood and into which she ushered them. Therein Tim in major-domo mode awaited. Reading from a card in his hand he pushed and pulled each one in turn, sometimes even two or three times, until this algorithmic approach succeeded. And finally they were all in their allotted seats as determined by Idris, with Ethel at the head of the table as was her *droit de seigneuresse*, where she had 'the boys' on either side of her.

Mungo democratically accepted his place at the bottom of the table. There was a definite slope to it, but whether that was a characteristic of the table or the floorboards could not be independently determined at this juncture. And anyway to talk about 'top' and 'bottom' was purely academic since the table was round. But still, Mungo was definitely not at the top.

Mungo and Ethel – separately – looked about the room while the others engaged in desultory (or in Dave's case) insultory conversation. So this was the old dining room, Mungo mused to himself. Chandelier could do with a bit of a clean, enough to flog it. At that moment Idris appeared at his shoulder and in her kind of whisper said:

"That big light's pure clatty by the way." Then she flitted away while Tim filled the glasses with what looked as if it was unfortified wine of two different hues.

Mungo, as he tended to do in company, withdrew into himself and looked about at his companions. Chelsea was seated opposite him and from time to time (actually most of the time), she rocked back and forth in great gales of whooping laughter (some would say 'cackles') at some Wildean observation of Dave. Dave, generous fellow that he was, tended to bellow these remarks to all and sundry, in order not to appear overly selective as to whom he included in his sphere of wit and influence.

As Chelsea rocked backwards, there seemed to be some articulated lever principle at work, for one of her legs tended to just brush against Mungo's. At first his reaction was to draw his legs away as his shins were feeling quite bruised after about five minutes of this. But then his fertile imagination (wrongly attributed to the *Right Side of the Brain*: recent research shows it to 'exist' in the landscape of neural networks at the cortical and sub-cortical levels), kicked-in.

Carefully he moved his legs forward under the table until he could just feel the merest brush – almost 'hush' – of Chelsea's foot and with a surge of creative energy unleashed inside the aforementioned neural network, he convinced himself that she was feeling him out deliberately and most provocatively.

And he tried to work-up indignation that the little minx (older readers) should be so bold in his own house, before her own Dave and under the nose of his Ethel, wife of several years, (and the Sartrams, for that matter). But this proved too much for his neural networks and instead they provided him with a vivid image of his baggy trousers and he fell into a very pleasant reverie as he watched Chelsea through hooded eyelids. Inevitably Mungo too began to rock back and forth on the legs of his chair in sync with Chelsea. Then he got a bit out of sync and in his haste to catch Chelsea on the downswing he went so far backwards that he and chair together tipped over and both landed on the floor. Fortunately his head cushioned the blow.

When he awoke there had been some movement about the table and the food had been scoffed. That went well he thought, as Idris and Tim busied themselves about the table doing whatever it is purveyors do when it is all over bar the tidying.

As his razor-sharp brain tuned into the conversations that were sprinkled about him, he heard a skilfully crafted variation of the usual hokum from the two A*ssie b*ggars who were deep in conversation with Tim who listened with head partially bowed in an almost servile stoop. Technically it was not a conversation as such, since Tim was not saying word one, while Brucie or the other b*ggar syrupped-on about how the great Sc*tt*ish working class had been the backb*ne of the E*pire and how humbling for them it was to meet one of that type in the form of Tim.

Tim stood like a member of his class and nodded gravely every now and then to show he was following their slowly enunciated simple sentences and the discourse contained therein. Then with a graceful bow he withdrew and as he passed Mungo said:

"Patronising b*stards."

Yes, Mungo thought to himself, it's good to see the classes mingle and engage, and to know that some of the working class saw through the whole *ph*cquing Human Comedy* (tr. loosely from Balzac) for what it was: a means of scr*wing the j*ice out of them.

But now, as in an over-hyped class-based soap drama (viz. *Do*nton A**ey* – a pale imitation of *Gosford Park* in which 'Dame' M Smith first perfected that irritating character that should in all truth have sparked class riots, except the rioting classes were watching the pap and eating Buffalo Wings), BUT NOW, when, as we say, the ladies should have withdrawn and the men could pass the port on the left-hand side (or was it '*Pass the Duchy on the Right Hand Side*'?) and smoke a good cigar and loosen their ties and cummerbunds, but now, there was some activity across the table from Mungo. Not in the shape of Chelsea's foot, for she had now turned her attention to Anita (at Dave's insistence, it should be said) while the bold blade himself had positioned himself by Anita's shoulder.

You will recall that Anita's perfect shoulder was, along with the rest of her divine self, encased in a Jenny Packham prom dress garnished with *bead with sequin embellishment and long waterfall tulle skirt, this glamorous dress is sure to make a compelling statement*. The important part being that while it concealed much it hinted at much, much more, for Anita had quite simply the loveliest shoulders ever discovered by *an elegant sheer mesh overlay.*

And Dave, a master of subtlety when it came to showing his appreciation of such beauty, was openly sniffing Anita all over her lovely shoulders, while Chelsea distracted her by making pouting motions and by running her tongue round her lips (Chelsea's own lip's at the moment, but the night was, as yet, young), and leaning towards Anita, Chels displayed in greater detail her bonny, boney, embonpoint.

For a moment Anita was totally fascinated by Chelsea's behaviour and exotic appearance, so much so that she thought that there must be a bluebottle in the room that kept buzzing her shoulder and hair (by *Taylor Ferguson*, Gift Vouchers available on-line), and so she flicked a perfectly manicured finger at the creature while her eyes were still locked on Chelsea, only to hear Dave curse as her nail cut into a spot on the bridge of his nose.

Anita looked from him to Chelsea and back to Dave: "Your… 'wife'? Is she you know… all right? She appears to be having some sort of seizure. Look at her cheeks and her tongue. That can't be normal behaviour or colours. Shall I get my husband to have a look at her?"

During all of this Mungo was quietly sipping a glass of wine that the two 'boys' had brought along. And he was thinking: there's something fishy about this. Doesn't taste altogether right. At which moment Tim passed him with some empties and Mungo voiced his suspicions to his sommelier. Tim placed the empties on a sideboard, made a brief inspection of the bottles and brought one of them to Mungo who examined the label (first donning his glasses of course – Poundstretcher x3.0 – his eyesight had deteriorated over the last several hours), then he slowly nodded and handed it back to Tim.

Mungo directed a laser-look of the utmost contempt at the two ingratiating b*ggars, strong enough to make them tremble in their tan brogues (*Loake*, £145 atow). But the signal somehow got mixed-up and one of them – Brucie perhaps – shuddered as if he thought that Mungo was coming-on to him.

And as for Mr Sartram, during all of this, he was trying to pretend to be interested in what the two Aussie boys were saying – he found them charming but shallow (among his almae matres, you will recall was Edinburgh Uni). But more importantly he was more than a little concerned with snatches of conversation he had overheard between Madame Laird and the boys apropos the house. For he and the memsahib had now set their little warm hearts on having it, for no other reason that it seemed a steal at the guide price and others wanted it too. The spirit of competition da... da... da...

Moreover, their surveyor (supplied by a very accommodating local firm called McGregor, Campbell and Glencoe) had assured them that the House Report exaggerated the faults and understated the rare quality of the fabric of the building and its remarkably intact original interior features. And there was a surge in interest in such properties in prime locations, and they were in short supply and as we said, it was a steal.

Mr Sartram (lots of letters) was a man for the moment. He saw a quick profit and like all the professions that serve humanity, he wanted it for himself (and the memsahib, of course). But d*amn it all, there was a distraction – that American Naval Officer (NO, not Richard Gere) fellow on the other side of the table seemed to be paying too much unwanted attention to his lovely Anita. But by the sacred tr*nk of Ganesha much worse was the fact that the officer's exotic 'wife' seemed to be… surely not! And worse, he had got a hint that these two charming but shallow New Zealanders were going to stiff him for the house. The gloves would need to come off!

Chapter 37

And they're off! Gloves too.

The decibel levels were beginning to rise when Idris poked her lovely head (strand of hair loose over one delicate eyebrow – Mungo would have paid good silver to brush that golden strand back behind her lovely bronze ear), through the hatch and rang a little pewter hand-bell.

Tinkle, tinkle, tinkle.

And just at that, Tim entered with two trays of remarkably appetising-looking *hors d'oeuvre*. In the silence that befell the room, the only discernible sound for a moment was of Dave spraying Anita with Salbutamol (or a cheap generic equivalent) and Mungo thinking: what a ph*cquing idiot.

But for all Dave was a complete idiot, and Chelsea had transferred her affections to Mrs Sartram, the Salbutamol or something was beginning to work on Mungo. And so he stood, and, steadying himself against the table while he recovered his legs, he limped to the serving hatch and beckoned to Idris who appeared drying her red hands on a pinafore. At the sight of that Mungo wanted to take her in his arms and, with a jar of Germolene that had been saved since the Korean War, salve her raw paws. (The list of possible side effects of this antiseptic cream which is used for chapped or rough skin includes (wait for it): *dermatitis, skin irritation and blisters.* On second thoughts, Mungo decided against the treatment.)

It should have been pointed-out earlier that there were two empty seats at the dining table – well there were, so there! And despite the odd movements of Dave and Chels in particular, there were still two seats vacant and to these Mungo now directed Idris and Tim. If this had been D*wnton A*bey, 'Dame' Maggie Smith would have keeled over and had a servant die for her. But here the only drama occasioned by this cavalier outbreak of egalitarianism on Mungo's part was that Ethel rose majestically from her seat (aided by the unseen and tasteful hands of her two 'boys') and threw down her napkin (which was a tea-towel bleached of all colour and depicting the New Forest in winter, covered totally in snow. From the ground up, and it was still snowing.)

Before she could utter a syllable, Mungo interjected in a voice that carried all the gravitas of his years:

"Stop right there, Ethel dearest."

He then proceeded to introduce Tim and Idris to the rest of the company, not just as the servants who had waited on them over the last couple of hours, but also as potential purchasers of Maison Laird (or was it Villa Laird?). Mungo rattled his wine glass with his hearing aid (a device he did not need – he only used its failure as an excuse in one extreme confrontation with Ethel that she had immediately seen through). He often wished he was deaf. At times like this especially, a legacy of his one traumatisingly disastrous public speech as Head Boy. (The H*rald had published it in full in the Readers' Funnies column, scooping The S*nday P*st for once.)

"Ladies and gentlemen, and I use the term inclusively," he said nodding at Dave and Ethel's two boys in turn, "we are gathered here this evening, and may I say thank you all for coming, yes, well, we are gathered here and we know what the object of it all is and so the moment has come where in pursuit of *equity* (Mungo had prepared this double entendre with great care in this afternoon's rehearsal), I now invite you to make your sealed bids. Here are the envel…"

And as he was preparing to take the envelopes from his pocket Dave bounded up and called out:

"April Fool you, Mungo." And as if on cue (which it was) Chelsea leaped across to her Dave and with one tug at a strategic point on his US Dress Whites, Dave was b*llock naked before them. EXCEPT for something that looked like a black leather finger guard cut from a small man's leather glove – but not worn on his finger. Dave had the courtesy to keep on his cap, which might have been in accordance with US Navy Regulations (or a homage to the final dance scene in *The Full Monty*) as far as they cover this type of situation.

And in a reciprocal procedure, and in the blink of several eyes, Dave had tugged away the pelmet (sk*rt) and *soutien gorge* of Chelsea who was left with only… well it was hard to work how, and to what, that cowgirl bootlace was attached.

They both proceeded to spray the room with Salbutamol while the others remained frozen in fascination (or in Ethel's case, undiluted horror), which is not a listed possible side effect of Salbutamol.

Eventually, Ethel pointed at Dave's finger thingy and said regally:

"What the d*vil is your friend displaying, Mungo?"

"I believe that's called a *thong*, my dear," he mumbled, wondering when Dave had become his friend.

"A *dong*, you say?" Ethel barked.

“That’s never a *dong*. A *dong*’s much bigger than that.” That sounded pretty much like Idris and this was confirmed when she turned to Tim and said with some pride, “Sure it is, big man.”

At which the Sartrams left with just a hint of *froideur* in their bearing.

[For the record: The steak pie was delicious. (“Home-made by the way. Tim rustled the coo himself, ha ha.”). The new potatoes, creamed cabbage and buttered baby carrots ideal complements. Even the non-vegetarian cordon-blue b*ggar seemed impressed and the other b*ggar had scoffed all his veg, asking for more.]

Chapter 38

A Recap and a Termination.

At which the Sartrams left with just a hint of *froideur* in their bearing and without even making their excuses. Yes we have already said that (we know) but what you do not, and should, know is:

1) They did take time to hand-out their business cards.

2) Dave and Chelsea had pulled at the Sartrams' main attire in a well-intentioned attempt to get the party going. They knew from their *previous* (in both senses of the word) that newcomers to the swinging scene tended to need a bit of gentle persuasion, and that as soon as they got rid of the *Alan Whickers* and down to the *dinkey-doos*, (no I don't know either: one author – *not* John) so too, like leaves in autumn, would their inhibitions be shed.

Dave was not to know that the *Jenny Packham* black jacquard prom dress does not come in *strip-o-gram* format, and ditto for Chelsea re Mr Sartram's *Dolce and Gabbana* two-piece (though perhaps this is a line these high-end *Matalan*'s should consider).

Anyway this little stramash came to an unsatisfactory end when Anita Sartram deftly slipped off one of her *Faye Chrystal* Embellished Point Toe Court shoes, (Black and Silver, £395 atow) and smashed the 9 cm (3.65 inches) heel into that part of Dave's body just beneath the clavicle. *Ouch*! (Disclaimer: It's important that the heel does not enter just *above* the clavicle in that wee sort of triangular soft bit, unless of course you are intending to do more than disable your assailant.)

At which point Dave came round to the view that this little bit of reciprocated violence was not the usual sign of affectionate arousal by a potential partner, not some novel variation on the mating rituals with which he was familiar and with which he had become a sort of cult hero of the demi-monde of 'swinger-city'.

And so, with good grace, he turned away from Anita – just in time, for she was aiming for the wee soft triangular bit *above* the clavicle. Her next shot only caught him a glancing blow on the *levator scapula*, which he could take all day. At which point Chelsea and Mr Sartram came out of an untidy clinch in a corner, and both rushed to their respective partners.

At which the Sartrams left with that previously mentioned hint of *froideur* in their bearing and without even making their excuses – though they did take time to hand-out their business cards as we said.

The rest of the evening passed in a whirl of misunderstanding, which is easily done in the circumstances. Who has not been at such an event where, though the details might differ, the intention by some who have mis-read the signals is clearly off beam?

Anyway, Dave was not easily discouraged, and after they had staunched the bleeding he had a go at Ethel while Chels turned her attractions on Mungo (bootlace not withstanding). But the mature-in-years couple it seemed, had forgotten to change into their *strip-o-gram* outfits and with one last surge of hope born out of despair the Ashley-Cole-Coles looked at each other, appraised Brucie and Dirk who were behind the piano, looked at each other again and shrugged their shoulders (*ouch*! for Dave), and made for the two colonials.

Brucie and Dirk separately and collectively had a pathological hatred of violence. *Violence* and *suffering* are the twin pillars of the *unconscious* (*Nietzsche*, 1887, in Jerry of course), not *sexual desire* as Freud wrongly averred around about the same time. And Brucie and Dirk tended to suppress their unconscious such that whenever confronted by either Nietzschean pillar, they gave vent to their discomfort of mind by acting in a gentle and pacific fashion.

What's this all to do with Dave trying to get the kegs off them (with Chels's assistance)? If we take Dave as representing 'violence' and Chelsea as 'suffering' in the Nietzschean scheme, then there was a situation in the drawing room of Mungo and Ethel akin to a powder keg (different kind of 'keg') next to a two-bar fire with or without the living flame.

So, as Dave from one end of the piano and Chelsea from the other closed on Brucie and Dirk, Brucie (or it could have been Dirk) held up a strong hand and gave a statutory warning that his hands were considered to be lethal weapons under the code of the *Hapkido*.

The way this came about was because there is a little known variant of *bonsai*, which Brucie had wanted to study at a gardening centre just outside Joondalup in his formative years. But the class was cancelled because it was condemned as anti-Australian by a national politician who would go on to rival T*ny A*bott in crassness and egotism. So, since he had paid in advance Brucie (for it was he after all), took the class in *Hapkido* (the variant that does not employ the knife or sword, but a little bit of rope is permissible).

ANYWAY, Dave thought this was just a little bit of gentle foreplay as he kicked the piano stool over in his eagerness to grapple with Brucie (or he would have settled for Dirk). But *grapple* is what you do not want to do with an *Hapkido-san*, since along with *joint-locks* (*ouch*!) and *throwing*, *grappling* is what gives *Hapkido* its distinctive flavour.

The outcome was as predetermined as if he, Dave, had been a *justified sinner* (Hogg, 1824), and so it was that he woke up b*llock-n*ked and tied to the nearest down-the-hill lamppost by what looked as if it could have been the lost cord of Mungo's dressing gown. Fortunately for Dave, Chelsea had gathered his kegs and had also dressed herself – in a rush it seemed, for she was wearing her *soutien gorge* where her pelmet had been, and her pelmet was now covering her *nichons.* The effect was not dissimilar to her original state of undress.

And so the dinner party ended as it had begun. It is for History to judge whether it was a success or not and whether there are lessons that can be drawn from it that have wider application – other than the obvious one: that if you think you're at a swingers' event ask to see the labels on the clothes before being first in the water.

Chapter 39

It's not good to talk... in the morning.

Idris and Tim were busy cleaning up the kitchen. Idris insisted on coming back early the next morning. She was particularly disappointed that her *Crème brûlée* (her signature dish – where did that phrase some from?) had been left lying unappreciated in the kitchen with the sudden end to the dinner party. She scraped the last sweet sweet-serving into the picnic carrier she had brought up the hill with her – Melissa just pure loved the stuff.

"Well?" she asked her husband.

"Well what?" Tim did not turn from the deep sink full of his dish washing.

Idris folded her hands until her glare was at last met by a reluctantly turning Tim.

"What can ah do?" Tim moaned. "What do you want me to do? It's nothing to do with us. They're adults. Look at them. Look at the life they've had compared with us. They've had it cushy. Now they get a wee bit of grief for getting too greedy. It happens to everybody. You can forget it, Idris."

"Oh aye, forget it. You're telling me that you're prepared to let that pair of... of Canadian t*ssers do that to them? You heard them as well as me. When they left. *'May have to* *reconsider our original offer. In a downwards direction, naturally.'* Ok. I'll forget it. Nothing to do with us. Aye right. When has that ever stopped you interfering? Like the time them Hutton juvenile delinquents were torturing auld Mrs McQueen's cat. Ye did'nae stop then and say: '*auld Mrs McQueen's had a better life than us, it's time her cat was tortured.*' Naw. Ye went oot there and battered sh*te oot the scum."

"For which I got arrested, got a six months' suspended sentence and a two hunner an' fifty quid fine. Not only that, I also got a doing from their relations, hence the knackered knee – or have you no' noticed?" Tim exaggerated his limp around his side of the kitchen.

Idris put on a seductive smile and sidled up to him.

"After which?" she asked as she stroked his non-designer stubbled chin.

"After which I got *my* relations and..." Tim laughed briefly. "And what a right doin' we gave each of them. And went back and redone the delinquent Huttons as well, just for afters. Since then? Respect. Nothin' but!"

The Walters were still in mid-clinch as Mungo crept fragilely into the kitchen. He walked past Idris and Tim, not seeing them at first. As he spotted them and not the kettle he so desperately sought, they looked up and separated.

"Sorry. Don't mind me. As you were. Not sure where I slept last night. Good of you to stay over."

"We didn't," Tim said.

Mungo never took this in as he went on, "Don't know what we would have... haven't seen milady by chance?"

"The chapel. She was there earlier," Idris said.

"Chapel? Do we have one of those? Must be going senile."

"That buildin' round the back wi' the pointy roof? Ah could hear her inside – sounded as if she was wailing, like you know, the Jews and the Arabs dae against that big wall on the telly."

"As seen on our big telly on the wee wall," Tim added almost to himself as he rummaged in the nearest cupboard.

Mungo wondered if the kettle was in there as he spoke to Idris. "Ah. Tack room, my dear. Ethel goes there to do her thinking in times of stress. All those old saddles and harnesses. Seems to invigorate her. The smell of the leather, the crack of the whip. Boarding school." Maybe fetch my baggy pants, he mused, but felt his temples and deferred.

"Ready for your tea, then? Paper's already here. I put both of them on your wee table in the big room. If the tea's stewed I'll brew some mair."

"Most kind, my dear, most kind. You wouldn't have any asp… Ah, excellent." Mungo smiled and took the two pills and glass of water held out by Tim.

Having swallowed his medicine he decided to take some more. "I… eh… didn't do anything last night, by chance? I remember little. I didn't, you know, upset anyone?"

"No. We were quite disappointed, eh Tim?" But before Tim could join his wife in the lie, a large claw appeared at the end of a larger index finger that now curled in the kitchen doorway beckoning Mungo to the drawing room tout de suite.

"Sleep well, dear?" Mungo asked up from the couch.

"Can't tell, was sleeping," Ethel replied testily, but as if her mind was on something else. She gazed out the window. "Mungo, you know how in all those dreadful radio plays you complain that there always comes a point where one character says to the other 'we've got to talk', and you always say that real people never talk like that? Well we have got to…"

"Oh b*llocks, Ethel." Mungo upped his whine and drooped his mouth. "I'm just about to read my paper. You're not going to insist on conversation, are you? Look at the time. No you can't but it's *morning* for C*rist's sake. Never a time for talk. Thought you would've had a surfeit of conversation with your homo friends."

Ethel in her perplexity and outrage was nearly lost for words. "'*Homo friends*?' What are you talking about?!"

"The queers. Whatsernames, Dark and Light. Bryce and Duke… the antipodean experts on every precious subject under the sun…"

"Mungo Laird!" Ethel felt cold outrage at this, then simply hot rage as she remembered most of what happened the night before. And all Mungo's fault. But she vowed to go with cold outrage (and never ever mention Mungo's four invited intruders ever again. A frisson of guilty pleasure fleeted past – the memory of young Dave Ashley-Cole-Coles' filthy demands of her.)

"You've finally and irrevocably flipped. This time you have gone beyond the pale and there is no way back. *Homos* indeed. My God! Not only is your language offensive – probably illegal. No one calls them *homos* any more, except themselves when they're fooling around with each other – though not in that way…" Ethel paused to give her best shudder. "But you are so, so wrong. Those two boys are paragons of masculinity. You saw for yourself what they…" She cut herself off, in danger of breaking a vow she had made to herself in the tack room never to think of those Londoners again. Then she saw what was eating away at her man: the green-eyed monster had taken hold of him.

"That what it is? You old fool! Jealous at your age. And not knowitalls – educated, knowledgeable, witty, experienced beyond their years."

"Homos, queers, queens, whatever. Doesn't matter a jot to me. Though must say never forgave them for expropriating the term 'gay'. Was my favourite word in all the world. Spoiled now. Why couldn't they have stuck to 'pansies'? Horrible little flowers… and then they sit at my table – our table – and regale me with their facile charms. Bore the ar*e off me – probably shouldn't say that – with their otiose information posing as knowledge, masquerading as wisdom. Do they think I give a stuff for climate change and recycled compost and the Marsh Arabs of Iraq? Was as if they were carrying a large sign that said: *look at me, I'm homosexual and proud, and I'm cleverer than you.* Clever? Didn't know what a *walloper* was if I recall. What normal man gives a t*sticle for all that Woman's Hour stuff? Eh? Tell me? And the wine? Did you see that bottle they brought? *Low alcohol*. Shameless. Who gives a rat's f*rt about these things? No, my dear, only women are taken in by the type." He paused and a hint of a smile played about his lips. "Got my own back with that rather indifferent Buckie, don't you think…? Poor month."

"Didn't stop you going along with their scheme. House off the market. Taking the sign away. And look where that's left us? Ruined." Ethel shot back, a quaver in her voice, no verbal arrows in her quiver now.

"Ruined? Ethel, my dear, my brain might be addled this morning, I admit I remember little of last evening, short-term memory lapse and such, but I distinctly recall that it was you who wanted to go along with their scheme to take it off the market. You said that I had no head for business…"

"And last night bl*ody well clinched that!" Ethel bit her tongue on another silent, self-promise broken.

"...and that it was a..." Mungo was determined. He talked over his wife. "Perfectly reasonable suggestion by Brycie and Dicky, that it would speed up matters etcetera, etcetera. Confess I went along with them taking the signboard away. Cuts down on the timeframe, you said. I trust you, darling, in all matters of a fiscal nature. You know I do. Now, what's all this nonsense about being ruined?" Mungo picked up the paper, turning to today's field at Ascot, a venue that had somewhat soured for him in recent years as it embraced the tidal wave of plebeian culture. He didn't blame Her Majesty for giving it a body swerve. Pert little thing she was, before she married the Greek.

Ethel grabbed the paper, ripping through the runners in the three-fifteen. "Mungo, can you cast your mind all the way back to the start of this conversation?"

"Let's see... in kitchen with Tim and Agnes... summoned out kitchen... by you... was ... yes...! No. 'Fraid I can't."

Ethel left the room, fuming.

She re-entered composing. "Mungo! We've got to talk."

Chapter 40

With one bound they thought they were free.

The Walters had long finished clearing and cleaning the kitchen.

Ethel and Mungo had had their few words – Mungo by far the fewest. They had just finished when Idris pushed Tim into the living room with his offer of help.

Mungo tried to refuse the offer. But an Idris-driven Tim had already spent some time on his mobile telephone.

“Enough, Tim, Idris. It is much appreciated but we are merely refusing to face up to the actuality: we’re doomed unless we go along with Bryce and Dirk’s blackmail. We’ve no option. Hammerhead are circling us in the water and the very thought is causing my g*nads to shrivel at a rate faster than justified by age alone. Tell you what, if we can get them to come our way just a little – a few thousand, say – we’ll claim a victory. Of sorts. What say you, my dear?”

“Tell me again, Tim… what did Val actually say when you told her about our Australian cousins?” Ethel asked.

The Walters’ next interchange was watched by both Ethel and Mungo as if it was a tennis match.

Tim served: “She said if you had properly checked by yourselves, you would have discovered that they were building a property portfolio all over the central belt on one basic principle: elderly house owners; in a rush to sell, for whatever reason. Their modus operandi never varies: they…"

Idris returned: "…they charm, they suggest that if the signboard is taken doon and the house taken aff the market…"

"…they will meet the price asked and complete quickly. Then…"

"…they go walkabout for a good few weeks and when they dae answer phone calls they…"

"…give reassurances that they intend to proceed, then a few more days of silence and then…"

"…the crunch – they claim their surveyor has telt them they'll need to spend a large sum on this and that and they…"

"…want to negotiate the price downwards to cover these costs. And…

"…by now the poor suckers – I mean sellers, are cracking up with fear and…"

"…will do anything to sell."

Team Walters paused for breath before Idris knowingly added, "And apparently, some *vendors*" (Idris liked this word because she felt it just about summarised how people can be duped by language), "even have them over fur their dinner."

Tim couldn't resist this chance, and addressed this one to Mungo. "And some *vendors* manage to top-up the balls-up by forcing them to sit down with competitors and try to start a live bidding war. So it's…"

"Game, set and match to the antipodean…" Mungo nearly completed.

"A*seholes," Idris finished instead.

"If only Val had thought to say," Ethel mused aloud.

But Tim answered her. “She said that she could not volunteer that information: client confidentiality – her firm does business with them. A lot nowadays apparently.”

“That’s it then.” Mungo had had enough. “We’re up against pros. We’re beaten. Tim, could you be so good as to make the call. If I hear one of their twanging voices again, I’ll probably v*mit down the phone.”

Tim made to lift the phone, but Idris stopped him with a shout.

“Tim!” She turned to Mungo, then Ethel. “Just give us a wee sec. Won’t be long.”

Idris drew Tim aside and they went into a huddle. Mungo noted that Mrs Walters was doing all the talking, her husband looking more and more resigned. For Mungo, a student of human nature in all its insane forms, he thought this another sign that class barriers were melting: there really was no difference in spousal relations between the classes. It was reassuring that working-class men were getting their come-uppance after centuries of marital oppression. He thought there might be a paper he could do on that theme, but not at this juncture as Tim, with a grimace that could have meant anything, spoke:

“Mungo, there is one other possibility. I have some pals, friends. Relatives actually – who might, just *might* mind you, might be able to help us.”

“In finance, are they?” Mungo asked.

“Sort of,” Idris snorted. “Aye, you could say that, I suppose. But cheap.”

“How cheap?” Ethel demanded – high finance being her forte. Low finance also.

Idris looked at Tim. "Oh, what would you say, Tim? The price of a drink? A really good drink..."

"...and a curry," Tim added.

"We're in your hands." Mungo rubbed his.

Tim still looked doubtful. "It'll maybe take a day to arrange."

"We have all the time in the world," Mungo lied as he put his arms around Ethel and rhetorically asked, "Wouldn't you say so, dearest?" [Parenthetically, he noticed that for the first time in many years – what astronomers call '*deep time*' – his hands could meet round Ethel. This worried him. It could only mean one thing: his arms were getting longer.]

Chapter 41

The law's a ph*cquing a*se – or, the shortest chapter yet.

The next night. Idris had climbed and Tim had limped all the way up the hill again. Idris and Ethel were sitting next to each other, almost cosily, on the couch, drinking tea. Mungo was staring into space trying not to check out Idris's little shapely legs as her husband paced up and down with his mobile phone in his hand.

After an eternity, it seemed, Tim spoke at the phone for the umpteenth time. "Ring ya b*s!"

It did. He checked the number on the display and nodded to the other three.

"That's them." He pressed a button on the phone and spoke sharply. "Aye, it's me. Who ye expectin' Craig Whyte? About time. Whit kept ye?" Then he listened for some time, only uttering the odd 'uhuh'. Mungo was amazed to see the change in Tim – no more the quiet little chap with the nice, understated limp that Mungo was trying to learn, who dogged Idris's steps like a... well like a faithful dog. Now he was exuding authority and purpose and... all the things that Mungo would like to exude including sex appeal to judge by Iris's coruscating eyes.

"Whit?!" Tim suddenly exploded. "Are you having me on, Gerry…? Aye. Well, could be. How can yae tell these days? Hang on ah'll check, hang on." He asked Mungo, "Our Ozzie friends, they're no' sort of?" Tim mimed a limp wrist and added, "Deep down under types?"

"I thought so. Ethel has a different view. Anyway, does it matter now? Was never that important before," Mungo said.

"Well it is now, Mungo." Then Tim returned to the phone. "Aye, they could be, it seems, Gerry. Is it really a problem?"

Tim listened for some time, his face registering increasing disbelief. "Whit? Say that again. Naw." Now he shook his head, smiling and scowling simultaneously at Idris. "You are kidding me, Gerry. Tell me you are. No? Right. OK. Ah'll tell them. Whit!? No I don't know a good Indian."

Tim terminated the call, shook his head, drew a big breath and blurted out as if releasing a lungful of poisonous gas. "There is a problem. The gist is, you cannot perpetrate or even threaten violence on gays or even on people you *think* might be gay. Seems there is *aggravation* involved."

"*Aggravation*?! I should blo*dy well hope that there is more than just aggravation – it's not violence otherwise," Mungo spluttered and rose from his chair.

"No, no. Keep yer hair on, Mungo. It means that the charge includes *aggravating factors*. A prison term is mandatory. *Hate crimes* they're called now."

"*Hate crimes?* All crimes of violence involve hate. And I hate them? Is that a crime? Never heard anything so absurd."

"It's a broad category – it covers not just gays, but racism, trannies, religions, eh… what else, oh, the disabled aye and some other minority groups."

"Minority groups? Racism? Alright then to duff up some elderly Scots but not someone from South Wales – windbags to a man."

"Aye. Well. Unless of course the Scot is gay, in which case it comes under hate crime."

"This way lies madness. Look, Tim, it's simple: we're having them beaten up not because of their race – though being Australian is provocative enough – or their religious beliefs or their sexual proclivities. We want them beaten up because they've cheated us out of our home. They've robbed us and there is no redress in law. OK, Tim, I'm not blaming you, of course, but tell me this: who can we legitimately threaten with violence – better still, actually duff up? There's no one left."

And then Mungo raised a theatrical finger in the air and reminded himself of Anthony John Hancock. "But wait members of the jury: what about the elderly? What about decent folk like us? Ethel and myself? Oh, yes you can threaten us. You can blame us for the ph*cquing mess the pension system is in because we have the audacity to live longer. Never mind that we paid into the d*mn thing for decades and now we are getting a niggardly sum in return. Blame us for 'bed-blocking'. Blame us for using the NHS. Yes beat us up. Abuse us with impunity." He paused, because Ethel had taken his arm and was stroking it in an insufficiently familiar way. He looked at her and gave a small smile, then said, "I rest my case."

Then he sat with Ethel beside him still clinging to his arm, his emotions in turmoil from a sense of triumph and pain in his righteous indignation at the injustice that had been heaped on his head and that of his consort.

"Ah… I'm no' sure about that: you definitely cannot refuse a job to an old person on the grounds of age. But it might still be okay to threaten them with violence – it's no' as if you're discriminating against them, is it?"

"Fine. Fine. Skelp the Aged! In fact, skelping's too good for us. Put us down. Send us all to that place in Switzerland. Give us a little nudge from this mortal coil." Mungo paused and waited for someone to contradict him. No takers. "That's it then: we'll just sit here for the next thirty years until those two conniving b*stards are as old as we are, having taken out Scottish citizenship in the meantime. Whereupon, we'll send the boys round – who'll also be old men by this time – round to deal with them. Ethel, Tim, Idris finished. Something will turn up. Let's have a small libation. Put away those tea cups. But before that, I suppose I should apologise for the use of that word."

"Whit word?" Tim asked

"You know. *Niggardly*," Mungo said.

"But there's nothing wrang wi' that. It's whit the Frenchies call the *mot juste*, or somethin'."

"Ah! I know that and you know that, Tim. But do the sheriff and the posse?"

Chapter 42

A Non-Inspector Calls – or a chapter even shorter than the previous one.

A big man all in black, from a too-small balaclava to not too-big boots (with reinforced steel toe caps) is in the final throws of tying Mungo to his favourite chair as he stuffs a gag in his mouth. He holds an eloquent masonry hammer and casually taps it into his other fist.

"Enough'th enough ya fly auld bathtard. Five weekth overdue with payment el numero uno. Thith will hurt you a lot more than it will hurt me. Now, betht foot forward ath Long John Thilver uthed to thay."

He now pulls Mungo's right foot out and assumes the recommended arm position (CIA Manual: *enhanced interrogation techniques*).

"Thith little piggy thould have paid the market prithe... on time... jutht to discourage the otherth (ath General de Gaulle thould have thaid).

As he is about to crush Mungo's toes with the hammer, Ethel appears in the doorway with a shotgun. And not just any old shotgun: this is the aforementioned Purdey (Favoured by the Royal Family!). It's the 28-inch barrel with sidelock ejector.

Mungo's eyes betray her sudden appearance and the big bad man turns.

Ethel fires. The big man collapses.

"Mungo! This thing loaded?"

"Not now, dear," Mungo mumbles spitting out the gag.

Chapter 43

Seven hundred and forty-five words (no' counting these).

The early eastern sun brought out the best of the motes through the living room feature window. The telephone rang. Idris appeared in her overall, her hair in a metal headscarf, one escapee lock dangling behind her as if looking for Little Bo Peep to catch up.

"Hello," Idris answered, her voice full of the joys. "Aye speaking. Melissa? Thought it wis you! It's been ages, hen. You goat the number awright then? You heard then? Aboot the hoose…? Aye… hardly believe it maself." She lowered her voice a little to just under euphoric. "Hang on a wee sec, honey." She walked over to stick her head into the hall to yell:

"Buckets 3 and 11 need emptied, Tim! An' walk on the joists – ah don't want you tae put your foot through the ceiling again – you wi' a bad leg an' that!"

She returned and picked up the old telephone that was twenty-sixth on her current list of things to change.

"That's him safely oot the road… naw, it wis easy wance ah'd made up ma mind. You know yer faither – never does anything unless you force him tae. Ah jeest sold the hoose from under him so ah did. Tae get him aff his e*se like. Your

Dougie like that as well? They're a' like that... aye, aye, naw. It was in baith oor names, so ah jeest forged his signature. Whit? Ye don't dae that? Ah dae it a' the time, for his invalidity an' the likes. Yae should try it. Wance yae've done it, it becomes pure addictive...

"Anyway. Wi' the money from the hoose an' his lump sum – ah forged that wan as well – ah paid Mungo. He's the auld fella that used tae live here – an' by the way: ah think he might have forged his wife's name, but who's lookin'? An' the balance we are paying monthly. It's ca'd 'rent-to-buy'. We should have paid it all off in... oh aboot another eighty-five years or so. It'll be worth it in the end. Listen, Melissa, doll, ah need tae go, yae'll need tae come up an' see the place. An' if yae want some tips on the financial front... free gratis?" Idris the recent ex-smoker still laughed throatily. "Still workin? Me? Ah'll never stoap. Ah've goat six jobs noo, no' countin' lookin after him... and forging his name." She laughed again deeply. "Aye... ah'll phone yae tae arrange things. See ye efter."

Idris hung up just as Tim came in. She looked up to admire the blazer that had seen better days and would now certainly see worse ones. He carried a cup in one hand and a copy of the *Metro* in the other (£0.00 atow) – never let it be said he did not contribute. He footsied the little table towards his chair as he addressed his wife, his voice concerned.

"Should you no watch your time? You'll be late for work so ye wull."

"Aye, where's ma handbag an' ma brolly. That wis oor Melissa... That wis oor Melissa by the way... ah said... oor docther..." her words now coming from her speeding mouth, now in the hall.

"Ah heard ye. An ah ken who Melissa is. By. The. Way."

The telephone rang. Tim looked and glowered at it. It rang and kept on. Idris shot back in, sculpted legs a blur, and pulled up just short of the insistent phone. She reached to pick it up after looking at Tim and shaking her head.

"No." Tim stopped his wife. "Don't answer it. It might be for me."

They both waited until the phone stopped ringing, but Idris busied herself plumping cushions and generally annoying Tim. He eventually had to stand and move to avoid her. The phone stopped but the pipes started. Idris put her hands on her hips to get Tim off the couch upon which he had just parked his a*se.

Tim sighed, rose, limped to the wall and kicked – with his good leg – the pipes into a silence now broken by his wife's instructions for his day ahead.

"Right, soup's in the pot, just light the gas. Don't put the pot in the microwave like the last time. There's a pie in the oven. Gas mark 5 for twenty minutes. I've left the beans in the can – you should manage that; it's a ring-pull. Think you'll be okay?" She kissed her hand and patted his head. "See ya the night."

Chapter 44

If we should live to be one thousand... or is there really no fool like a really old wan?

The low sun flickered through the imported eucalyptus on the petite patio-come-terrace. It seemed to shimmer and flare and reflect the warmth and sinuous rhythms of Stan Getz's *Menina Moca,* the seductive sounds of which emanated from the interior of the small villa. The waves – a mere senescent stone throw away – slapped gently on the pristine sand. There were no wind chimes this time round.

Mungo and Ethel in full evening dress, with the skill and athleticism of a youth they remembered but never had, were carried away on the hypnotic runs of Getz's sax, Steve Kuhn on piano, with the inimitable Laurindo Almeida on guitar. In this one piece they had recaptured the years they never had, and Ethel was once again the *menina moca* she never had been. But memory is a strange organ upon which all tunes and histories can be written and re-written: sometimes for the bad, sometimes for the good. Sins are not forgiven, but wiped away; slights are not remembered or are invented (for the counter-view of memory see JR Searl, OUP, 2002).

ANYWAY, the music stopped. The youthful couple reluctantly let loose their hands and stepped back a pace and the young gentleman bowed gracefully and the young lady, her face flushed and glistening charmingly in the rapidly setting sunlight, curtsied to her partner. Then they moved towards each other and Mungo took Ethel's hand again and led her over the terracotta tiles to the small wrought-metal table. He indicated her glass as they sat.

"Another, my dear? Before lights out?"

"Why not, Mungo? But just the one."

"Buckie coladas, Mourinho!" Mungo called to their houseboy who, ever attentive to their needs, stood in the shadow of the patio doors.

They fell into a contented silence broken only by sounds of the warm Iberian night and the gentle surf on the beach. Each idly perused their reading material.

Mourinho quietly slipped the drinks on the table, taking the empty glasses away.

"Obrigado, Mourinho," Mungo said without looking up from his 'Abroad' *Daily Mail*.

"Obrigada," Ethel whispered, her head still in her magazine.

These were two words of the total of three words of Portuguese that Mungo and Ethel knew and felt they needed. They had only learned them as a courtesy to the locals. Certainly not for Mourinho who had once been an interpreter employed at an apparently quite well-known Spanish Football Club – though the name meant nothing to Mungo when Mourinho had mentioned it at the interview.

Ethel put down her magazine, looked at her husband and after a moment's hesitation she spoke:

"Mungo, ever wonder what the others are doing?"

"Others, Ethel? What others? There are no 'others'."

"Well, yes, but I was thinking ... Idris and... Tim and... and... I can hardly now bring myself to use their names ..."

"Ah, Bruce and Dirk. Or was it Bryce and Derek? Yes. Tim and Idris. Yes! Meant to say. In the mail this morning."

Mungo took an envelope and a postcard from his jacket pocket (Oxfam Shop on Byres Road; trousers from British Heart Foundation shop, just next door). He passed the envelope to Ethel.

"From Buffy. Cheque for ninety-nine euros. Made out to bearer. Think I'll try that little town up the coast."

"Well, this time don't use the tartan balaclava." Ethel tossed the cheque on the table and looked across to Mungo who waved the postcard.

"Idris and Tim. Should have said, card from them." He read the card to himself for a moment then said, "Look. Quaint. A sepia print of the old town. Or is it a true colour print? No matter."

"How are they? What do they say? Any word on Tim's knee?"

Mungo turned the card over again in his hand and read aloud, "'*Wish we were there*'."

A disbelieving Ethel took the postcard to find that Mungo was not being facetious. She read on as Mungo continued blithely.

"Wouldn't concern myself overly with Light and Dark... the ersatz Colonial cousins. Resilient. Bounce back. Ten years down the line, why, could be rehabilitated. Visiting professors of entrepreneurship at some third-rate uni, I shouldn't wonder. Insiders at Holyrood? Headlining reality television? Advisors on penal reform. Born again Christians. Someday the slate will be wiped clean, for those two." Mungo paused, happy that

Ethel had happily returned to her magazine and was sipping her cocktail.

"It's the great flaw in our system. Rehabilitation. Prefer Yank's system – three strikes and you're for it. They'll be out in seven at most."

"But how? How did you manage it, Mungo?"

"Manage it, my dear? You give me too much credit. Law of unintended consequences." Mungo rose, glass in hand and took a sip, then breathed deeply of the perfumed air – the reek of burnt chicken piri-piri reminding him of Glasgow on a Friday night.

"After they tried to screw us, I learned from a slightly remorseful little bird, let's call her Val, that your boys were having a liquidity crisis. So, in the spirit of forgiveness I introduced them to that charming young lady, Meg, from Hammerhead. Resourceful lass, damned good brain too. One wave of her personal organiser, and Bruce and the other b*ggar had more cash than there were investment opportunities in a decidedly slack market. The gist: they rewarded each other for the years of hard work and self-sacrifice – skunking the vulnerable can be quite exhausting, one imagines. Meg then produced the micro-print of their agreement with Hammerhead. And that was that."

"And that was that? But Mungo, we had the same type of deal with your Meg, and we didn't end up in… you know…"

"The *merda*, (no *s required for foreign swearies; it's one of the things that made The Empire…and the Pavilion) I think is the word you are seeking Ethel. Mmh? Ah, didn't I say? Well Meg, she presented our boys with the killer deal. I don't have all the details, involved a quick trip to Bangkok – or was it Bali?

No matter. And the importation of specially scented talcum powder. Except it wasn't."

"It couldn't have been much worse." Ethel laughed and took another sip of her colada.

Mungo laughed in harmony, saluting with his own. "Indeed it could have. Could have been us." He chuckled some more. "Still, in a sense they got part of their wish: the experience of gracious living in an old country house. By all accounts Castle Huntley is one of the more salubrious of her majesty's penitentiaries. I imagine with their charms, both boys will be very popular. Yes, very popular indeed. It all strikes me as a sort of metaphor for the food chain – or vice versa, if that is not too judgemental?"

"Let's banish them from our minds." Ethel paused and looked up at her husband who was deep into the Codeword in the Abroad Mail Puzzle Pull Out Section (he had finished one once, with only minor cheating, and was determined to double that before he tipped over someday on this very glorious terrace).

Ethel threw back the last of her last cocktail, for this day. "Mungo dearest, one other thing puzzles me." She waited until he looked up and over at her over his skinny little specs. "I've been doing some calculations, and even after we received the money for the arrangement with Idris and paid off your friends at Hammerhead, well, taking into account the loss we had to take because of the Antipodean squeeze, I find… oh, never mind, doesn't matter… thing is we're happy. Happier than we have ever…"

"No, carry on, dearest. What is troubling you?"

"Well, just that we still appear to be short some seventeen-thousand eight hundred and twenty-nine pounds or so? I was wondering: how did you do it?"

"Ah dear Ethel, there's the rubadub. Thing is, you rightly pointed out, more than a few times, that I lacked business acumen. So... jumped along to a three-day risk management course. Local Disney-college. The days you suspected me of a late-life crisis and that I might have taken up charity work? And what do you know, passed summa cum harry lauda. Would show you the beautiful diploma – real parchment, colours you would like: swirling cream, ink of deepest indigo, signed by some bod or other. Anyway, can't show it, Polly chewed it first time I showed her at her new home. She seems happy enough. Almost as happy as us."

Ethel considered all this then blurted, "Mungo, how the hair-oil did the diploma solve our little shortfall?"

"Oh sorry, dearest. Thought I'd explained. Met this charming girl, on the course. You would really have liked her: decent school, proper uni, low heels, and so on. Anyway, she put the whole thing together." Mungo fumbled in first one, then two, then three pockets.

"Wait, let me show you. Really neat." He held up his hand and between his thumb and forefinger was a plastic card. It shone, glistened almost in the setting sun – which was taking a long time to dip over the horizon for some reason (probably curious).

"Here's the chap: *Atlantic Ocean Finance*. Everything taken care of: *one simple phone call, debts consolidated, one monthly payment. No loan too small, no debt too large*. Neat, eh? All we need to do now, is live to three hundred or so."

Epilogue

Thanks to Idris (no' tae mention Tim).

You still here then?! (Dear Reader). Have you nae joabs tae go tae?! No like me. See me. Ah've goat seven noo, no' counting apparently huvin' tae talk tae youse...ach well ah'll make it quick...

I know most of ye prefer a happy ending. Well ye'll be glad tae know that auld Ethel did'nae kill the cop. She'd been on the sherry trifle and missed him by a mile. He pure sh*t himself though. Then hud a heart attack. The fright killed him. That and the smell... well that'n the everyday Scottish diet... coupled with typical sedentary polis lack o' lifestyle..."

"Look ah really wull huv tae go, ye cannae hear that lovely racket but that's ma Dobermans, God love them, eatin' the chickens again... God love them...Aw naw! An' the f*cking ponies..."

THE END

Appendices and references

Appendix 1. How Sitting Bull might have looked had he stayed at Villa Laird:

From the expression on his face one might infer that he was a Bon Accord supporter and not at all impressed by Gilbert and Sullivan's efforts at musical whimsy. Those that knew Mungo and Chief Sitting Bull often remarked on the family likeness. Apart from the fact that one of them had been dead since 1890, the best way to tell them apart was that Mungo never wore his hair in pigtails.

- Digital ID: (digital file from b&w film copy neg.) cph 3c11147 http://hdl.loc.gov/loc.pnp/cph.3c11147
- Reproduction Number: LC-USZ62-111147 (b&w film copy neg.)

(Library of Congress)

Appendix 2. Guards at Nullson Cattle Show with visitor.

Friday and Saturday nights tend to get a bit boisterous.

Photo by Margaret Duignan

Appendix 3. Competitor at Nullson Cattle show – selfie.

Photo by John Duignan

Appendix 4. Drawing room inventory:

1 *Piano (grand) – Brinsmead, John (Not Stanley!), circa 1890*; available on E-bay, any reasonable offer; buyer to collect.

2 *Leather club chairs – raw sienna patina, with particularly thick leather and stuffed with horsehair. Circa 1920.* Of uncertain manufacture – possibly Wade. A few animals were harmed in the production; some evidence of singeing if sought for; pleasantly pungent aroma of cigar and fortified wines on first entering the room.

1 *Leather sofa – Berrington style, scroll arm with some studs still in place.* Similar in patina to the club chairs though not part of a suite. Not suitable for vegetarians or vegans.

1 *Standard Lamp (Silk shade); Unknown manufacture; ReUseIt* label on base.

1 *Mirror: Over-mantle type; Circa 1900; Bastard Georgian/Regency style.* Some chips and cracks result in a charming shabby look, enhanced by singe marks at the lower edges and what appear to be fortified-wine spatter down one side of the glass and gold-leaf frame.

2 *Side tables*; mismatching of uncertain manufacture with ReUseIt labels on the underside that can only be spotted from the recumbent position on the floor.

1 *Carpet Ziegler Persian* (Copy – had it been genuine their worries would have been over); 18' x 10' approx. Some wear

and fraying at the edges give it a charming shabby look as do the burn marks and stains of a veritable cocktail of wines and spirits of diverse provenance.

1 *Tiger skin rug (genuine; head intact, gaping jaw as if taken by surprise) preparation attributed to Gerrard and Son.* Circa 1920. (An animal was definitely hurt in the production of this item.)

Miscellaneous: Coal bucket (brass); Living Flame coal-effect gas fire (damaged); sideboard (one door missing; one drawer jammed closed) converted from a genuine Welsh dresser, but no relation to the slate on the roof. Aspidistra in large black CI pot (some evidence of use as ashtray).

Appendix 5. *A very short treatise on the role of methadone as treatment in the community for heroin addiction and Mungo's Principle of Equivalence with special reference to Nardini's Fish Tea.*

The comment by Mungo *vis-à-vis* those unfortunates who are recipients of a daily dose of methadone courtesy of the much-maligned NHS, might suggest a certain distaste, even cynicism and a lack of compassion by the old fella. But in fact he had given quite some thought to this state of affairs and had even done some research – going further than seeking Ethel's views on this or listening to her shout at the telly.

On the one hand it greatly angered him if he happened to be in Lloyds Pharmacy (next door to Iceland) or for that matter Boots (no apostrophe), wanting to buy a pack of three – no! Only jesting: those days were long gone. SERIOUSLY. Say he was wanting to purchase something for oh... let's say fungal-nail infection (not that he ever had any problems with his nails or fungi outside of the garden – in fact more than once in his youth young ladies had commented on his nails as being his strongest feature).

But anyhow: he's in Lloyds waiting his turn to be served by one of those lovely girls in their dark green tunics – pity about the trousers – when N*cky Cl*gg (real name) comes lurching in and goes straight into the wee cubbyhole at the back of the shop as if he has trodden that path many times before (he has), and he is exercising his human rights (he is), whereof he partakes of a nice little jigger of the green stuff. And minutes later the bold Nicky bounces out sunbeams streaming from every orifice (that Mungo can see). Now that does get on Mungo's t*ts.

It is not the principle of the thing, the dispending of a very tasty heroin-substitute to heroin addicts that gets on Mungo's t*ts. It is QUEUE-JUMPING that tips him over the edge. In this respect this can be seen as the manifestation of his social class and bloodline – at least one of Mungo's ancestors on the distaff side was of the Anglo-Saxon persuasion. And we know what the English think of 'queue jumpers' (and the Dutch and French, who not surprisingly are among the worst culprits when it comes to this social disease). Hanging is too good for them. Make them wait in line.

As to the principle of free daily methadone, the fact that it did not make one ph*cquing bit of difference to their heroin consumption was neither here nor there for Mungo. To him it was just like free school milk that the children of the plebeians had in his day – it made not one whit of a difference to their health. They still grew up fat and uncouth, with a lifelong distaste for milk. No. It was not the... the fact that methadone did not do what it did not say on the big green jar; it was simply that it was SO UNFAIR AND DISCRIMINATORY.

His argument was simple: these poor people who were heroin-dependent (lads and lasses) were simply a different sub-set of the same population as himself and his beloved Ethel IN THE SUBSTANCES THEY ABUSED AND WERE DEPENDENT UPON.

Is that so hard to understand? Ethel and Mungo and a fair little proportion of right-thinking people in this fair country are hooked on alcohol. Well with weather and politicians like... take your pick... is it any e*fing wonder? They needed it to function in the same way that those junky-types (judgemental language, he adopted when he got a little bit angry when trying to get this point over to obtuse doctors, nurses and do-gooders like his own children) needed their daily fix of heroin.

As soon as you accept that ***principle of equivalence***, Mungo argued – to himself because no one listened to him ever – then you must admit that alky types like himself and Ethel were being discriminated against. And it would be a simple matter to end that discrimination. No, *don't do away with methadone; but give a little jigger of set-me-up for the day in a glass of whisky being dispended by Lloyds, Boots or your local pub of choice.*

Every morning! It would get them out their beds (and their dressing gowns, slippers and goonies before mid-day if there was a nice wee goldie waiting on the NHS and dispensed by angels in dark green tunics (pity about the trousers) or blue and white (Boots) or wee, old men in long dirty aprons (the pub).)

Consider also the positive effect on the economy. The industry would get a boost. As it is, the pharmacy chains are in clover with the methadone programme; so the pub chains would support his proposal he was sure – though in the case of The Counting House in George Square, Glasgow, the addicts might die before they were ever served.

To this end Mungo had dashed off his proposal and sent it to various respectable newspapers, academic journals and industry organizations. This provoked a diverse response. He noted with interest that the *BMJ* was now using a different firm of solicitors (the other one probably having skipped with client funds in the way of these types). The *Angling Times* carried a vigorous debate among those members that could write. Overwhelmingly the angling community supported the proposal – which in itself is not surprising given that they are half-cut most of the time and keep the hip-flask industry in business.

Interestingly he had a response from the *Defence League for the Rights of Heroin-users and Methadone Suppliers*. While the author acknowledged the force of Mungo's analysis, he, or she, said that Mungo and his ilk were favourably benefited by a type of discrimination: *Free Bus Passes within Scotland*!

Ha! Mungo went to himself. The correspondent had fallen into the trap set for him. He had obviously never used a bus pass.

Take the idylls that they think the oldies have going to say, Largs. They get up in the morning – or afternoon – and on a whim say, "Let's go to Largs and have the '*Senior's Choice 'The Traditional Fish Tea* at Nardini's' (ignoring the questionable, potentially supernumerary and erroneous apostrophe, Fish & Chips, Tea, Bread and Butter. Delicious and at time of writing £7.50. The menu requests: *For the over 60s only please!*).

You pick up the bus from Paisley Cross having duly noted the clean-up of the Town Hall, the beautiful Abbey (tomb of Marjory Bruce therein) and the High Street which has some of the best buskers in and out of Peru, and possibly remark that the cooncil have made a valiant but failed effort with the chewdy gum on the trottoir. You clamber aboard the bus (McGill's number 904; but don't expect Big Sandy to be your driver – he's got enough on his plate and it aint the Fish Tea

Special). And if you don't already have a bad hip or knee you stand a good chance of getting one or both from tripping over the sticks, crutches (is that word allowed?) and zimmers blocking the passageway.

And if the ambulatory aids don't get you, then your eardrums will take a pounding from the shrill, croaky hubbub of girlish voices with sandpaper accompaniment – and that's the men. Word of advice – even if you don't use one, take a stick! Even if it's just for defensive purposes.

ANYWAY, you get to Largs and you all make a mad limp to Nardini's (the big one, not the one on the corner at the pier – though you will have directed some of your fellow-travellers to that one, in order to gain advantage). When you arrive you pass through the ice-cream parlour and are directed by a sign to move to the centre of the dining room where you will be greeted and taken to a table when one is free.

There are two things you can do now while waiting: admire the décor and see if you can spot Hercule Poirot, who must surely dine there; and the other thing, and much more pleasant, is to admire the lovely girls who serve there. They are simply the most charming young things in the west of Scotland. Beautiful and friendly with it and they treat the elderly as if they are humans worthy of consideration.

Later, having noshed the quite delightful fish tea (bread+butter+tea included) you get back to the stop for the bus home (901). The stop at the railway station. And this is where your heart sinks. For there is now a baying mob of the elderly who are arguing over the queue. Who was there first and the likes. The best thing you can do is to nip down to McCabes Bar (25 yards on the left, same side as Railway

Station) and have a few in there AND – b* ggar the cost – TAKE THE TRAIN BACK!

Thus is the refutation of the 'benefits' enjoyed by the elderly through the bus pass.

FOOTNOTE: For those readers who have been living as recluses, methadone as dispensed looks a bit like *Night Nurse* or *Fairy Liquid (Original)*, but twice as effective, and very nice too. Yum, yum. Said to go well with a Fish Tea.

Appendix 6. Tasting notes on Buckfast Tonic wine.

They exist but as we are now at Appendix 6 and have now been partaking of tonic wines of different vintages, they have been misplaced. HOWEVER for the discriminating reader it should be noted that *Buckfast Tonic Wine* comes in two main variants: that sold in the UK has a marginally higher alcohol content than that sold in the Republic of Ireland, but less caffeine. In addition, the UK recipe Buckie has some vanilla content while that of the R*I has no added vanilla. And as most of you will know, *Buckfast* sold in the UK comes in the endearingly familiar green bottle while that of the R*I comes in a brown bottle. It is also worth noting that the alcohol content of both main variants is less than many 'prestigious' fortified wines such as Harveys Bristol Cream or Taylor's Port. So there!

Appendix 7. The politics of Buckie – or how to become High Commissioner for Australia, Malawi (naw ta) or just to get in the papers at election time.

Helen Liddell, former Secretary of State for Scotland, called for *Buckfast* to be banned in Scotland; Cathy Jamieson MSP suggested retailers should stop stocking it in Scotland. Other 'Scottish' Labour politicians queued-up to bad-mouth the tonic wine including Jack McConnell (First Minister of Scotland – whatever happened to that High Commissioner to Malawi gig, Jack?). Andy Kerr, Scottish Executive Health Minster said... Enough. You get the gist.

The monks of Buckfast Abbey and the licensed producers and distributors of their product point out that the areas allegedly associated with anti-social behaviour linked to *Buckfast* consumption, have been economically deprived for decades and that *Buckfast* represents less than one percent of the total alcohol sales across Scotland. Mungo and Ethel Laird have never been charged with disorderly behaviour, have never threatened firemen on bonfire night, and excepting Ethel shooting at and missing a moonlighting cop, have never under the influence of *Buckfast Tonic Wine* assaulted police officers going about their duties. Whether or not that suggests that the aforementioned politicians are a bunch of opportunist t*ssers is left to the intelligent reader.